Discovering Ataraxia

DISCOVERING
A TARAXIA

NANCY GRAVATT

NEW YORK

LONDON • NASHVILLE • MELBOURNE • VANCOUVER

DISCOVERING ATARAXIA

A Novel

Published in New York, New York, by Morgan James Publishing. Morgan James is a trademark of Morgan James, LLC. www.MorganJamesPublishing.com

Proudly distributed by Publishers Group West®

Morgan James BOGO™

A **FREE** ebook edition is available for you or a friend with the purchase of this print book.

CLEARLY SIGN YOUR NAME ABOVE

Instructions to claim your free ebook edition:
1. Visit MorganJamesBOGO.com
2. Sign your name CLEARLY in the space above
3. Complete the form and submit a photo of this entire page
4. You or your friend can download the ebook to your preferred device

ISBN 9781636983165 paperback
ISBN 9781636983172 ebook
Library of Congress Control Number: 2023944998

Cover and Interior Design by:
Chris Treccani
www.3dogcreative.net

Cover Illustration by:
Samantha McInnis

Morgan James is a proud partner of Habitat for Humanity Peninsula and Greater Williamsburg. Partners in building since 2006.

Get involved today! Visit: www.morgan-james-publishing.com/giving-back

To Emily and Serinda, who shine light upon my life.

Table of Contents

CHaracter LIST

Meg	Mother of Allie and SJ
Will	Father of Allie and SJ, succumbed to color cancer
Allie	Daughter of Meg and big sister of SJ
SJ	Son of Meg and Will and brilliant brother of Allie
Aunt Agatha	Meg's mother's sister who left her home to Meg
Russell	Nerdy friend of SJ
Mrs. Longwood	Literature teacher at Lakeshores Middle School (MS) and advisor for *Aviso*
Ben	Editor of the school newspaper, *Aviso*
Jenna	Fellow student at Allie's school
Lola	Jenna's best friend
Grace	Friend of Allie's at school
Stu	Fellow student and friend of Lola and Jenna
Dak	Basketball player and friend of Grace
Sophia	Student on Allie and Ben's math team
Mr. Lemmel	PE teacher and coach at the elementary school
Mr. Lozano	Math teacher and math team coach at Lakeshores MS
Mrs. Durwood	Cheer team coordinator at Lakeshores MS
Angela Anderson	Principal at Lakeshore MS

CREATURES OF ATARAXIA*

Graham	Sheep member of the Guardians' Council, father of Luke and Delilah
Molly	Wife of Graham and mother of Luke and Delilah
Solomon	Owl and chairman of the Guardians' Council
Luke	Son of Graham and Molly
Delilah	Daughter of Graham and Molly, believed to be dead
Ethan	Son of Zion
Justin	Brother of Katy
Daphne	Honey badger, mother of Squeaker
Squeaker	Honey badger, living in the Abyss

OTHER GUARDIANS' COUNCILMEMBERS

Zion	A stately tiger
Moriah	A graceful white dove
Lucius	An ox
Ellie	A shy cream-colored deer
Albert	A sly and entertaining hyena
Helen	An attractive, bushy-haired fox
Orion	A stately skunk
Jake	A tall, skinny wolf
Lilly	A fierce honey badger
Aurora	A giraffe gazelle
Katy	A talkative Kodiak bear

Nancy Gravatt

creatures of Malvelnia

Wendigo	King/Leader of the Overseers
Eris	Wife of Wendigo
Estrelle	Conniving daughter of Wendigo and Eris
Kibou	Fun-loving son of Wendigo and Eris
Ashok	Evil vulture brother of Wendigo
Simon	Chief heralder for the royal family
Devon	Monkey spared by Zion
Diego	Chief spokesman for the crocodiles of Malvelnia
Phinehas	Crocodile captain serving Diego
Diablo	A huge, intimidating python

outliers, fairy creatures of the ABYSS

Gavril	Son of Whitney
Seraphine	Sister of Gavril
Whitney	Mother
Jude	Father
Dustin	Older son
Squeaker	Brave honey badger
Glowerth	Foster father of Squeaker
Magda	Foster mother of Squeaker
Cedric	Son of Glowerth and Magda
Lomar	Father of Jalen
Jalen	Son of Lomar

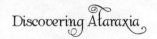

CREATURES OF THE ABYSS

Abaddon	King of the Abyss
Daisy	A hippo
Lorna	Spirit 1 of the Abyss
Gaffy	Spirit 2 of the Abyss
Myrna	Spirit 3 of the Abyss

SCHOOLS

Lakeshores Middle School (LMS)

Lake Bluff Elementary

Ataraxia (definition): tranquility of mind and spirit

They had as king over them, the angel of The Abyss,
whose name is Abaddon and in Greek is
Apollyon (that is, Destroyer).

—Revelation 9:11

Chapter 1

THE ABYSS

A s tiny Delilah peered over the edge of the cavernous hole in the earth, she let out a shivering sigh.

Oh dear, she thought. *I can't even see the bottom. There's only blackness covered in mist! I don't think I'll survive this descent.*

The grizzled orangutan, Simon, stood behind her, nudging her forward. The punishment for communicating her heartfelt desire to return to her family was banishment by the royal family who had adopted her, forcing her on this trek to the Abyss. Few survived the trip downward, according to vulture lore. Even its name conjured up terror. Since no creature had ever returned from its depths, its fate was considered forever sealed. Because of the steep incline of the precipice, a narrow winding path had been dug into the wall of the Abyss by countless creatures, each etching a portion of the pathway into the cliffside as they made their way downward.

Peering upward, Delilah barely caught sight of Simon gazing over the edge. In the damp mist, the little lamb shook her soft white curly coat, with its perfectly circular whorl of extra-white hair crowning her head, and struggled downward, one tiny hoof at a time.

Fifty yards below, as she rounded a precarious turn, Delilah heard a strange humming noise—one she had never heard before. With every step, the droning hum grew louder. She stopped still and did not breathe, listening intently. It was at that moment she realized it was the deafening roar of thousands upon thousands of bees.

1

As she had inched downward and her eyes had adjusted to the darker environment, she had noticed a few large bees, perhaps oversized bumble bees, she thought, flying overhead and then disappearing somewhere in the shadows. But as she descended further, she could now make out several huge hives wedged into the sides of the cliff. To her dismay, they did not appear to be bumble bees. Instead, they looked like a breed of giant hornets. They were frightening in their numbers. Delilah slowed down her breathing and her steps to a level and cadence that rendered her nearly motionless. She knew to survive, she would have to move forward in this stealthy manner, tiny step by tiny step.

Delilah remembered a time when she and her vulture brother, Kibou, were rambling in a green pasture, and a giant hornet that looked just like these had spotted them, and for no reason other than its mean temperament, dive-bombed the pair. As they scrambled for cover, the hornet zeroed in on Delilah and stung her fiercely on her back leg before flying away.

Poor Delilah was sick for several days from the power of the hornet's potent venom. Mud packs helped ease the pain, and gradually, she recovered. But that frightening experience was etched in her memory. At this moment, it was nearly paralyzing her with fear at the prospect of being observed. One stumble, one misstep might alert them to her presence. There was no doubt in her mind that multiple stings from just a small segment of the hive's inhabitants would end her life.

As she shivered on the side of the precipice, her mind flashed back to her strange arrival at the home of Kibou and the little vulture's imperial family. She vaguely recalled emerging from Simon's smelly brown sack, only to be embraced by the baby vulture, Kibou.

Who could have imagined that two animals who were so different would bond? But Kibou pecked for a moment at her white bundle of fuzz and then snuggled up, making a warm pillow for himself while Delilah fell asleep next to the soft feathers of the baby vulture. Kibou looked so happy that his parents did not remove the lamb, lest they wake him from his contented slumber.

Over the coming weeks, the two became close companions, playing together and snuggling up every night, falling asleep to each other's heartbeats. Perplexed, the parents discussed this unexpected development, then decided to allow the baby lamb to stay with Kibou rather than snuff out its life and eat it.

Nancy Gravatt

Their haughty older daughter, Estrelle, wanted nothing to do with the lamb. "How can you even consider allowing that white fuzzy thing to remain in our midst?" she cackled. "You should get rid of her at once, before Kibou gets more attached."

They considered Estrelle's advice but realized the two kept each other content, which allowed the parents to go about more important business in their kingdom without worrying about Kibou. For one thing, they had been hearing the Guardians' Council was planning a meeting for the next month, and they needed to do some surveillance.

Unbeknownst to Delilah, she was sheltered by royalty: King Wendigo and Queen Eris.

Wendigo was known for his far-ranging vision when out searching for carrion. He was also greatly feared by the Guardians because of his reputation for having powerful talons, swift speed, and an insatiable hunger to support his gargantuan size. His partner, the haughty Queen Eris, was smaller in stature but tougher by temperament. While Wendigo snacked on dead animals, Eris was known, with the support of her handmaidens, to swoop down on small, defenseless animals, killing and then devouring them. She had a mean streak that caused her to urge Wendigo on to more evil actions than he might initially imagine doing.

With their combined power and Eris's self-serving tactics, the pair had ruled the Overseers' kingdom for the past ten years.

At one point, a giant Python, Garrett, had attempted a coup to dethrone King Wendigo, but Eris got wind of the plot. Through surveillance, they knew of Garrett's favorite spot in the river to catch his preferred lunchtime treat, the tasty black-toed lizard. Securing the support of several fierce crocodiles in exchange for giving them authority over the Indigna River region, Wendigo and Eris were victorious in having Garrett killed and decapitated, his head delivered to them to verify the operation's success.

Delilah's state of protection was short-lived. The small lamb had recurring dreams of a family she could not fully remember. But dream-like visions brought faint recollections, fleeting images of a plump, softly bleating mother licking her curly coat and of a deeper yet stuttering voice urging her to stand up as she lay unable to move. She had slipped into a coma-like state, but Delilah was not dead; she had merely fallen into a temporary state of paralysis, which led to her family's conclusion that she was stillborn, and eventually, the orangutan's possession of the knapsack that he delivered to King Wendigo.

3

As the days went by, the visions grew stronger in Delilah's mind and in her heart. A huge desire welled up within her to find that soft, round, loving mother from whom she had been taken.

"I want to find my real mom," Delilah confessed to Kibou. "You can see I'm not your real sister, right?"

Kibou blinked and violently flapped his small wings. "Nope! You're my sister," Kibou said. "You must put those strange thoughts out of your mind. If our parents hear about it, they'll be angry!"

Despite Kibou's best efforts to persuade Delilah to forget those urges and visions, the next afternoon, when Wendigo and Eris arrived with food, the words poured out of the lamb as she asked them for permission to leave to seek her birth family.

"What?!" shrieked Eris. "After we've given you a home and everything you could want! What a miserable ingrate."

"Now, Eris," Wendigo soothed. "It's natural she might wonder where she came from. Perhaps we should let her go search—"

Estrelle, eating nearby, shot a piercing look at her mother. "Listen to this wretched creature. She is not worth another moment in our presence. Banish her, Mom! You know where to send her." And as she spoke, a snide screech emerged from her black beak.

"Estrelle is right!" Eris said in vehement agreement, emphatically flapping her wings. "Wendigo, send for that messenger of yours, Simon, at once, and have him take this ungrateful wretch to the Abyss. Let her search for her family there."

Large tears rolled down Kibou's cheeks. He knew when his mother ganged up with his sister, his father always caved to them. He fluttered up next to Delilah, heartbroken at what he realized would be her imminent departure and likely death.

Simon arrived the next day to take the lamb to the terrifying place where Eris and Estrelle believed she would never be seen or heard from again.

These thoughts and memories raced through little Delilah's head as she continued her creep downward beneath the hive-encrusted cliffs. An event of great fortune for Delilah occurred at that moment, one that she did not even realize was happening. A black bat had strayed from its habitat, a nearby cave carved into the side of the cliff another hundred feet below. It was hungry and happened on one of the giant hornets unawares, grabbing it with its sharp claws and biting its head before consuming the rest of it for an afternoon snack.

Unfortunately for the bat, it did not realize its predatory behavior had been witnessed by several other hive-dwellers. They spread the word, and in a fleeting moment, a swarm of the nasty winged creatures was heading like a missile toward the bat. Trying to evade them, the bat made several high swoops before careening down, trying to hit them and knock them out.

But being spiteful and given their numbers, the hornets regrouped and attacked the bat, covering him and stinging him repeatedly as he emitted several high-pitched screeching sounds. They made quick work of him as the bat succumbed to their venom, his limp body careening downward to disappear in the dark mist.

All the while, Delilah had quietly edged farther and farther on the path. Soon, she had safely moved below the area of the hives, picking up speed the further she got from them.

The Abyss was a strange geologic phenomenon. No one knew exactly how it had come to be. Because it was several miles deep, with a relatively small opening at the top, it generated a gray, cloudy mist that prevented anyone from truly seeing how far it went. As Delilah continued her journey, the mist surrounded her. It felt cool and clammy. She was exhausted after what felt like an eternity of creeping on the narrow ledges, making her descent excruciating. Every muscle pulsated from her tensing them in fear. Her agonizing descent continued for several hours.

Unable to see more than a dozen feet ahead on the path, she was suddenly taken aback, feeling cobwebs brushing her face. She shook her head gently at first and then more vigorously as the strands became thicker and more abundant. As she struggled forward, she realized the web was sticky, and the strands were gripping her legs and neck.

"What can I do? I'm frightened! Can anyone help me?" she cried out.

As she wiggled and fought the thick web, a monstrous gray and black spider twice the size of the lamb emerged and stared at Delilah with close-set, beady red eyes. Delilah shrank back as it slithered toward her, stroking her face with its black furry legs. Skillfully, it spun threads and wrapped them around Delilah. She wiggled and yelped, putting all her energy into trying to break the threads so she wouldn't become a mealtime treat for this giant arachnid.

Delilah did not notice, but as the spider spun and she struggled, the lamb was no longer standing on the pathway. She was now suspended in midair, hanging within a ball of thread as she fought to free herself. The lamb's sharp hooves proved to be successful in cutting more and more of the threads while the huge spider had moved back to encase a more compliant creature—a small sparrow that had lost its course and flown into the very center of her giant web.

With a final burst of energy, Delilah swiped several of the sticky threads still binding her. Her body slipped downward. As a final thread broke, she began a rapid fall into the dark unknown. Hurtling downward, Delilah created an image in her mind's eye of a lovely mother ewe saying goodbye to the daughter she loved.

Spray from a huge waterfall showered her as she landed in a deep pool of clear water. She felt a current carrying her swiftly as she surfaced, and she caught her breath. Then, astoundingly, Delilah found herself in the middle of a river. The deep waters had broken her fall. Fighting her way with all the energy she had left to get to the riverbank, Delilah waggled her legs in all directions, somehow getting two legs caught in a huge vine extending over the edges of a mound of moss, mud, and vines. Squirming forward, she managed to crawl onto the riverbank. Throwing herself on her side, Delilah lay with huge gasps, gradually regaining her breath.

"Oh, my!" she bleated. "Where am I?"

Chapter 2

PICTURE WINDOW TO ANOTHER WORLD

Present day, October in Lakeshores

Allie's Toulouse-Lautrec night light threw a soft glow in her new bedroom. As she lay on her side gazing at the painting on the wall, she could have sworn she saw one of the large sheep move slightly in the foreground.

"You are really losing it, girlfriend," Allie said to herself. "It's a painting, not a TV screen!" Still facing the painting, she tried to imagine where that grassy meadow existed. Maybe it was a place back in her home state of Virginia. Her mind drifted to the time her mom and dad had taken her and her brother on a scenic drive through the foothills of the Blue Ridge Mountains, where rolling farm country melted into more rugged terrain on sharply winding roads with the occasional warning sign to beware of falling rocks.

A sudden movement from inside the painting jolted Allie's eyes back to the sheep. What the heck was going on?

Allie crept out of bed in her flowered PJ pants and tie-dyed T-shirt and slid over to the wall on which the painting hung, donning her bunny slippers with the pink-nosed toes and canvas soles on the way. She heard a faint voice . . . was it in her head? Or was the voice in the room? No, it was too muffled to be in the room, almost as if it were coming from within a dream.

"C'mon! Step in and join us. We've been waiting for you. B-b-but hurry, we have to get to the meeting!"

Startled, Allie rubbed her eyes. Maybe she *was* dreaming. She could swear it was one of the sheep in the painting talking to her.

"Yes, *you*, Allie. Come with us. J-j-just take a big step into the grass, and we'll show you the way."

Allie hesitated, then decided maybe she was sleepwalking and would play along with this peculiar dream. The bottom edge of the painting was about two feet from the floor, so she pushed her hand-painted toy box over in front of it. Climbing onto it, she raised her slippered foot and stuck it headlong into the painting. She felt a strange suction sensation pulling her forward through a clammy gray substance— something between Jell-O and slime, with a consistency that swirled around her and spit her out with a giant sucking noise onto the grassy knoll.

She thought it was the lushest, darkest green grass she had ever seen. She sat there in a state of shock while putting her senses on high alert. Was she still alive?

Allie took a deep breath, smelled the sweet clover and lilac around her, and was relieved that her lungs seemed to work fine. She reached out her hands to feel the grass. It was cool and damp. Blanketing the hillside, the grasses were bordered by the noisy waters of a bubbling brook that meandered past foothills, which turned into craggy cliffs off in the distance.

She struggled to her feet, staring in disbelief at the sheep family facing her.

"Great. You can come with us now," the tall and very curly-haired ram bleated.

"Graham, are you sure you know the entire way to get there?" the second sheep, a ewe with a roly-poly body, asked, gently batting her eyes.

"Of course, of course, Molly," Graham blustered. "I've b-b-been there many times before. Everyone—I mean practically *everyone*—told me they would be there. We need to get walking right away. We c-c-cannot be late for the beginning of the meeting. I'm speaking! C'mon Luke," he said to the midsize ram lamb chasing a dragonfly from a daffodil. "No more time for play. We've got to get moving."

"Who are you?" Allie finally blurted out. "And where am I?" Her voice rose in a tense crescendo as she stood, mouth gaping, still wondering whether this was a dream.

"I'm Graham," the ram said matter-of-factly, "and this is my family: Molly and our son, Luke. We're on our way to an important meeting. We invited you along

because I thought m-m-maybe there's some way you can help. I don't know why I thought that, but something told me you could."

Allie, who had no idea what Graham was talking about, was fascinated that the trio was speaking. Talking sheep! How utterly strange! But off they trotted on the winding pathway with Allie following closely behind—to where, she did not know.

As they walked, Allie's mind wandered to her new friends, Grace and Ben. She had weathered the move to North Carolina, and despite being slow at getting to know people, she had already managed to find two awesome friends in just the first two months.

I wonder what Grace would think of this outlandish place, Allie mused. *Would Ben even believe her if she told him about it?* Maybe, but she didn't know him well enough yet to be sure.

Her brother, SJ, who was quite peculiar, didn't care as much as she did about making friends. He considered Allie his best friend and confidant. They could tell each other anything and always cheered the other one on. But even SJ was not going to believe it when she told him about *this* adventure.

Then a fearful thought arose: *Would she be able to find her way back to see her family and her friends?* She decided to file this thought away for the moment since Graham was leading the way at a fast clip, and she now had to run to catch up.

Chapter 3

GETTING SETTLED

August, two months earlier

R ain pelted the car unmercifully as Meg strained to keep the aging gray Volvo on the road. She glanced in the rearview mirror. No movement in the back seat from the kids as they slumbered through the storm. Allie— Alexandra Kyra Lee—had her head buried in a pillow, her straight black hair with its dramatic blue streak sticking out of the pillowcase's folds. Meg's son, the speed Meister—Spencer Jonathan Lee—with his head snuggled into the blanket covering Allie, was lightly snoring. His light tan rimmed glasses were still perched on his head, a tribute to the basketball great he admired, Kevin Durant.

After seven years of trying to make ends meet in the expensive northern Virginia suburbs of Washington, DC, she had pulled up the stakes and headed south after an unexpected turn of events produced a house for the widowed mom and her two children in a small town in North Carolina. With the lower cost of living and no more mortgage payments, it was as if fate had handed her a new beginning. Still struggling to get past losing her husband, Will—even though four years had gone by since his death—Meg needed this chance to move their lives forward in a new direction.

Her mind wandered back to those difficult days when Will's health was rapidly declining. Will, her pillar of strength, had been diagnosed with stage IV colon cancer, a shock to their happy lives. The treatments had taken their toll on his six-foot-two frame, and the new experimental drugs they tried had failed. SJ was six when Will succumbed to the cancer; and Allie, who was nine, had taken it especially hard. She had always been close to her dad. He was "uniquely handsome," Meg often said of Will, with his mix of Native American and Chinese heritage. Allie, who had inherited his shiny black hair, had recently added the bright blue streak for artistic effect.

Meg tilted the rearview mirror her way and took stock of the woman staring back. Attractive in a down-to-earth way, Meg looked a youngish thirty-eight. She combed her fingers through her auburn, naturally curly hair and forced a big smile to check her teeth. Will used to tease her about her slightly prominent overbite, but it was a feature, he later told her, that endeared her to him. "It feels like you're always getting ready to break into a smile," he said.

Will and Meg had met in college at George Mason University in Fairfax, Virginia, where he studied economics. Meg had taken an econ class as an elective while working toward her communications degree, and that's where she'd met Will. She had spotted him at the end of the row she chose to sit in on the first day of class and noticed his striking good looks and quick smile. The next time the class met, Meg purposely chose a seat one down from Will. Meg broke the ice by asking to borrow a pen, then struck up a conversation with him at the end of class. Before long, they were both showing up a few minutes early, which evolved to coffee after class, and, as they say, the rest is history. They were soon inseparable; five months later they were engaged.

They naturally complemented each other. Will had a wonderfully dry sense of humor splattered with sarcasm, along with a set of corny jokes he loved to tell and retell until Meg knew all of them by heart. Yet, even with their repetition, it was always Will who laughed the hardest after he hit the punch line.

Meg, on the other hand, was quieter and more thoughtful—the practical one of the family. She often pondered their goals, their future, when they would start a family, and how they would possibly pay for those far-off college bills, seeing that tuition and fees rose every year. She was the one, after Allie was born, who set up a 529 savings program in Allie's name. She was also more emotional, something she tried to hide, even going to another room if she started tearing up about something she heard on the news.

Will was spontaneous and always lots of fun to be around. People gravitated to him because of his quick sociability. Extremely well read, Will could speak to just about any topic a new acquaintance might mention. Meg marveled at his encyclopedic memory. She worried, now, if she would ever make friends again because, in her mind, Will was the one who had always attracted them.

As she headed down I-95 in the rain, Meg's mind wandered to the new town, new home, and new life that lay ahead. Who would have imagined her spinster aunt, who had always been fond of Meg as a little girl, would quietly leave the aging Victorian white elephant on Main Street in Lakeshores, North Carolina, to her niece?

As she drove, Meg thought back to the visits she had enjoyed with her tall, awkward, but awesome Aunt Agatha, when she was a girl. Agatha always had a twinkle in her eye for Meg and a riddle for her to solve. She felt children let their brains waste away in front of TVs and computer screens, so she always had a brain twister for Meg to figure out. (This one when Meg was seven: What word contains twenty-six letters but only three syllables? Answer: Alphabet!) She laughed, remembering silly Aunt Agatha's brain twisters. Yes, Aunt Aggie had been a special, one-of-a-kind aunt.

Whenever they talked by phone, her aunt was always reporting on a new item she had purchased for her home. From the Capodimonte Rococo chandelier in the dining room to the unusual paintings throughout her home, each item had been thoughtfully selected by Agatha.

Even the clerk at the small neighborhood grocery store knew about Agatha's art collection since the eccentric spinster had been renowned throughout the area for gallivanting around the country to estate sales and auctions, where she searched for unique pieces to adorn her home.

"One of the charms of Aunt Agatha's house is the artwork she installed over the years," Meg had told Allie. "We are *so* fortunate to be able to enjoy these because each one reflects a unique element of her taste and personality." Allie had agreed. Meg was amazed her unconventional aunt had bequeathed this home, with its antique décor and paintings, to her.

Early September in Lakeshores

Allie had always viewed the arts as a window into another world, especially after her father's death. Allie often escaped through sketching her own drawings,

ones with unusually colored birds and butterflies flitting over rainbows toward a golden horizon. She preferred those hope-filled places to the cold, lonely spot her dad's departure had left in her heart. She had withdrawn more within herself in the years following his death and only now, four years later, was she emerging from that dark cloud, seeking to open her mind and heart to the new possibilities ahead. It was really hard, but she was trying.

The painting in her bedroom had intrigued Allie from the moment she saw it. Right after they arrived, Meg told the kids they could look around and decide which bedroom they liked for their own. They had dashed upstairs. The moment Allie saw the bedroom with the mural-sized painting, the tray ceiling with its fancy white moldings, and the alcove with rounded arches where her bed could fit, she knew it was made for her.

A huge grassy hill rose from the bottom of the painting with a path winding off the frame in the upper corner. There was also a weeping willow to the side and several sheep grazing in the upper middle section. As she gazed at it, she imagined herself skipping up that pathway with hope in her heart. Silhouettes of birds danced across a violet sky tinged with golden streaks. Allie, who loved art history, thought the painting had an ethereal quality that reminded her of a painting she'd seen at a gallery in Washington, DC.

There's something magical about this painting, Allie thought, *but I can't figure out what about it makes me feel that way.*

Aunt Agatha had told Allie's mom a little about the painting—how many years back, when she acquired it, it had a story. Then Allie's mom told Allie it was one of several items an antique dealer in Connecticut had acquired from an estate sale by the daughter of elderly parents who had moved their household decades earlier from England. The antique dealer said the daughter had told him, unlike any of the other estate sale items, this painting had a mysterious history.

It had been sold to the woman's mother by a roving troupe of actors passing through the town in which they lived. The town, located in Essex, featured many buildings and castles from medieval times. The actors were down on their luck and needed to raise some cash. At that time, the town was holding an open market in the central square, so the troupe secured a booth.

They rolled up in a horse-drawn wagon out of which they pulled all sorts of items to sell. Among them were a book of potions, some hand-hammered brass pots, several musical instruments, and three paintings. The daughter said her mother loved the large, mural-sized painting with the sheep grazing on the hillside.

When she asked the actors its price, she was astounded at the high amount they were seeking to get for it. The reason, they told her, was that the painting had been acquired from a magician's home and was rumored to have "magical qualities." They said they did not know what they were, but they concluded the painting was more valuable because of them. This story further intrigued the woman, so she paid the price they were asking and brought it home.

It also captivated Agatha's imagination. She purchased it without hesitation, after which she arranged with the dealer to have it shipped to her home in Lakeshores, North Carolina.

After it arrived, it immediately found its place on the wall where Allie was now admiring it. The walk-in closet, which could double as a secret hiding place from her brother, sealed the deal. She shouted, "This one's mine!"

Spencer, or SJ, as the family called him, did not care. He was much more enamored with the bedroom at the end of the hall with built-in bookshelves that would handsomely house his Lego creatures, science books, comics, action figures, and dragonfly collection. Plus, it had an awesome view out the back window of the rolling cow pasture that backed up to their yard. SJ decided at once that this move was a good thing!

Chapter 4

THE NEW SCHOOL

The alarm blared just as Allie strode through a house with hundreds of doors to rooms of assorted sizes and painted in distinct colors. She lurched sideways in her bed to hit the snooze button as her mom came by the kids' rooms to make sure everyone was up and moving.

Allie rolled over, keeping the pillow over her head. One eye peeked out from under it. A few weeks into the school semester, she feigned illness that Monday morning claiming she was sick to her stomach so her mom would call the school and let her stay home.

Allie did not like the new school. She had been apprehensive about making friends and sure enough, a bunch of the girls in her class were already in a clique and had no trouble letting her know she was not part of it. That was OK at first because Allie was absorbed in figuring out where to go for all her classes, who her teachers were, getting the required supplies, and just making sure she got everywhere on time. But once routine had set in, Allie found her early attempts to strike up conversations with a couple of the girls in her homeroom met with limited success. Jenna, a gregarious blonde with long braids, seemed to be the one who a lot of the girls tagged along with during lunch. Allie decided to seek out a conversation with her one morning.

"So d'ya know who I should talk to if I wanna get involved working on *Aviso*?" Allie asked Jenna.

"Truthfully," Jenna said as she rolled her eyes, "I have no idea." (This seemed strange since her friend, Hannah, was a reporter for *Aviso*, the school newspaper).

"You could ask Mrs. Longwood, but I don't think they have room for anyone new." She said the word *new* with a touch of disdain in her voice.

Jenna's best friend, Lola—petite with oversized hazel eyes and light brown hair cut in a bob—was in earshot and nodded her head in solemn agreement.

The cheery, slightly rotund, gray-haired Mrs. Longwood taught English literature to both grade levels at Lakeshores Middle School. She was also the teacher-advisor for *Aviso*.

"Well, I'll have to talk to Ben Lopez, the editor of the paper," Mrs. Longwood told Allie, "because he already has his staff set for this year unless he changes his mind and decides there's a need for another reporter."

During class that day, Allie noticed Jenna and Lola whispering and staring her way, then smiling and laughing. She wasn't sure if she was being paranoid, but it felt a lot like they were talking about her. And not necessarily in a positive way. Allie, like her mom, did not easily warm up to new people. She thought it would take her a long time to feel even slightly comfortable in this new school.

Allie could not decide whether she wanted to write for the paper since what she really loved most was drawing. Maybe they could use an illustrator or someone who could do cartoons, she thought. In her childhood, her mom had taken her to the National Gallery of Art in Washington. There, she had fallen in love with the work of Henri de Toulouse-Lautrec, a nineteenth-century French artist who drew and painted pictures of everyday people, not the wealthy class but common people. A little mental cartoon shot up in her head of two gossipy girls in dirty urchin outfits with large mouths and the letters *J* and *L* beneath them as her lips curled into a slight smile.

Tall and willowy, Allie, thirteen, was wise beyond her years. Since her father's death, she had felt like she needed to be an anchor for her mom, but also a watchful big sister to her little brother, SJ. When she smiled, her almond-shaped, green eyes crinkled into slits, "just like your dad's," her mom always told her. Her jet-black hair fell softly and hung below her jaw, with one side frequently slipping forward to cover her right eye.

When she thought about her dad, Allie's heart ached. She didn't understand why God had allowed this gaping hole in her life, but she rationalized it, believing he was too good for this world. He must be an angel now, watching over her. That thought gave her comfort.

Later, in PE, Allie found herself feeling again like an outsider. The girls had to pair up for a routine skills test, and everyone rushed to pair up with someone they already knew. That left Allie arbitrarily paired up with Grace, a skinny Black girl at least four inches taller than most of the other girls and an inch more than Allie.

"Must be tough, first week in a new school," Grace offered.

"Yeah, totally," Allie nodded. "It'll take forever to feel like I fit in here."

"Oh, not to worry," Grace smiled. "I've lived here all my life, and I still don't feel like I fit in!" And with that, Allie had a new friend. They laughed and headed off to take the skills test.

While Allie was hiding in her bed, at nearby Lake Bluff Elementary, SJ and his classmates were taking the President's National Physical Fitness test, which tested for strength, balance, flexibility, and speed. Even though SJ met part of the time in a classroom for kids with special needs, everyone competed when it came to this event. The fifth-grade boys lined up, toe to the line, as the starter's pistol erupted with a bang!

Several taller boys led off the pack at a quick pace. SJ could see at four hundred meters into the 1600-meter race that they were not going to be able to keep up with the pace they had set. He had always been the swiftest in the family—at just about any activity. Speed was his forte. When he was just a toddler, Allie had shortened Spencer Jonathan to his first and middle initials, SJ. His parents liked it, so it stuck. That was what everybody called him, except for teachers at the new school, who would read off the roster, "Spencer Jonathan Lee," after which he'd raise his hand and say, "Just call me SJ."

Ever since he was little, SJ had a funny habit of twirling a lock of his hair between his fingers. When Allie first asked him why he did that, he looked at her weirdly, as if to say, "What are you talking about? I'm not doing anything."

On another occasion, when she teased him about it, SJ told her it made him feel calm. After that, she never brought it up again. If it made her little bro feel happy, that was good enough for her.

Now running outside on the track, the wind ruffled his auburn curly hair, a trait from his mom, as he cranked up the pace and slipped ahead of the pack. Slim, but with strong, muscular legs, he had the perfect build for running. Three-quarters of the way around the track, SJ led by three meters, and by the end of the race, it was no contest. It was a record time for the school's fifth-graders. SJ threw up his arms to celebrate, adding a couple of happy dance moves to finish. Even though he squabbled with his sister over dumb stuff like most siblings, SJ could hardly wait to tell Allie about the race later.

Chapter 5

ALLIE

Allie was thankful her mom had let her stay home that day. As she lay in bed, she daydreamed about one of her favorite places to visit as a girl: her grandparents' home, her dad's parents. They lived in an outlying neighborhood of Chicago, so living in the East, she didn't get to visit them frequently, but when she did, they always took her to interesting places. The Art Institute on Michigan Avenue, with its famous Georges Seurat painting, A Sunday on La Grande Jatte, was one of her favorites. Another was the planetarium.

Her grandfather Lee, born in Taiwan, had met her grandma when she and a group from her Midwestern church had traveled to Taipei, the capital of Taiwan, on a mission trip. They were scheduled to stay for the summer to teach English to young Chinese adults and share the gospel. As it happened, her grandfather, who was trying to improve his English, turned up in Winona's class. He was immediately attracted to this charming young girl, with her chocolate-brown eyes and olive skin, reflective of her Native American heritage.

Her grandfather's Chinese name was Guangyuan, but after they migrated to the United States, his American name became Gordon. Winona was "Winnie" to all the family; Allie called her "Grammy." It was from this interesting blend of ethnicity on her father's side that Allie had inherited her straight black hair and slanted almond eyes, while it was from Winnie that she got her lightly olive-colored skin and artistic talent.

Winona, which means "first daughter," had displayed her artistic abilities as a young girl, taking a sketch pad with her most everywhere she went so she could record her observations. Usually, it was in pencil, but as she got older, she sometimes fiddled with pastels.

In college, she majored in art and discovered the joy of sculpting as well as the beauty, yet difficulty, of watercolors. Incredibly talented, Winnie exhibited her work at her university's art shows where fellow student, Elaine McAdams—whose goal in life was to write children's books—enlisted Winnie for her first project as a book illustrator. The matchup was fortuitous as they went on to watch several of their children's books published.

As much as Allie had inherited talent in the arts from her grandmother, she got a dose of her personality from her grandfather, who had passed his on to both her father and her. Like her dad, Allie had a stoic element embedded in her mentality along with a wry and sometimes sarcastic sense of humor.

"I wonder why girls are always expected to chit-chat about unimportant stuff," she once said to her dad. "I'd rather talk about the deeper things in life that touch my soul, like a rescue dog that needs adopting or feeding the birds in winter." Will looked into her eyes and said, "You keep being exactly who you are, Allie. You will find others along the way who appreciate you just as you are. There's no need for you to be anything other than that."

Her dad, William Gordon Lee, "Will," had more of his mom Winnie's sociable personality, with the humor woven into it, but as her father had often told her, Allie was the embodiment of her grandfather's persona. She used her words sparingly, but when Allie spoke, she always had something worthwhile to say. Her stoicism had helped her navigate her way through losing her dad, although it was something with which she still struggled. It also helped her with the move, being compelled to adjust to a completely different, less diverse community unlike transient northern Virginia, a veritable melting pot of cultures and nationalities. At its core, Lakeshores had a preponderance of families who had been there for decades, content with the familiarity of sameness.

It was no wonder Allie found Lakeshores a difficult environment to adjust to. It was imbued with cliques—middle schoolers who had hung out with the same friends since kindergarten—many who would not have been able to tell the difference between a Monet and a Picasso. Of course, Allie's personality didn't lend itself well to quickly making friends. In this area, she was more like her mother. She was reserved until she got to know someone better, which worked against her social acclimation, fueling her loneliness. But Allie was not one to sit and feel sorry for herself. She could easily escape into her imagination, occasionally daydreaming her way through a class. At home, her journal was her friend with whom she confided. She addressed each entry to her dad because he was the person she had always been able to share any of her thoughts with.

In third grade, for example, she had an entire fantasy story, which she wove while gazing out the window during the boring review sessions of math basics since she already knew the math by heart. In her imagination, she saw a gorgeous palomino stallion wander into the field next to the school building. It paused to munch on the tall grass and then kneeled and lay down to rest in the cool greenness. No one in the class noticed this development, so when the bell rang for recess, Allie dashed to be the first one out the door to slide onto the back of the stallion, and as her classmates shuffled outside, they gaped at her. Then the horse would rise and gallop off with Allie atop, holding tightly to its mane. The daydream was so real to Allie that during recess, she would gaze longingly, watching for her imaginary stallion to appear.

Since moving, Allie had begun a new project, a book she was writing accompanied by her own illustrations. On one of her visits to Grammy and Grandpa's, she had curled up in her favorite spot at their house, a cushioned window seat in the guest bedroom where she always stayed, and read *The Donkey and the Bluebird*, a fanciful McAdams-Lee book in the collection her Grammy had illustrated. That was the inspiration for her new endeavor. As she worked on the book, she tried to process some of the behavior she saw at her school and record her thoughts in her narrative.

She had never before experienced the insularity she found at Lakeshores MS— nor the outright bigotry. More than once she had overheard Jenna and Lola use the word "chink" when talking about her. She pretended not to have heard, but she felt they had purposely spoken loudly enough that she would. Similarly, she had seen and heard racist comments circulating on social media. Again, it tended to be a few—those among the popular crowd at Lakeshores who retweeted ridiculous rants about immigrants "invading" the country. It likely reflected the fact that the city's ethnic makeup had been gradually shifting over the past decade. But again, the authors were some of the children of old-line Lakeshores families. Allie felt it was a combination of ignorance and meanness.

Still in her PJs, Allie ambled downstairs. She heard her mom in the kitchen as the teapot whistled.

"Where do kids around here come up with these mean comments about people or groups they don't know anything about?" she complained.

"What d'ya mean?" her mom responded.

"Well, just now, I saw this girl from my school, Lola, post a selfie on Instagram. It was of her and the cheer squad at practice, with a thumbs up for their successful squad. She added, 'Let's set the tryout standards super-high so we can keep it that way!' And then she posted a photo right below that from tryouts today of four girls, three of them Latinos, and one kind of heavy, clearly body shaming them and inferring that these girls would not meet their standard. It just makes me sick to my stomach that she's so narrow-minded . . . and happy to shout it out on social media!"

Meg paused a moment.

"Well, it's an opportunity for you," she finally said.

"Opportunity?" Allie rolled her eyes.

"Yeah, an opportunity. An opportunity to demonstrate otherwise. A chance to show people that tolerance and grace toward others is what God intends, not divisive, hurtful behavior."

Allie shook her head and closed her eyes for a moment. Then, as she reflected on her early days at the new school, a tear escaped from the corner of her eye, sliding down her cheek.

Apparently spotting it, Meg asked, "Okay, what's really going on? Has someone been mean to you? You know I can't stand bullying or any kind of cruelty middle school girls are famous for. Man, when I think back on the girls I knew in seventh and eighth grade, how petty and hurtful they . . . well, all of us could be—it could bring me to tears. But you know, everyone was so insecure. Instead of trying to help each other through that phase, some kids would put down other girls just to make themselves feel better. But, when I look back, the few kids who were brave rejected that kind of behavior. I wish I could have been braver, but I was pretty quiet in those days."

Then Meg did something that surprised Allie. She grabbed her daughter's hand and said a quick prayer.

"Lord, God, I claim right now that your justice would prevail and that you would show Allie how to reflect your Light, your Truth, to those around her at the new school." Then, just as quickly, she let go of Allie's hand, gave her a hug, and headed off to her office.

That night, Allie updated her journal.

Hi Daddy,

I don't understand people who want everyone to be the same, who see beauty as only one way . . . who make fun of kids who are different. I call that boring!

Different can be exciting—the unknown waiting to be discovered. A painting with wild unexplained splotches of chartreuse and blue and yellow can be as enthralling as a perfectly structured real-life picture of wildflowers in a vase.

I'm going to ask God to please open my mind to the new people around me and open my heart to the possibilities of being a friend, even though I hate to make small talk! I promise I'll work at it.

Love,
Allie

Chapter 6

MeG

It was another school day, and Meg had plenty of work to do after she got Allie and SJ off to the bus. Back when they lived outside of Washington, DC, Meg had developed a thriving business, built around her communications and marketing skills. Writing had always come naturally to her, whether it was a business plan, a magazine article, a biographical profile, or a speech. Her talents were in demand in a city of policy wonks, elected officials, and oversized egos. It was an ideal career as she raised her kids because so much of the work could be done at home and on her schedule. She was a bit of a perfectionist, so if it meant staying up 'til 2 a.m., working on a speech to get it right, she did it.

Thus, when Meg launched the plan to move to North Carolina, she first talked to each of her clients to assure them there would be no lag in her work for them. With so much work being done remotely, no one cared exactly where her home office was located, as long as she continued to deliver the high-quality communications services she was known for. That work arrangement had become the norm during the pandemic a few years before. And with the kids a little older now, Meg figured if an occasional trip up to DC was required, it would not put much of a crimp on the family schedule.

"Rise and shine," she yelled into SJ's room as she stuck her head in the door and flipped on the light switch. Meg still habitually picked out a shirt from his dresser and left it on the chair. Today, she also left his underwear and slacks she had washed and folded last night before she went to sleep.

She heard Allie in the shower, so she headed back downstairs to make lunches. She insisted on sending healthy lunches for the kids instead of having them eat the school lunch. "Too much starch and sugar," she complained. "You need good brain food." That included lean turkey and Swiss cheese sandwiches, baggies of carrot and celery sticks, and a whole grain fruit bar of some sort. Unbeknownst to Meg, SJ usually threw out the veggie sticks at school in favor of chips from the vending machine.

Meg and Will were believers, people of faith. They had always brought Allie and SJ to the small church they belonged to back when they lived in Virginia. So now, without Will, she would need to find a church for her family in Lakeshores. Before turning to the article she was drafting for a magazine, Meg began searching on Google for churches a reasonable distance from their home. Doing all these things by herself without Will was hard. But Meg was someone who didn't give up easily. She would put her best efforts into helping her family feel like Lakeshores could be a welcoming place for them.

Chapter 7

New Friends

Showered, Allie threw on her outfit and headed out the door with SJ trailing behind. Allie shifted the heavy backpack on her back. She hated all the books she had to cart around, but it was better than the twenty-four-plus months of remote classes she'd had to live through during the pandemic. Real-live people were better than talking heads on a laptop screen. *I am thankful to God that we are on the other side of that nightmare,* she thought.

Allie frequently talked to God about everything in her life. But she had not talked to Him for more than a year after her dad's death. So many families in their church had prayed for Will when they found out about his cancer diagnosis. Allie felt she had prayed more than all of them. And yet . . . he still died. She had been angry with God for that long, painful stretch until, in a remarkable dream one night, an angel had spoken to her, telling Allie she would see her dad again one day. She felt something inside of her shift from this newfound sense of hope. Her art became more infused with light and a new sense of optimism. From that point forward, she resumed her conversations with God.

She picked up her bus at the same corner as her brother's; it arrived after SJ's. But she had always enjoyed that brief time in the morning to hang out with him and catch up. After school, they both had to do homework, and dinner was not a suitable time for brother-sister talk the way they liked to do when they were alone together.

They also laughed a lot at the silliest things, like the way their cat "hid" on top of SJ's bookshelf in plain sight. He would not move a muscle for fifteen minutes while he stared intensely at the terrarium bowl where SJ's pink-toed tarantula crawled. Thankfully, he kept a screen across the lid. Then Mr. Quiggle would go into stealth mode, climbing down onto the desk, and from there, onto the windowsill, thinking no one saw him. They would watch and giggle and then go back to their conversation.

Sometimes they did their own version of fitness routines, including one where Allie would lie on her back and balance SJ up in the air, with his stomach on her feet while he did rapid arm and leg movements. They measured how long they could do this with SJ's running watch; their longest record was 1:50—until they started giggling, causing Allie to wobble and SJ to leap off onto his feet.

A twenty-minute bus ride later, Allie was deposited in front of the sprawling, tan brick buildings that made up Lakeshores MS, along with the thirty-three other kids who rode her bus. She saw Ben Lopez in the distance and waved at him. He was easy to spot with his dark hair shaved with a distinctive pattern on the sides and some longer thicker hair on top tied in a ponytail. His bright purple backpack helped too. A few weeks ago, he had signed Allie on as an illustrator for *Aviso*. In the process, they had become friends. He was the only person who called her "Al."

It's because he treats me as an equal, she thought happily. *Like one of the guys.*

Ben had transferred in the year before when his family moved east from Texas, so he knew how hard it was to break into a new crowd in middle school. He hated cliques of any kind. The oldest of six kids, he was also good at handing out assignments. As editor of the paper, he championed equal treatment for all students, including expanding school awards to allow for more individuals to be recognized for a wide spectrum of achievements.

"For students who come from varied backgrounds, like where English is a second language, the school should find ways to recognize their achievements, such as an award for strong communication skills, an award for improved writing composition, an award for unique family history; those should be just a few examples to consider," he had written in a recent editorial, urging the school administration to consider ways to encourage more than just the usual students who earned top grades. It was a timely topic given the community's changing demographics—added to the established Caucasian families was a mix of African Americans, Asians, and a rising Hispanic population, along with segments of mixed race.

Allie was too far away for Ben to see her as the first bell rang. Thankfully, they were heading for the same class: Advanced Algebra I. As she got settled at her desk, she continued sketching an illustration she was working on for *Aviso*.

Allie's desk was in the second row along the left side of the classroom. As they waited for Mr. Lozano to arrive, Allie heard whispering behind and to the right of her. She glanced over her shoulder. Jenna was chatting it up with Lola and a large, slightly overweight boy who sometimes hung out with them. Then she saw they were pointing to a girl in the front row, Sophia. She was quiet, with long, coarse black hair, pink glasses, and sequined slip-ons that looked more like slippers than shoes. Despite the girls in the back gossiping about her in stage whispers, Sophia never looked back—not even once—nor did she flinch or indicate she was aware of what was going on.

Mr. Lozano strode in as the second bell rang. Tall, slim, with dark short hair, a prominent nose, and a touch of debonair about him, Mr. Lozano was universally considered by Lakeshores MS students to be one of the best teachers at the school. Even for kids who came in fearing mathematics, Lozano had a way of making it fun. He cracked jokes, told funny stories, mostly about himself or his kids, and recruited a lot of kids for Math Olympiad, a math contest geared to middle schoolers. But he was not a pushover. He checked homework every class just to see that it was done and demanded respect from his students. No talking was allowed while he was speaking to the class, and the room was to be left clean and tidy for the next incoming class.

"Stewart, I'd like you to start us out here by coming up to the board and solving a word problem," Mr. Lozano said, gesturing for Jenna's pudgy friend to come up to the front of the room. Stu ambled up, his jeans slung low on his hips to show off the Tom Ford label on his skivvies. "And I want everyone at the same time to try to solve the problem at your desk." While Stu worked the problem, Allie noticed Sophia had already finished and had put down her pencil.

"No, that doesn't look exactly right, Stu. Let's try redoing some calculations here; that looks a little bit off," Lozano said. While he was adjusting some of the figures on the board, Lola, who was sitting directly behind Sophia's desk, stretched her foot forward. Below each desk was a rack to set books or supplies, and when she had arrived, Sophia had set a stack of several heavy books on the rack. Smirking, Lola got the toe of her shoe far enough to push sideways the top two books, which went toppling to the floor to the right of Sophia's desk. Startled, she leaned forward to retrieve the books and set them back on the rack. One of her idiosyncrasies was that Sophia had to have everything in perfect order. She could not tolerate anything being in disarray, and of course, Lola had observed that and was using it to her advantage. Sophia turned in her seat to see who was behind her. Lola stared at the blackboard, pretending not to notice Sophia's penetrating stare.

"There," Mr. Lozano said. "Thanks for your work there, Stu. You were a little off, but thanks for being brave and coming up here." While Lozano chattered away, Lola snickered to Jenna about Sophia. Allie glanced over at them and shook her head in disgust. Just because Sophia was a little different in her looks and ways, these bullies, as Allie pigeon-holed them, were ganging up in a ridiculous display of juvenile, rude behavior. It reminded her of what her mom had said about middle school girls and their need to feel better about themselves by slighting others.

"Okay, class, let's focus!" Mr. Lozano quipped. "I'd like to cover several topics before we talk about this year's Math League at the end of class." He moved on to discuss inequalities, exponents, and radical and rational expressions at length, after which he assigned homework with examples of each for Thursday's class. With five minutes left, he turned to the topic of the Math League.

"This term, I'd like to see three-person teams compete against each other to determine who will go to the state, regional, and maybe even the national competition. We'll use the relatively friendly competition within our class to start the process," he explained. "And since this is the only advanced eighth-grade math class here at Lakeshores—and we have twelve of you in the class—I'd like you to create your four teams so we can launch the first round of competition next week."

Allie glanced around and saw Lola, Jenna, and Stu already signaling to each other. She also noticed Lola give her a glancing stare, then narrowing her eyes slightly at her with a frown. She saw Sophia turn slightly in her seat, squinting as if shielding her eyes. Allie waved at her and, pointing to herself, raised her eyebrows in question as if to say, "Wanna team up?" Sophia responded with a shy smile, nodding her head up and down. At the same moment, Ben, who happened to sit two seats back from Allie, hit her with a spit wad to get her attention. Allie looked back, surprised. She never expected him to want to team up with her since they were still getting to know each other. Little did she know, Ben had developed a bit of a crush on her, which, of course, he had not revealed. Guys were not given to talking about those kinds of things, especially not thirteen-year-old boys. He motioned, pointing to Allie and Sophia and back to himself, with a quizzical look, turning his head to the side. Allie gave him a quick thumbs up. He grinned back. Their team was set!

Chapter 8

Ataraxia

Present day (October): returning to Allie's otherworld adventure

As Allie trotted alongside the sheep family, made up of Graham, the ram; Molly, his wife; and Luke, their son, she noticed something fluttering ahead on the path, creating a sizable dust cloud. At first, she thought it was a small dog. But as they got closer, she realized it was a funny-looking bird that appeared to have injured its wing.

Molly gasped, "It's a vulture!"

Based on the little that Allie knew about the bird kingdom, it appeared to be a juvenile vulture. With its inability to use the injured wing, the unfortunate creature was spinning and sputtering around in the dirt. By the time they reached it, the bird was exhausted. It croaked as if trying to say something, but no words came out.

"Could I borrow your scarf?" Allie asked Molly, who had a scarf fashioned from vines and long clover stalks slung loosely on her back and shoulders.

Graham gave her a penetrating look.

"Vultures are the Overseers here," Graham said. "They are *not* our friends, and they might not take kindly to you even touching one of their children."

"But look at the pitiful thing," Allie said. "He's all tired out from trying to recover. There's no way he'll be able to fly anywhere for a while. He might die of thirst or exhaustion if we just leave him here like this!"

Molly leaned her head down so Allie could untie her scarf, and the resourceful girl managed to slip it under the worn-out fledgling while tying together the corners to create a sort of back sack.

"Don't you worry, Molly," Allie said. "I'll tend to him. Hopefully, with some water and rest, he can try out his wings later." Allie had a strong caretaker instinct within her that had led to numerous critter adoptions over the years. So tending to this scraggly vulture was natural.

A squawky voice emerged from the scarf.

"I hit a tree branch and hurt myself. I am so tired. Thank you for stopping to help me. My parents are going to be so worried about where I am."

"What's your name?" Allie asked, peering into the back sack at the homely bird.

"Kibou," the creature squawked. "What's yours?"

"Allie," she said. "Short for Alexandra. My brother could never say it when he was little. Allie was easy. Everyone calls me that now."

"We need to let the Heralders know," Graham said. "Those monkeys spread the news around our kingdoms. But we must make sure they know he's all right, just a minor injury. And that we'll care for him until the Overseers collect him."

In another half mile, the travelers came upon a station, a place with large boulder-sized rocks piled up and monkeys moving throughout the natural tunnels and crevices the rock formations created.

Graham beckoned a large chimpanzee over, one who seemed bolder than the rest as he stood on a huge rock overhead, his eyes scrutinizing the group before him.

"I have a message for the Overseers," Graham said. "We found one of their young ones on the road. He was unable to fly. B-b-but we're taking good care of him," he stammered, a hint of fear in his voice. "T-t-tell them to find Graham for his safe return."

The gray monkey nodded his head. "No problem, Mr. Graham. I'll share your message with my boss, Simon, when I see him, but I'm on an errand right now. I'll remember to tell him what you said."

The monkey, Devon, was a regular part of the Heralders squad, but his priorities always revolved around himself first, so he decided he would try to get word to Simon by the next day. Today, Devon was on his way to a mango grove he had discovered—one with the lushest, most delicious fruit he had ever tasted . . . not to mention that the last time he was there, a cute girl chimp had playfully thrown a mango at him. He wanted to have a mango feast, but he also wanted to see if his mango-tossing friend might show up again.

Having shared their message with Devon, Graham, Molly, Luke, Allie, and their little back sack friend tootled on down the path toward the meeting place.

Ahead, a small herd of deer merged onto the path from the woods. All five were heading in the same direction, which included a buck, two does, and two juvenile deer with spots still fading from their rumps. Further in the distance, Allie thought she could make out two rabbits hopping along, all on the same path they were on.

"We haven't seen anyone in your world for a long time, Allie," the ram said as they walked together. "When I saw you, I felt in my heart that we needed you here with us. I'm not even sure why, but that's why I called you. We are facing serious issues here in our kingdom, and your steady spirit of calm strength is something we need. That's why I called out to you and invited you to join us in Ataraxia. We are pleased that you are here with us."

Allie nodded her head as she listened, feeling curious and yet strangely exhilarated. But how did this stately creature know about her, never mind his positive view of her character? She had no sense of how her presence might be a help, but she waited to see how events would unfold.

On either side of the path, Allie saw a rocky, cavernous terrain with an occasional monkey popping its head out of the rocks to watch the group pass by.

Graham pointed to a natural shelter created by hedges and vines overhead, which they were rapidly approaching. "That's a wayfarer's station," he said. "Remember, Molly, that's where we stopped last month when we came this way to bring your sister those healing herbs," he said.

"Let's stop for a short rest, puh-leeze, Graham?" Molly pleaded. "I just *have* to rest these tired feet." Slim legs supported Molly's considerably plump girth. Graham nodded in assent, so the group moseyed over. In the middle of the protected structure were hay and grasses indented by others who had paused here over the weeks. Molly plopped down with a sigh. Luke pranced over to a grassy spot for a snack, kicking up his heels on the way. Not yet a year old, he had a lot of energy to burn. Allie took a seat on a boulder that sat right outside the shelter while she set her back sack down and untied the scarf to check on the little vulture.

"Oh my, it was dark in there!" Kibou exclaimed. He fluttered around in the hay, still unable to raise one of his wings, which was tucked close against his side. Allie saw a creek in the woods nearby. Glancing inside the shelter, she saw a giant hollowed gourd, which she grabbed up and ran over to the creek, lowering it into the cool water until it was nearly full. She carried it back to the porch, offering some first to Molly and then set it down on a low, flat stone so the little vulture could drink to his heart's content.

Gurgle, gurgle, glug. He stuck his beak in the gourd, guzzling, then throwing his head back repeatedly until he had quenched his thirst.

"That's good; that's good. Now what's there to eat?" he asked, scanning the area where they had stopped.

It didn't take long for Kibou to spot his lunch. A family of moles lived nearby. They had dug below the ground a sizable home with several rooms. Out of a recent litter, one tiny mole had been too weak to survive. The family brought it outside in the sun in hopes it might revive. Now its body lay in the shade where it had taken its last breath that morning. The timing was perfect for Kibou, who quickly consumed the small carrion and then nestled down on the scarf for a short nap.

Refreshed from their stop at the rest station, Graham, Molly, Luke, Allie, and Kibou—back in the back sack—set off for the meeting. Allie could tell from Graham's impatience with Molly that he was nervous about reaching their destination. The sky, while it was still the middle of the day, had darkened slightly as clouds skittered in and out of the grayish-blue expanse, beckoning the small group to hurry. As they rounded a sharp curve in the path, Allie saw a sight unlike any she had ever seen: a sweeping amphitheater hewn in rocky cliffs by nature's forces. Covering the slabs of rock that edged the arena were animals of varied species gathered in groups, heads together and murmuring, the result being a dull cacophony that echoed off the rocks.

"Yes, that's it." Graham motioned to Allie. "L-l-let's see who all has arrived."

The path on which they had been traveling had grown wider but now narrowed slightly as it led directly into the main entryway of the arena. Allie's eyes widened, taking in the sight of rabbits, deer, tigers, raccoons, squirrels, a colony of beavers . . . all filing into the amphitheater. Overhead she saw bluebirds, doves, cardinals, a pair of blue herons, warblers . . . all fluttering and then settling on ledges around the semi-circular theater.

It seemed Graham was right; every possible member of this kingdom was arriving for the meeting. She thought this must be how God had originally created the creatures: to live in harmony with each other. A verse from the Bible, from the book of Isaiah, came to her mind—one that her mom had taped on the wall in her office:

The wolf will live with the lamb,
The leopard will lie down with the goat,
the calf and the lion and the yearling together;
And a little child will lead them (Isaiah 11:6).

At the center of the arena, several huge boulders leaned against each other. A few oxen had pushed one of the boulders so that it lay across the others, creating a dais. Allie was curious to know what Graham would have to say or what the meeting was being held for, but she figured she was about to find out.

Chapter 9

THE GUARDIANS

S olomon banged the gavel for the meeting to begin. Allie looked up startled at
the noise, but also at the tremendous size of the owl who had swooped from
a high ledge to alight upon the podium. As he waved his majestic wings to
quiet the noisy chattering, she thought they must stretch at least seven feet wide—
the largest owl she had ever seen in her life, including the great horned owl she
remembered seeing once at the zoo.

Solomon was the oldest and wisest member of the kingdom, according to
Molly. His large black and dark-gray head was streaked with pale gray feathers,
revealing his senior status.

"We're here today to discuss a grave issue," Solomon said, "emanating from the
dark kingdom of Malvelnia. The Overseers, led by King Wendigo, have announced
a new system they plan to put in place whereby each one of us in Ataraxia will have
a number, a way to classify us. If you remember back to the Days of Fear, we had
to take extreme measures to force the Overseers to stop attacking our young. That
is when you unanimously gave us the name 'The Guardians.' Implicit in that was
our Council's commitment to watch over the well-being of our community. Yes,
we were ultimately successful in getting the Overseers to amend their ways, but it
was costly," Solomon said, shaking his head as he looked downward. "Very costly."

Allie surveyed the rocky arena and saw animals and birds alike nodding their
heads in agreement. She noticed tears in many eyes, and turning her head to Molly
next to her, saw the same emotion: a look of grief with a teardrop emerging from

the corner of her eye, now rolling down her furry cheek. She could tell this other kingdom, Malvelnia, had some power over Ataraxia. But why, she wasn't sure.

"Out of that conflict emerged the system of the monkeys serving as Heralders, messengers to inform the Overseers of the locations of our dead. We also agreed to provide them with a certain volume of other food sources so we would never again experience the heartbreak they caused in those days," Solomon said. "Now, this has worked reasonably well; I think most of us would agree. Yet it is not free of heart-ache, and it does not mean the threat no longer exists. We were just able to mute it.

"But now," he continued, "I fear this system to classify each one of us will be used against us, perhaps to turn us against each other or to infiltrate our lives in new and dangerous ways. I've asked Graham, one of our elected leaders, to share his thoughts about this measure," he said, looking up and nodding at the ram. "Graham, if you could come forward at this time."

Graham looked particularly elegant, Allie thought, as he stepped forward to the platform and turned to address the crowd. A stately figure, he spoke with a con-vincing tone of authority. Yet she could tell the widespread respect among his lis-teners was because of his humble spirit.

"F-f-friends and neighbors," he began. "Solomon, as always, has w-w-words of wisdom for us today. We have all lived here together enough years to recognize the Overseers are plotting something. While w-w-we don't know fully what that is, but certainly, any change in the rules of the kingdoms has implications for every one of us. In this case, creating a more robust system to keep track of each of us, our families, our locations—sounds extremely w-w-worrisome, indeed.

"You elected me as a member of the Council of Ataraxia to help watch over your safety and security and to never let us fall back into the b-b-barbaric ways that existed during the Days of Fear. Today, I believe we are facing a new threat. We must have a plan of action and a w-w-way to convince the Overseers they are moving in the wrong direction," Graham said, shaking his head back and forth to underscore that thought. "We prefer harmony to conflict. Unfortunately, Mal-velnia prefers conquest over cooperation. We must show them Ataraxia's spirit of peacefulness is not a sign of weakness.

"To d-d-do that, I'm going to invite one of the most prominent members of our governing Council to speak to you. Zion, please join me here," he said nodding in the direction of a stately tiger with piercing blue eyes who was already making his way forward to join Graham.

As Allie watched, the dynamics confirmed her earlier thoughts. Clearly, in this kingdom, the creatures were far advanced from the society she knew where owls, sheep, and tigers would never stand peacefully next to each other. Here, it seemed predators were a thing of the past. Yet the overwhelming fear of the Overseers she felt rippling throughout the amphitheater belied that notion. Two different powers were in play, and she could feel the tension of their conflicting designs.

"Recently, the Heralders called on each of us who serve on this Council," Zion said. "Their purpose was to deliver a decree from the Overseers, a decree that requires all of us to be assigned and marked—branded—with a number. They say it is to help leaders of Malvelnia monitor all the activity throughout the land. However, as Graham said, we have great trepidation about this message. To make matters worse, they are urging anyone aware of resistance to the decree to report that member to the Heralders. And those who willingly step forward to obey will be rewarded.

"Such a system is clearly designed to turn us against one another," Zion continued, his voice rising in anger. "We must make a unified stand against this outrage. I propose all members of the Council meet to discuss a strategy before paying a visit to Mount Kukulkan to present our opposition to this decree. And we must discuss alternate ideas should we fail in our quest to squash this unreasonable decree." With that, Zion leaped gracefully down from the dais to let Graham continue the meeting.

"We agree," shouted several skunks in unison. An older one in the group nodded. "Yes, members of the Guardians' Council need to go there right away," he shouted, "to let them know we will not comply!"

"Yes, take action immediately," a gazelle called out.

"Take action now," others repeated.

"Put a halt to this intimidation," a large hyena chimed in. "Stop them; stop them now!"

The chant caught on and voices rang out in unison: "Stop them, stop them now! Stop them, stop them now!" The chanting continued until Solomon raised one wing, motioning for silence.

"Is there anyone o-o-opposed to this course of action?" Graham asked in his best and loudest voice as he looked out over the multitude. Silence ensued for a moment; no one signaled dissension.

"We are in agreement then," he stated. "In the meantime, I urge all of you to resist any efforts by the Overseers to launch this system. We will reconvene soon to inform you of the results of our meeting. I'd like to ask members of the Council to join me in the corner of the big rocks so we can discuss our next steps."

With that, Solomon adjourned the meeting. As the crowd dispersed, no one noticed a slithering movement and the two dark shadows on the ground sliding hastily away from the amphitheater.

Chapter 10

DELILAH

A few months earlier, the origins of the lamb

Molly lay on her side, breathing with heavy sighs in a bed of hay and leaves. She had been in labor for several hours and was nowhere near delivering her baby. Big brother Luke's arrival had been surprisingly easy, a sturdy lamb who was a welcome first addition to Graham and Molly's family.

Graham nuzzled Molly, feeling helpless. She groaned and tried pushing again, with no success. Sweat poured down her face. Between stretches of pushing, she paused, closing her eyes to rest.

Several hours later, she was finally able to deliver the lamb. Undersized, the lamb appeared lifeless. Molly licked her over and over, hoping to revive her. She had already selected a name for the fragile creature: Delilah. The tiny lamb had a distinct mark, a swirling, perfectly round whorl on her forehead that created a clockwise circle in her snowy white coat.

"Delilah, please take a breath, for me, for your mom," Molly said. But the body lay still.

Luke huddled close to his father, not fully understanding the cruelties that life can bring.

As was the case throughout the kingdom, the Heralders quickly heard the news. In a world where the Overseers had appointed the monkeys as their chief channel of communications, the Heralders maintained a grasp on what transpired in every corner. Word spread that Graham and Molly's newborn might not have survived. For the Heralders, this was the kind of rumor around which they sprang into action. One of their number, Simon, a particularly tall, reddish-brown orangutan, his once vivid coat now graying and covered with hairless patches because of battle scars, headed to Graham and Molly's shelter.

Molly continued licking the tiny lamb without success. She bleated soulfully to Graham.

"Our baby did not make it," she wept. "I cannot bring her to life."

"Oh dear, it can't be." Graham nuzzled Molly gently. "Try to rest, dear Molly," he soothed. "You need to sleep now." Exhausted, Molly, her heart heavy, let her drooping eyelids close. She fell into a fitful sleep. Graham quietly pulled palm leaves over the tiny lifeless body of their daughter.

When Graham saw Simon's stark silhouette from a distance, he felt a tightening in his throat. A tear escaped from the corner of his eye. He knew the reason for the messenger's visit.

Simon issued a perfunctory greeting to Graham and peered into their abode. Molly had awakened but continued her soulful mourning as she lay on her side. He heard Molly as she cried, "My poor Delilah, my poor baby lamb." Simon saw the small, motionless bundle in the corner. A few minutes later, Graham, with a grim look on his face, followed Simon as the Heralder departed the sorrow-filled space with the small lamb's body, still wrapped in palm leaves. Then, tipping his head to the side in acknowledgment, Simon placed the body in a dirty sack he had brought with him and left.

Simon, along with other monkeys, was in charge of delivering the dead bodies of Ataraxia's departed to the vultures, part of an unsavory agreement the vultures had forged years ago. The dead were delivered to Mt. Kukulkan where the royal family and their vulture team decided which vultures deserved which deliveries for future meals.

As he loped away, there was a faint stirring, unnoticed, from the bundle he carried.

Chapter 11

THE AGREEMENT

Present time in Ataraxia

Allie, Molly, and Luke waited patiently while Graham and the twelve other members of the Council discussed their plans to meet the Overseers at their headquarters. Such meetings had been arranged in past years, but this one was particularly urgent, given the decree issued and the unanimity among the kingdom to defy it.

The central base of the Overseers was located on Mt. Kukulkan, a plateau-like section of mountainous terrain, which made it a great lookout point for the vultures and their allies. Its geographic location, with a huge sea located just beyond the mountains, was such that much of the year it was dark, cloudy, and damp. That, along with the unyielding style of the Overseers, had earned their region its foreboding name, Malvelnia.

"I don't understand," Allie said. "What did they mean by the Days of Fear?" She examined Molly's gentle face, which had assumed a pained expression as soon as Allie uttered the phrase.

"It is a time that none of us like to speak of." Molly grimaced. "In those days, the vultures roamed the lands in search of weak members of our kingdom—the old, the sickly, or those who were injured. No one was safe. Those dear to us could be grabbed, taken away, and devoured by those heartless creatures. Every family has a story. We all felt the most unimaginable fear living in those times.

"That's when the Council was formed, the one meeting as we speak," she said. "The fear, the panic, the sorrow was so great that the Council declared war on the Overseers. No longer, they agreed, could these cruel masters inflict such pain on our families. That's what led the Council to be called the Guardians—because they felt they had to guard and protect the rights of the many creatures who had been living harmoniously until those frightful days."

"You must have had some success, right?" Allie asked. "After all, you have some powerful creatures among your Council . . . tigers, hyenas, oxen!"

"You would think so," Molly said. "But those vultures had quietly been securing support from those who could really hurt us. Alligators, constrictors, pythons . . . every kind of slithering serpent and roguish reptile joined them. And then, as you already know, the monkeys saw the chance for a key role that might earn them some rewards from the Overseers as their mercenary messengers! Some of the meaner, mutant members of the insect kingdom have also helped maintain a horrible place we try not to speak of," she said, referring to the Abyss without naming it.

Allie nodded, wondering where the lions were in all of this. She had not seen any lion at the summit and none at the Council meeting, so she asked Molly about it.

"Unfortunately, the lions choose to remain neutral," Molly said. "They are strong enough to look out for their own, so they choose not to raise the ire of the Overseers. They've let everyone know they will not take part in any conflict or pick sides.

"A horrific battle was launched after seven families lost loved ones in a single day, all snatched away by the Overseers. It was horrible, calamitous! The Guardians tried to use a strategy built around the different strengths and capabilities of our warriors. The Overseers used the serpents for stealth attacks and the monkeys for constant updates. They consider the monkeys to be carriers of the truth. We view them as messengers of doom with their own self-serving agendas. Their largest fighters, the crocodiles and the constrictors, brought brute force, but our warriors took out many of their numbers.

"As the toll of lives continued daily, the Overseers called for a meeting during a truce that both sides had sought," Molly explained. "The Council stood up to them and did not back down. Graham and the others insisted the attacks on the most vulnerable in our herds must end! They argued back and forth for days. Finally, Solomon was able to broker an agreement: the vultures would no longer attack us if we would agree to turn over a portion of the grain and fruits from our fields and our dead to them."

Molly shuddered at that final thought, something that still haunted her whenever she thought of her tiny daughter who had not survived. Allie put her arm around Molly and hugged her. She had only known this sweet creature for a brief time, but she loved her kind and gentle spirit.

Then they heard the Council meeting end, and Graham headed over to tell them their plans.

Chapter 12

THE PLAN

A s she stood watching the meeting, Allie shifted her gaze around the interesting group that made up the Council. She saw it comprised thirteen members, a number chosen, Graham later told her, to prevent any tie when voting on critical matters. Three of them Allie already had heard speak at the meeting: Solomon, the most senior member, Graham, and Zion. The other ten included Lucius, a huge and muscular ox; Eleanor (known as Ellie), a shy, cream-colored deer; Albert, a sly and entertaining hyena; Moriah, a graceful white dove; Helen, a bushy-haired fox with striking white, orange, and black streaks, which she enjoyed displaying; Orion, a regal skunk; Jake, a tall, skinny, gangly-looking wolf; Lilly, a handsome yet fierce honey badger; a beautiful gazelle named Aurora; and Kodiak, a friendly and talkative bear. The members of the group could not have been more different, but because of that, their strengths and weaknesses complemented each other. Allie listened as they developed their plan.

"It's clear the true agenda of the Overseers with this number system is to exert their control over our kingdom," Jake muttered, shaking his stringy tail. "Especially because they could try to turn us against each other through the fear and uncertainty such a system would produce!"

"How do you foresee that?" asked Ellie. "Perhaps it's just information they want."

"Yeah, information they'll use to heighten their power and advantage over us," Kodiak said. "I heard those monkeys chattering about it. They could not be happier because, as messengers, it will make them more important to the Overseers. It will make it that much easier to report on us, putting our families in danger."

Zion nodded his graceful head. "I agree. Rather than allow this idea to develop any further, we need to meet with them to see if we can nip it in the quick of the feathers." He paused and scanned the eyes of the members of the Council.

Allie thought Kodiak was right. The system the Overseers wanted to put in place would impose a threatening control over Ataraxia. She hoped Zion would urge them to take swift action to resist it.

"However, if there is no willingness by the Overseers to back down and abandon this idea," Zion continued, "we need to have a plan in place. I recommend we be ready with a surprise attack. They will not expect that from us because we have always been so tolerant and peaceful. But today is a different day. It feels like we are on the verge of changes that could shake our world. Instead, we need to shake theirs!" Zion saw his words were met with approval as heads nodded.

Allie was surprised to hear the dove, Moriah, who appeared to have a gentle nature, speak up quickly. "I am ready for our winged group to provide surveillance and gather intelligence to help the cause. I remember the terror of the Days of Fear! Never again!"

As Allie listened, Moriah set the plan for a contingent of doves and catbirds to make numerous "stealth" flights over known habitats of the Overseers. Secretly, they would keep track of the numbers at each location, from the crocs and boas in the Idigna River region to the monkey caves and vulture centurions around Mt. Kukulkan. Each day, they would return to update the Council members so the Guardians could fine-tune their plan.

She heard them agree that Solomon, Graham, and Zion would call for a meeting with the Overseers. Simultaneously, the Council outlined a plan for a stealth attack should the meeting fail. Their goal would be to take Mt. Kukulkan by surprise, subdue the leaders, and compel them to abandon their goal of subjecting the Ataraxians to being marked and numbered. This attack would not be easy, but Allie could tell they were wisely devising a strategy based on the variable strengths of each group within their kingdom.

Knowing the snakes and serpent allies added strength to the Overseers, Solomon proposed that one of their ranks—the honey badgers—form a frontline attack on the snakes. Honey badgers, fearless despite their modest size, were renowned throughout the kingdom for their ability to take out snakes five times their size with their shrewd battle tactics and sharp teeth.

They would be positioned on the edge of the Idigna River Valley. No one fully knew the number or size of the serpents, but the hope was the winged contingent could gather helpful specifics to empower their attack.

Solomon directed the hyenas to surround the monkey caves to wait for the attack signal. Simultaneously, he directed, honey badgers would be at the front, followed by the leopards and oxen, who would head for the Idigna's riverbanks, while the skunks, wolves, and tigers would prepare to climb Mount Kukulkan, where the trees on the huge plateau were home to the royal vulture family and the Malvelnian's inner circle.

Chapter 13

The Plan Takes Form

Moriah and her winged posse sailed noiselessly over the caves of the monkeys, the swamp, and the Idigna River Valley. As they traveled, they made note of the number of Overseers they could spot. With tall grasses in certain areas, shrubs, and trees, it was especially difficult to spot snakes, whether black snakes, boas, pythons, or other species. It became easier as they soared over the dryer plains, out of which sprang the unique plateau known as Mount Kukulkan. It was not really a mountain, but because of its strange geographical protuberance, it was considered among the animals to be a mountain.

As they continued west, they noticed a gathering at the farthest side of the plateau, near an altar that had been erected from rocks and stones in honor of King Wendigo. Here, the doves could see the king and Eris, his wife, and various leaders from the ranks of the Overseers holding some sort of summit—an important one by the looks of things—as representatives of all breeds of Overseers appeared to be consulting with the royal couple. In number, Moriah could make out about fifty, but as they circled higher in the air to avoid being spotted, she noticed hundreds of snakes slithering up the east side of Kukulkan. Crocodiles clambered up behind them, while a sizable group of monkeys, gorillas, and orangutans held court from a rocky cliffside near the altar.

Little did the Guardians realize, but two well-camouflaged snakes had been privy to their Council meeting at the amphitheater the day before. This summit was in reaction to that. Wendigo had already received a message from one of the Heralders that Zion, Solomon, and Graham from the Guardians' Council wanted to meet with him. But he was sly enough to know that when they found out the Overseers were not going to back down from the decree, a challenge would follow.

"Thank you for gathering here today!" boomed Wendigo. "The Kingdom of Malvelnia welcomes you, and I, Wendigo, along with my beautiful wife Eris, are delighted at this impressive turnout."

Plumping out her full plumage while displaying her formidable talons, Eris nodded her sleek, bald head in agreement with her husband. While she was not as gargantuan in size as Wendigo, her piercing expression, along with her razor-sharp talons, struck a note of awe (as well as fear) in the crowd as they listened.

However, "beautiful," the term Wendigo used to describe his wife, was quite a stretch given the homely appearance of vultures. Typical of the breed, their large bulky bodies, featherless heads, and hunched shoulders might defy the term "attractive" to observers. Some vultures, like Wendigo himself, were huge, with wingspans of as much as ten feet. Wendigo's face was a pinkish-red color with large folds of puckery skin hanging from the sides of his bare head. His large black beak was strong and heavy for tearing hide, muscle, and even bone.

"I think, perhaps, this is by far the largest crowd that has ever gathered on Kukulkan," he screeched proudly. "But I should not be surprised. I do not call upon you often, but all credit to the Heralders for spreading the message swiftly of the need for this summit.

"Here's the issue: we are expecting members of the Guardians' Council to arrive in a short while to ask us to put aside our decree requiring all of them to be marked with a number so we can get a sense of the size of the population east of the Idigna River. We all inhabit this world, and all must contribute to our well-being.

"Lately, the Guardian ranks have not done that," he snorted. "They are focused on their concerns and are not living up to their place in this land. That rankles me. We need more workers to support the goals of this kingdom! Those mongrels and renegades have done nothing. That is why I am committed to putting this numeric system in place. Once we have a sense of the numbers and breeds available to us, we can figure out how to best engage these assets." The king spoke possessively of Ataraxia, although for years, it had existed as an autonomous kingdom, overseeing its affairs.

A murmur of approval rose from the crowd. The leader among the crocodiles, Diego, opened his jaws wide in roaring accord. "Enlist me to enlighten those peons," he said. "I know I can persuade them to cooperate." To underscore his statement, Diego flipped his gigantic, armored tail back and forth.

47

"What do you think, Simon? Are you ready to move your group into action?" Wendigo boomed.

"Absolutely, your majesty." The orangutan bowed obsequiously. "The Heralders will play an indispensable role in this ambitious plan," he shouted to Wendigo and the others near the front of the gathering. "Once the branding tool is ready, we will make sure every family east of the river and the caves are counted and marked! Of that you can be sure—yes, you can be sure," he repeated as he rubbed his leathery hands together in anticipation.

But Wendigo and his crew incorrectly assumed that the peace-loving nature of Ataraxia meant they would accept such an invasive directive.

Chapter 14

THE MEETING

Zion and Graham made their way up the trail to Mt. Kukulkan. They had already agreed they would treat King Wendigo respectfully. But they would remain firm in their message: the Ataraxians would not agree to the system Wendigo was proposing. The Council had been unanimous. Zion shook his regal head as Graham chattered.

"But w-w-what will we do if Wendigo rejects our message outright? How will we respond?" Graham said with a hint of fear in his voice.

"Graham, my friend, our mission is to represent the feelings and position of our community. There's no room to back down, but as fellow Councilmember Orion insisted, we need to look for ways to forge a peaceful solution to this untenable decree."

Zion spoke with authority, yet Graham knew at heart: this creature, gracefully powerful as he tramped alongside the ram, was merciful. He recalled years ago when the rambunctious son of a Heralder, Marvin, had ventured into the grasslands of Ataraxia, running and chasing after one of Zion's cubs. Zion, who was nearby, heard the cub racing back to his mom, Athena.

He could have taken out Marvin with one strike of his powerful paws, subdued and killed him for the threat to his family. But instead, Zion confronted Marvin, scolded him, and then, with a roar, chased him back toward the caves from which Marvin had strayed. Now an adult, the once mischievous Marvin maintained respect for the clan of tigers that roamed the grasslands, not forgetting that act of mercy.

As the pair reached the top of the plateau, they saw Wendigo's elaborate tree palace in the distance. It was an impressive structure. Hundreds of vultures had joined in the construction of the sprawling center of power, which, because of gigantic banyan trees in that section of the plateau, enabled them to build a massive entry room that led to a series of living areas, including Wendigo and Eris's throne room, elaborately decorated with colorful tapestries woven from plant fibers and colorful, mineral-laden stones that glinted with every hue of the rainbow in the sunlight. Thousands of branches and twigs had been flown in by his loyal winged subjects to create the palace from which Wendigo and Eris reigned.

As they neared the entrance, they heard fluttering above, looking up just in time to see Solomon arriving. The three had agreed to meet there when the sun reached its highest point. At the entryway, they were met by Simon.

"Gentlemen," he said, "King Wendigo will meet you at his meeting place in the rocks. It's just a short distance to the east. Follow me." With that, the long-limbed orangutan scampered ahead of them, occasionally glancing back to make sure they were following him. Solomon sailed above, spotting the rocky area ahead where he could see the Malvelnian leader and a wake of vultures spread throughout the craggy rocks, peering out toward the arriving visitors.

"King Wendigo," Zion said, giving a slight bow of his head as he stood before the giant vulture.

"Th-th-thank you for agreeing to this m-m-meeting," Graham stammered.

Solomon, who had sailed into the rocky enclave as Zion bowed, positioned himself on a flat boulder closest to where Zion and Graham stood.

"Please, make yourselves comfortable," Wendigo grunted. "I've asked these members of my royal entourage to be present as witnesses to our meeting. I understand the Ataraxian Council met and you are here to deliver feedback to the decree that I have issued?"

"Yes, you are quite right in your understanding," Zion said. Graham thought Zion's voice had a booming timbre that gave added authority to his message. "As you know, our Council speaks on behalf of all the residents of Ataraxia. Ours is a peaceful land, one built on mutual trust among our citizens and a council that addresses troubles or disagreements within our community. In that way, we are able to maintain harmony despite physical differences, from inhabitants of the grasslands to the pastures to the forests." Solomon nodded in solid agreement, interjecting his concurrence.

"When we received word of your decree from the Heralders, we were surprised. I might even say shocked! Following the violence of the Days of Fear, we believe the truce that was forged serves the needs of Malvelnia while minimizing the cost to Ataraxia. It has been a workable solution. We've respected the boundaries of Malvelnia. To my knowledge, we have never attacked or abused any of your subjects. On the contrary, as agreed, we have provided you with carrion and other sustenance from our lands.

"But now, you have proposed something unacceptable. Our Council was unanimous in rejecting this proposed system to count every Ataraxian, which would require, in your words, 'a branding of every citizen.' We have acted in good faith to provide benefits to our Malvelnian neighbors. But this! It is not going to happen."

Standing beside Zion, Graham was nodding his head up and down, but as he watched King Wendigo's face, he saw a look of scorn developing that caused him to shiver. Zion saw it too and stepped forward as if to counter that shadow of disagreement he saw building on the vulture's countenance.

"I see," Wendigo snarled. "But I must insist on the enforcement of my decree. You see, just as you have met with your councilmembers, I have met with my inner circle. We all agreed that Ataraxia is not contributing to the well-being of our world. Yes, you honor that agreement you mention, but your citizens prosper from Malvelnia's willingness to generously allow you to reside in some of the most fruitful lands. Why should we continue to do that?" he said, shrugging his huge gray shoulders and spreading out his wings to their full ten-foot breadth to accentuate his question.

"If you refuse to take this message back to your citizens, we will be forced to detain you!" Wendigo shouted. "On the other hand," his voice softened into velvety coddling, "you could lead the way and demonstrate ease in complying with our request. Make yourselves an example by allowing us to brand you and then return home to show how easy it can be to accommodate this modest decree. It's that simple, and it won't hurt at all," he lied.

Simon hopped up and down in anticipation during Wendigo's response. The king had appointed the Heralders as the crew who would enforce the branding process, and as their chief, Simon would be in charge. He had been working on the branding tool.

Using minerals gathered from the ground, the monkeys had been able to heat them over a fire and create bands that would be placed around the legs of any flying creatures, each marked with a unique number. For the larger animals, the monkeys would shape the minerals while hot into a unique number symbol. They would heat it before applying the the symbol to each Ataraxian's hide. Throughout the process, the Heralders would oversee the recording of every citizen, assigning them a number as they did.

Despite quivering in his hooves, Graham spoke first.

"Ah-ah-absolutely not, King Wendigo. With all due respect, we cannot do such a thing. You h-h-heard our council's response. We can neither agree to the branding nor tell our citizens to comply."

"Graham is correct," Solomon agreed. "We must find another course of action that might satisfy Malvelnia. But we ask you sincerely to cast aside this misguided decree. There's plenty of time to find a compromise."

"I agree with my colleagues," Zion said. "We ask for a period of consideration while both kingdoms discuss an alternate plan."

"At this time, we request that the decree be put on hold," Solomon said. "We will return to Ataraxia with a plan to meet again following the next full moon."

No sooner had Solomon uttered those words when the three saw hundreds of wings hover menacingly above them and heard loud slithering noises. A torrent of snakes swirled around, over and under their feet, and as Zion and Graham fell over on their sides, huge ropes woven over weeks of work by the monkeys were wrapped around their necks and bodies, tethering them tightly to boulders. Simultaneously, a cloud of vultures dropped a net from their talons—also the handiwork of the monkeys—over Solomon's stately body, preventing him from using his wings to escape.

Before the meeting was ever held, King Wendigo had already prepared for this capture, knowing it would send an immediate signal back to Ataraxia that it was futile to rebel against his decree. Contrary to Solomon's words, the branding *was* going to happen. Simon and his crew would make sure every citizen of the tranquil kingdom knew it was only a matter of time. And they would begin by branding these three Guardians to show Ataraxia what was in store for them all.

A team of Heralders led by Simon gathered around Zion, Graham, and Solomon to taunt them, chattering, pointing, and jeering at the trio.

"Be brave, friends," Graham shouted to Zion and Solomon. "This too shall pass." He had often whispered this to himself over the years whenever he faced difficult trials. Now, he spoke it to encourage his friends despite the bleakness of the situation.

Nearby, within the meeting place, was a partial cave in front of which was a barrier. They dragged the three prisoners there to be guarded by Diego and two other crocodiles. Diego snapped his jaws ominously, a warning to the prisoners about what would happen should they try to escape.

Moriah and her surveillance party had heard the commotion earlier. Flying at a remarkable height, they had spotted Wendigo's evil capture of the leaders of Ataraxia. Already, they had turned and were heading at top speed to report the developments to Albert and Lilly, two of the councilmembers who lived close to the Idigna River and, thus, were first in the path of their return flight.

"Despite the promise of a safe meeting for the exchange of ideas between the two kingdoms, Wendigo has broken his word," Moriah blurted out. "Our brave leaders have been captured and are being held at the far side of Mt. Kukulkan, guarded by none other than that frightening character, Diego! What should we do? Oh my, what *should* we do?"

"The first thing we must do is let the other councilmembers know. What Wendigo has done is beyond reason! We will have to move up our plans," Albert said, referring to the large-scale battle plan the members had drawn up before deciding to seek the meeting with Malvelnia.

"Agreed," echoed Lilly. "Moriah, you go on to alert the others. Tell them we need to meet immediately at the grove by the amphitheater where we have met before. Tell them to get there as fast as they can! The first priority will be freeing our Council leaders. Then we will launch the attack for which we have already been preparing."

With that, Moriah and the doves flew on to alert each member of the Guardians' Council, while Lily and Albert discussed a stealth mission to free Zion, Graham, and Solomon.

Chapter 15

SJ

There was no doubt in Allie's mind: SJ was brilliant. She remembered when he was two years old, SJ was already reading and trying to write on his toddler whiteboard. With his shock of wavy auburn hair and bright, wide-set eyes, he was an adorable little brother. In the Lee family, SJ took after their mom in looks, although his slightly slanted, brown eyes revealed a hint of his Chinese heritage. Allie sported her father's straight black hair, noble brow and nose, and a clear indication of Chinese ancestry in her almond-shaped eyes. Their mom thought Allie even walked with Will's gait. SJ's reddish-brown hair was wiry; he had his mom's prominent front teeth and freckles on olive skin paler than his sister's. No one would have guessed at first glance that SJ and Allie were siblings.

But he also had serious quirks that concerned Allie's parents. They would hear him talking to himself in his bedroom, often repeating the same word or rhyming phrases, but when their mom took him to story time at their local library, he jammed up and would not utter a word. He displayed some nervous behaviors when he became anxious, twirling his hair around his fingers and staring straight ahead, sometimes with a slight twitch in his shoulders.

Allie and her parents also noticed that he was awkward making friends outside of the family. And he had difficulty displaying his emotions. He often soothed himself to sleep at night by rolling from side to side, and at times, despite his high intelligence, he seemed to have a short attention span at learning a new skill or reading a story with his mom. She would be three pages into the story, and he'd take the book out of her hands and drop it, *plop*, on the floor. Just like that. On

the other hand, as he got older, he excelled at certain things, since he could become singularly focused on what mattered most to him.

When their parents took SJ to a children's behavior specialist, he was diagnosed with ASD, autism spectrum disorder. His was a mild form, allowing him, according to the specialist, to be fully functioning throughout his life but would need therapy, or special ed programs, to learn skills that would help him navigate the challenges he would face, especially in the social realm.

The specialist also observed that SJ had a high IQ and the ability to block out distractions to focus on what he considered top priorities. Interruptions, loud noises, conversation . . . they were just a background buzz if, for example, he was putting together one of his gigantic Lego creations.

Once Allie overheard her parents talking about SJ in hushed voices. She caught bits and pieces—that he was "on the spectrum" and might need "special classes" at school—but has "incredible potential," she thought she heard them say near the end of the conversation. But if that was the case, why did they sound worried? Allie knew SJ could be weird at times, but he was also kind. He used to run outside to get the paper on the driveway when Dad no longer ventured off the couch in the morning. He would delight in handing it to him with that goofy look on his face, the one with a half-smile *and* a furrowed brow, so you couldn't tell if he was happy or sad.

And when Allie spotted a sparrow that had hit the windowpane and was flopping below in the grass, SJ was the one who ran to get a shoebox. When he arrived with the box, he'd already put a soft velour cloth on the bottom to set the sparrow upon. Two weeks later, their mom bawled him out for losing his new blue shirt, which was when Allie realized where the cloth had come from for the injured sparrow's temporary home.

Allie could tell that SJ loved his big sister. He would go and sit on the floor in her room, endlessly twirling his hair through his fingers while she sketched and never say a thing. She not only did not mind, but she valued that both of them could be perfectly content together without uttering a single word. They could also disagree on things like most sisters and brothers do, but it never resulted in a wedge between them. She felt protective of him and thought maybe she was one of the only people who really knew her brother and how unique he was. In her mind, SJ was pleasingly different from anyone else she knew.

Their mom was particularly happy, once they moved to Lakeshores, that she was able to enroll SJ in the special ed program. He came home to tell her he had made a friend, a boy who rode on his bus. "That's fantastic, Speedy!" their mom had told him with a fist bump. "I like a man who's not only speedy on his feet but quick at making new friends."

SJ and Russell both were in Lake Bluff's special ed class for kids in fifth grade. Russell, or "Russ" as SJ called him, had Asperger's, specifically, and met SJ on the first day of school. Big for his age, Russ had sandy-red hair and eyes that blinked frequently, a mannerism he'd developed early in his life. Russ had never had much interest in making friends at school, in part because kids did not treat him kindly. They made fun of his monotone voice and the awkward gestures he sometimes made while trying to keep physical distance from other kids. Along with Asperger's, Russ had an anxiety disorder that caused him to avoid physical contact with others as much as possible.

Allie guessed it was because of the boys' similar social difficulties or just because they understood each other's differences that they hit it off. When SJ pulled out Yoda from his backpack to show Russ his favorite action figure, that sealed the deal. Russ, who seldom smiled, gave a quick grin of approval as he rattled off a handful of facts about Yoda. They were soon not only fellow Star Wars nerds but friends.

Allie knew that like Russ, SJ had not made friends in his early grade school years but given his closeness to his sister and his general disinterest in socializing with other kids, he seemed perfectly content with that. However, she could see this new dimension in his life gave SJ a needed boost as he adjusted to the new school. It made him happy too, he told Allie, that when the squad of mean kids (Lake Bluff, like every school, had a share of its own) made rude remarks about Russ, he could support him by shaking his head at them to show that their barbs meant nothing to them. In SJ's mind, those guys were just goons who didn't know any better, so he shook their insults off as easily as a retriever coming in from the rain.

That day, however, things took a not-so-nice turn. After SJ had joined Russ on the bus, he immediately heard some wisecracks coming from the back of the bus. On the morning run, Scotty, a slightly overweight sixth grader, sat in the back seat with Aiden, another sixth-grade boy, wearing a pair of Air Jordans and a smirk on his face. Aiden, with his deep brown hair and classic good looks, was always the leader in his cadre of friends.

"Your mother dresses ya funny," Scotty yelled from the back row, directing his insult toward the two boys. The bus driver glowered in the rearview mirror at Scotty.

"Yeah, where'd ya get those sissy shoes?" Aiden scoffed, staring at SJ's foot that extended into the aisle.

Now truthfully, there was nothing sissy about SJ's checkered Vans. Allie told him they were absolutely dope. That was good enough for him. A few taunts from those losers did not even rattle him a bit. He looked at Russ, shrugged, and ignored them. Of course, this was not the result the tormenters in the back row were trying to get.

By the time they reached Lakeshores, Scotty and Aiden were cooking up a scheme to teach those fifth graders how to show their upperclassmen some respect. That year, the fifth and sixth-grade PE teachers had decided to develop a competitive event to challenge the students. It was being held under the banner of the Annual Field Day Event, and it would feature competitions for boys and girls separately in several categories, including shot put, long jump, high jump, and several running events: the 100-meter, the 800-meter, and the 1500-meter.

Aiden and Scotty had plotted that morning on the bus to prank Russ and SJ. For what reason? No better reason than having fun at the expense of two socially maladjusted classmates, which they falsely thought would affirm their superiority. Russ, who was big for his age, would take part in the shot put. SJ's speed had already been established in the Presidential Fitness activities that week; he was signed up to compete in two of the running events: the 800 and the 1500-meter.

Once the guys went into the locker room to get ready for the field day events, Aiden and Scotty were going to create a distraction that would give them an opportunity to put some Icy Hot inside Russ and SJ's gym shorts. The timing was crucial as they would need the lockers to already be open so they could access the boys' gym clothes before they got back. They decided to set a containable fire in one of the large trash carts that sat inside the locker room near the door.

As the boys spilled into the locker room, Aiden quietly lit a newspaper on fire and dropped it into the cart, which had some empty cardboard cartons in it, along with assorted food wrappers, paper towels, and other flammables. Then Aiden quickly scooted over to his locker. Nearby, Scotty, who was in the same aisle of lockers as Russ and SJ, saw the smoke rising. "Fire!" he yelled out. Most all the boys around dashed in the direction of the smoke to see what was going on. Mr. Lemmel, the sixth-grade PE teacher, came running from his office, saw the smoke, and went to grab the extinguisher.

As all this commotion continued, Scotty was secretly squeezing gobs of Icy Hot on the waistband and inside SJ and Russ's gym shorts. He did it quickly and deftly and then returned them to where he'd seen them lying when he'd rushed over to do his dirty deed. Once accomplished, he slipped around the corner in time to see Mr. Lemmel dousing the flames with the fire extinguisher as all the boys cheered. It was out so swiftly that it never set off the smoke detectors, which would have triggered a fire drill for the entire school.

SJ and Russ were on the outskirts of the crowd of boys, and as the noise quieted, Mr. Lemmel asked if anyone had seen how the fire started. Since it had been a stealth mission, no one had noticed Aiden igniting the fire.

"Get back to your lockers," Mr. Lemmel barked, "and be outside in five minutes sharp!"

Everyone filtered back to their gym benches to finish getting ready. Scotty rushed back so he could catch the next act, his phone in his pocket, ready to capture a photo of it. (Kids were not allowed to have their phones in school, but they regularly kept them with them to locate their rides home and for situations just like this.)

SJ and Russ rushed to get on their T-shirts and shorts. As they pulled them on and started to stuff their regular clothes into the lockers, SJ let out a "*Whoop*," and a terrible look of pain crossed his face. Russ spun around to see what was up before he felt a searing, stinging sensation at his waist and upper thighs.

"Hellllp!" Russ screamed, running around the locker room and suddenly tearing off his gym shorts.

SJ realized they had been pranked about a minute after he had pulled up his gym shorts and felt the waves of the burning sensation under the waistband and on his upper thighs and butt where the Icy Hot had connected with bare skin.

Fortunately, they were over his underwear, so once he ripped the shorts off, there was some immediate relief. Russ ran to Mr. Lemmel's office, who had not yet gone out on the field. As he frantically described the pain from his gym shorts, Mr. Lemmel grasped what was going on and grabbed Russ a pair of shorts from the supply in his office.

"SJ needs some too," Russ blurted out. A hole in the back of his underwear had made the experience particularly uncomfortable for Russ. Mr. Lemmel planned to interrogate the boys later about who was behind the prank.

Mr. Lemmel spotted SJ, walked over, and without a word, handed him another pair of gym shorts. Around the corner, in the next aisle and unseen by Mr. Lemmel, Aiden and Scotty were laughing and high-fiving each other. Scotty had captured some of the commotion on his phone, which he planned to laugh over later with Aiden.

Poor Russ was so upset by the incident, he told Mr. Lemmel he needed a pass to the nurse's office. There, he asked the nurse to call his mom. In tears, Russ, his mouth a tight, straight line and his face pink and puffy, sat and waited to go home. He did not care much about missing the shot put, but SJ knew he felt embarrassed and was sad to leave SJ to do the field events without his friend there to root for him.

Fully recovered by now, SJ headed out for the field day events. He was not about to let anyone prevent him from competing in the running events, especially bullies who had just ruined his friend's day.

Chapter 16

THE RACE

More boys were signed up for the 800-meter race than for the 1500-meter. There were two heats for the 800, with nine runners each and just ten on the list for the 1500-meter. All were a mix of fifth and sixth-graders. SJ was signed up for both.

Over on the far side of the field, boys were warming up for the shot put. Another group, closer to the track, was doing some practice runs for the long jump, getting a feel for landing on the takeoff board and lunging forward into the sand-filled landing area. Alongside the main track, the runners were doing some short sprints, leg swings, high kicks, and lunges, all the moves Coach Lemmel had taught them for getting limber before a run.

The first heat was the slower of the two. Coach had SJ's group scheduled for the second heat. The best eight times would run in the final. SJ stood by the track, quietly surveying the first grouping as they got into position, everyone with a toe on the starting line.

The starter pistol fired with a deafening clap and off they shot. SJ squinted to see how they were doing as the group rounded the first full lap. They had quickly spread out, with three boys close together in the lead and the others scattered at increasing distances behind the leaders. Scotty was about sixth in the slower heat as the boys rounded the second lap, heading for home. SJ noticed only the three leaders pushing hard in the final fifty meters, trying to snag a fast enough time that would ensure they made it into the final heat.

"2:48!" yelled out Coach. "2:55 . . . 3:02 . . ." He rattled off the times as each boy crossed the finish line. Some were still fifty meters back and bringing up the rear. The final runner finished at four minutes flat.

Coach's assistant, Myra Phillips, who volunteered during PE for service points, jotted down the times. Then Coach yelled for the next heat. That was SJ's signal to line up. There were more sixth graders in this heat given that a year made a difference for many in their physical development and thus their speed. SJ was ready. The pistol cracked, and the pack was off.

During the first lap, the group looked like an inverted pyramid with the fastest racers out front, followed by slower pairs, and with the slowest couple of boys bringing up the rear. But as they completed the first lap, it had thinned down to the fastest four boys, with two at the front followed by SJ and Aiden, who were running in stride.

SJ saw that it was time to make a move and get ahead of the two front runners, so he swung out into the third lane, and he cranked it up a notch, easily moving ahead of them. However, Aiden took advantage of that movement to advance as well, ending up almost elbow-to-elbow with SJ. As they closed in on the finish line, SJ ramped up to his highest gear, finishing first with Aiden a hair behind him.

With all the times recorded, Coach called out the names of those who had the fastest times for the final heat. Six of the boys who had just run would be in the final, along with two of the best times from the previous heat. SJ clapped, his spirits and adrenaline buoyed because he was in the final 800. He had a chance to make his mark. Plus, he just loved running. When he ran, he soared in a world of his own, deeply breathing the air into every corner of his lungs. Sometimes, he felt it was the only time everything seemed to fall into place and make sense in his life. It made him feel great; it gave him joy.

Coach allowed some time for the guys who had run in the second heat to have a brief rest. SJ stood staring blankly, twirling his hair around his fingers. As he watched the boys across the field competing in the shotput, he thought of Russ, hoping he was okay. He knew Russ had been really upset.

As his mind wandered, he wondered who had pranked them. But SJ was without guile; he didn't really care and had no desire to seek vengeance. It just wasn't in his DNA.

Some gray-tinged clouds appeared off in the distance, affirming the chance of rain that had been forecast. But for now, it was a typical, slightly muggy day—not ideal for runners but cool enough to counter the humidity.

With the shotput and long jump events concluded, Coach called for the runners to line up for the final 800. SJ sized up his competitors as he put his right foot on the line. All the fastest were sixth graders except for him. Aiden, Robert—a curly-haired redhead who joked a lot—and Jon, a muscular Black miler who also excelled at the 800, were his main competition. SJ was confident he could live up to his reputation. He was the fastest fifth-grader at Lake Bluff, and here was a chance to prove he was the fastest boy at the elementary school. Period.

SJ blinked as the pistol went off, lunging forward quickly. He wanted to clear the crowd early and try to stay at or near the front for the first four hundred meters of the race.

Directly in front of him, Aiden had also jumped off to a fast pace, with Jon to his right and Robert next to SJ, who was running on the inside lane to the sixth grader's left. The four runners maintained their spots as they cleared the first 400 meters. The other four runners were staggered behind the leading pack, but the distance between them and the front runners was deepening.

Suddenly, Aiden bumped elbows with Jon, which, in that minuscule moment, was enough to throw Aiden slightly off balance. He fell. Jon and Robert cleared around him to the right, but SJ was right behind, with no room to maneuver. As Aiden went down, SJ fell forward, doing his best to go into a somersault, hoping he might regain his footing. He glanced at Aiden, paused, stuck out his hand, and jerked him upward.

"C'mon, man! We gotta finish the race!" SJ yelled, as two more boys passed by the pair.

Sparked by SJ's assist and the sharp tone of his voice, Aiden yelled, "Right!" as they both steamed into breakneck speed, trying to make up the impossible distance. Over the next two hundred meters, they caught the two who had passed them and headed toward the finish line. Robert finished first, Jon second, and SJ third, with Aiden right behind him.

"2:30!" Coach yelled out as SJ crossed the line. It was 2:32 for Aiden. A respectable time, but not what SJ had envisioned. As SJ loped over to the grass alongside the track, Aiden's eyes followed him. As SJ sat down to do some stretches, he couldn't have guessed that a quick thought passed through Aiden's mind: He knew he had not been a winner that day on the track or inside the locker room.

The bus door creaked open as Allie hurried down the steps. She headed home at a brisk pace, wondering if SJ was already there.

"Hi, Mom," she yelled to her mom, who sat before the computer in her home office. It was a lovely nook off the kitchen, painted a warm lemon yellow. The bright white wood trim at the doors and windows, along with white semi-sheer curtains, made the small room a welcoming spot for work.

"Hi, sweetheart," her mom yelled back.

Allie realized her mom was likely halfway through a speech she'd apparently tackled that morning and knew she wouldn't want to break her flow. Her suspicion was confirmed when her mom said, "We're gonna do pizza tonight. I'll take a break later, and we'll order it when SJ is home."

Allie ran upstairs and threw her bookbag on the old toy chest that had her name painted on it in lilac letters. The colors had faded slightly, but now she used it to store photo albums her mom had put together with favorite pictures of her and her dad, as well as records of the many day trips the foursome had made while creating memories Allie held onto fiercely. The zoo (a favorite of SJ's), the National Gallery of Art (where Allie had fallen in love with Toulouse L'autrec and other Impressionists), the East Wing with its monolithic Calder mobile, and the Air and Space Museum, her dad's favorite, were just a few.

As she hung up her jacket, Allie heard the back door slam. That would be SJ. She heard him greet their mom and then fast steps as he scampered up the stairs.

"Guess what?" he asked before he stared at Allie.

"OK, what SJ?" she answered. Despite the way SJ's face did not exactly register emotion like others, she could tell he was excited by the way his eyes sparkled.

"I won the 1500-meter race! Beat a bunch of sixth graders too," he said with delight. "It was the last event of Annual Track Day, and I won it!"

Allie did a quick fist bump followed by their secret dap, a ritualistic series of gestures they'd developed over time, mimicking some of their favorites among NBA players. Their dad had been a fan, even taking them to a couple of Wizards' games, so they held on to a love for the game with a deep sense of loyalty.

SJ proceeded to fill Allie in on every detail of the day, from the locker room prank that ended with Russ going home to the mishap with Aiden during the 800-meter race, and to his clear victory in the 1500-meter event, where he finished one second ahead of Jon, previously the fastest at the 1500-meter at Lake Bluff ES.

"You are superhuman, SJ," she said as they scampered downstairs. "And guess what? We're ordering pizza tonight, Mom said, so it will be our celebratory pizza party for your amazing race!

"Mom, should we get the usual?" she shouted.

"Sure thing, guys. Two larges: one pepperoni and one vegetarian, hold the green pepper! I'll take a break when it arrives. . . . I'm on a roll, so I'm gonna keep writing."

The pizzas arrived thirty minutes later. Meg wandered into the kitchen to be regaled by Allie retelling SJ's incredible race story, with a few added flourishes and high-fives for SJ. Allie had a flare for the dramatic, loving to retell family stories, each time embellishing the details. But SJ was the one to tell his mom about the locker room prank, which he guessed was cooked up by Aiden and Scotty.

"That's outrageous!" Meg said, grimacing. "That's unacceptable. They're trying to intimidate you and Russ. I feel like I should report this to the school," she said, eyeing SJ.

"No way, Mom. That would make it way worse. I'm fine. I recovered and didn't give them the reaction they hoped for. I just feel bad for Russ. I'll talk to him tomorrow on the bus. Coach Lemmel said if something like that happens again under his watch, there'll be suspensions for the perpetrators. And he said he'd find out who they were. I think he already has a suspicion about who it was too."

Meg looked closely at SJ's face and his expression. She worried about him, but she remembered when she and Will had discussed his autism diagnosis, they agreed not to be over-protective. They knew he would face some rude kids because he was a little different and, as she saw now, even bullied. But that was to be expected, so they agreed to be observant but not overbearing. They had even prayed about it.

Remembering now, years later, their prayer for SJ, she decided not to go into "fierce mom mode" but instead, follow SJ's suggestion to leave things be.

"Okay, I hear you, sweetie. I'll step back for now. But if these guys escalate in any way, you let me know right away," she insisted.

She got a fist bump from SJ for that before he wolfed down another slice of pepperoni pizza.

"We'll clean up, Mom," Allie said, "and then we both have homework we have to get done."

Meg nodded. "Yep, I've gotta get back to my speech. I feel surprisingly good about what I've got drafted so far, so I'd like to try to complete at least a rough version tonight. I can always edit it tomorrow."

Allie threw out the empty pizza boxes while SJ wrapped the remaining slices in metal foil—easy microwavable meals for the next day.

Chapter 17

BENEATH THE MIST

Delilah arrives in a new land

Recovering from her rapid descent through the Abyss, Delilah gradually opened her eyes to fully take in the setting in which she found herself. For a moment, she wondered, "Am I in paradise?"

The water was so clear that she could see the shiny pebbles of many colors at the bottom of the streambed. Palm trees lined the riverbank as a waterfall tumbled from the cliffs above, foaming over the rocks as it plunged into the river. The splashing, rumbling noise of the water was strangely comforting.

She heard another sound, almost like giggling; a light, airy voice that sounded downright gleeful emanated from a cave in the rocks. Suddenly, a creature scurried past the lamb so quickly that Delilah did not see who or what it was—only a flash of tan and brown. She decided to raise herself from the mossy bed where she had been resting to see who had dashed past her.

Hesitantly, she tiptoed toward the source of the noise, drawn to discover what it was, but at the same time, feeling fearful. As she stared into the entrance of the cave, the pounding of her heart echoed in her ears. She strained to hear the noise. *Ah!* There it was again. It not only sounded like giggling, but she could now deduce it was laughter!

Peering more deeply inside the cave, Delilah could only see dark shadows. After walking inside, two sets of eyes materialized, and as her eyes adjusted to the

dark, she saw the outline of two creatures, small in stature and like no animals or birds she had known before. Once her eyes adjusted to the dim light, she saw they had tan bodies with brown fur covering the lower and some of the upper parts of them, and from their shoulders sprang translucent wings. Unlike Delilah, they stood upright on strong, hoofed back legs, while their front legs were more like arms.

"Who are you?" Delilah asked timidly, unsure if they were friendly creatures, although they did not seem intimidating as they peered back at her.

"I'm Gavril," the slightly larger of the two creatures said, "and this is my sister, Seraphine. We saw you on the riverbank and wanted to talk to you, but we weren't sure if you were friendly or not. We're supposed to be collecting berries for our mom," he said and then smiled with an expression so kind, Delilah immediately felt entirely at ease.

Seraphine moved closer to Delilah, staring with curiosity. She put out her hand to pet Delilah's curly white coat. The lamb drew back in fright but then realized she was just as curious a creature to Seraphine as the pair were to Delilah, so she walked forward and let the angelic creature feel the softness of her wooly coat. The sprite let the lamb nuzzle her gossamer wings for a moment. They both smiled and then spontaneously laughed at each other's shyness.

The lamb explained to her newfound friends how she had been banished from her adopted home at Mount Kukulkan and forced into the Abyss by Simon, the royal vulture family's chief messenger. The story spilled out as Delilah shared how she had been taken away from her birth family to be adopted unexpectedly by a vulture's family.

The angelic creatures fluttered their wings as they listened to the lamb.

I don't know where this journey will take me, Delilah thought, *but perhaps these gentle creatures will help me find my way.*

Chapter 18

ALLIE RETURNS HOME

Present time, as Allie departs from Ataraxia

While Graham had bid his farewells to the many Guardians at the meeting, Allie told Molly, with some urgency, she needed to return home. "I'm anxious my mom will be worrying about me," she said, "and my brother SJ will expect me to help him tomorrow with a project he's working on." For the last couple of days, Allie had been helping SJ build a display for his science fair project. She was applying some of the lettering while he finished writing up the conclusions. He was trying to develop a fluoride battery, which he believed could surpass lithium-ion batteries. Not something the average fifth grader would be examining. But his condition gave him the ability for the intense and singular focus required for such an advanced endeavor.

On top of that, Allie had an illustration she was working on for *Aviso*. Her developing friendship with Ben made it more important to her not to disappoint him. She also wanted to talk to Grace, whose opinion she respected and who was becoming a friend she could trust.

As Allie rushed, tracing her route back down the path and beyond to the field where she had first found herself when she had arrived in Ataraxia, she realized she had no idea how she would return home.

"What can I do?" she panicked. "I have no idea what phenomenon brought me here."

Arriving at the expansive field filled with clover and fragrant wildflowers, Allie wandered through it, trying to find the exact spot where she had entered this magical realm through the picture in her room. That's when she saw a wide, flat tree stump, which she had not noticed before, and sat down to catch her breath.

As she sat, she heard a voice within her, a voice she had only heard once before, and that was a year after her dad had died. Grief-stricken, she had been struggling, wondering how life could go on without him. That was when she heard that soft but clear voice, as if an angel was standing beside her. It was a voice of comfort—gentle in tone, yet with authority. "Take heart, daughter. For you will see your father again one day. Be comforted."

Now Allie was again hearing that same gentle but clear voice speaking to her. "All you need to do is close your eyes; think about the people you love most and your desire to be with them."

She closed her eyes tightly and focused on the image of her mom and her brother. Her mom was in their big country kitchen, washing berries, with her wiry hair pulled back in a clip that left wavy strands flying. SJ was upstairs in his room, peering over an energy chart for his science project.

She kept her eyes closed and took a step imagining she was ready to walk down the hall to SJ's room. At that moment, she felt that same, strange sensation she had experienced when she first arrived, as if she were being pulled through squishy Jell-O. Then suddenly, a *pop*, and she found herself sprawled on the rug, back in her bedroom.

Allie glanced at the glowing face of the clock perched on the small bedside table. It was dark outside, the same as when she had first put her foot into the picture. And unless a day had passed, it appeared that her adventure in Ataraxia was on an entirely different dimension of time and space. She tiptoed down the hall to SJ's room. He had a digital clock with not only the time but the date. Peeking into his room, she stared at the clock.

Unbelievable! It was still Wednesday night, the same night and the exact time she had left. Somewhat exhausted from the miles she had walked while also meeting and talking to so many amazing creatures, Allie walked back down the hall, grabbed her journal, and flopped down on her bed.

Dear Daddy,
    You won't believe this, but I've just returned from an entirely different world. I met the most wonderful family of sheep and lots of their

friends—all different breeds of animals who live in harmony in a land called Ataraxia. It is almost too much for me to explain. And all the animals talk, just like us!

It's so hard to believe it happened, but I had to tell you first. I'm not ready to tell anyone else about it, not yet.

The weird thing . . . just like we have bullies here who put down others and take advantage of them, there are other creatures who want to assert their control over the citizens of Ataraxia. I'm thinking maybe I'll tell SJ about it. We could go back there together and help them.

I'm so tired now. I have to go to sleep. But you'll hear from me again soon.

I love you always and forever,
Allie

As she curled up in her bed and pulled her covers to her chin, her mind was filled with thoughts about the new friends she had made. Who would ever believe her? She was doubtful that Ben, or even Grace, would understand. No, as she slipped into a deep dream, she thought the one person to whom she would tell everything at the right time about this new world was sleeping right down the hall.

Chapter 19

THE OUTLIERS

Now that Delilah's senses had adjusted to this unusual environment, she asked her two new friends where they lived. Gavril and Seraphine explained that their homes were hidden on the outskirts of a territory completely different from the idyllic setting into which Delilah had fallen. Their family was part of a community of Outliers. They were an assortment of those who, over the centuries, had somehow survived the descent into the Abyss. Their appearance had evolved, including developing gauze-like wings, creating a more agile means of navigating the smooth-surfaced cliffs and the fertile river crescent yet maintaining a dependence on foods from the ground.

They were cliff-dwellers, which as Delilah would learn, was a crucial factor in their self-preservation. The conversation continued as the three rounded the bend to arrive at a clearing.

Delilah caught her breath as she surveyed the scene. Stretching in a sweeping row to the south were the cliffs that Gav (as she now called him) and Seraphine had described. They were breathtakingly beautiful. A pale topaz color, they reflected light emanating from the east. Luminescent colors of orange, cream, and silver streaked the walls of the cliffs, caused by minerals that glazed the surface of the rocky terrain. The steep descending walls of the cliffs had been hewn over time by a large body of water, producing the smooth, almost glassy surface.

In ominous contrast was the territory Delilah saw lying straight ahead as far as the eye could see. An expansive, dark swampland engulfed the horizon. Huge trees loomed over the murky waters. They looked to Delilah like monstrous giants with broken limbs weighed down by cascading tufts of green and black hair. On closer examination, the tufts appeared to be moss overgrown with black lichen. Rotting logs crisscrossed the swamp, creating walkways for those who ventured in, though some might easily collapse under even a lamb's weight from decay.

Gav and Seraphine urged Delilah to turn southward and follow them to their home, a much cheerier prospect. As they neared the cliffs, Delilah saw there were pathways cut into the cliffside—narrow but adequate, allowing her small frame through to follow her friends. She also saw more of these fairy-like creatures busy about their cliffside homes, some arriving with the food they had gathered, others leaving on their errands. None appeared frightened by little Delilah, albeit she did attract some curious stares.

Soon, they reached the pair's home, an inviting nook. Nature's elements—the wind and long-ago high waters—had scooped out large areas within each dwelling, which created places to eat, meet together, and rest. There was even a small cubby-hole at the top of their home that served as a lookout. Delilah was relieved after all that had transpired in her eventful day that Seraphine showed her a small resting spot, softened by grasses they had gathered that were now dry yet that still had a sweet fragrance. Delilah lay down and shortly fell into a deep sleep.

Several hours later, she awakened to a bustling household. An older brother had arrived after a day spent collecting a variety of nuts and small pumpkins, which their mom was cleaning and mixing for their dinner.

"We're happy to welcome you, Delilah," Seraphine's mom said. Whitney, as she was called, displayed the same huge blue eyes that her daughter had inherited and a broad face enhanced by highly arched blonde eyebrows.

"The children told me they found you on an island in the clear brook! That's amazing. So many who have been exiled to the Abyss do not survive. And no wonder," she exclaimed, "given the murderous hordes waiting to trap their prey on the way down. We've been here for many generations, but we know the stories from the few who have survived—at least that part of their journey. How did *you* survive?" she asked the diminutive lamb with an air of disbelief.

"A poor, unfortunate bat saved me," Delilah explained. "He didn't know it, but the distraction he created by eating one giant hornet for his morning snack drew the swarm to him, allowing me to creep silently downward. Pitiful creature . . ." She sobbed at the memory. Delilah was an emotional being and even though bats were not the friendliest of creatures, she was saddened that his life was lost while hers was spared.

"Then I stumbled into a gigantic spider's web," she continued. "Never had I imagined a spider that large. It came to wrap and secure me in its sticky threads, but again, I was saved by another poor creature who unwittingly flew into her clutches, distracting her before she had fully bound me in her web. I was able to wriggle and cut my way out—after which I fell. I have no idea how far it was," she said, "but I fell into a waterfall that ended in the most beautiful, crystal-clear pool, somehow escaping injury. And then, thanks to your children, I was able to revive. I still can hardly believe it all happened!"

Then Delilah told Whitney the entire story about Kibou and her brief adoption by the vulture family, then her recollections of her birth family whom she wanted to find. "But now, I think I will never be able to find them," she said as a tear rolled down her fuzzy cheek.

"You might be wrong about that," Whitney said. "I know about Ataraxia, your homeland," she smiled. "But the journey to get there is nearly impossible. It would require crossing the swamplands," she sighed, "and I do not know any who has successfully done it. But of course, if they did, I could not know for sure. But certainly, it would be too much for a wee one like you to go by yourself. It's because of the swamplands that our community forged our homes on these cliffs where we are safe from marauders."

Delilah wanted more details.

"To begin with, entering the swamplands is fraught with danger. Those swamp waters are full of slithering creatures of many types. Some want to nibble at your ankles. But the big ones would rather have you for lunch! Nevertheless, *if* you were able to cross the swamplands, there is another challenge even greater. On the far side of the swamps is an area of tall grasses and hollow trees where the Great Snakes reside. They are huge, many ten feet or longer. They are lazy, sleeping a lot throughout the days," she said.

"But when they become hungry, they lurk in the weeds, waiting to attack. They have been known to consume much larger animals than a wee little lamb. One creature who survived the journey into the Abyss, a handsome and swift leopard, never made it past the Great Snakes.

"It is rumored that Abaddon himself, the ruler of the Abyss, attacked and squeezed the life out of that leopard in less than a minute, after which he consumed him whole. Abaddon is a monstrous type of python. He can be identified by his dark red and brown diamond mark right on top of his head. He's rumored to be at least thirty feet long. Everyone is afraid of him, even the snakes themselves!"

Delilah's eyes grew wider and wider as she listened to Whitney. Inside her head, she fretted "What can I do, what shall I do?" as the story continued.

"The final passageway to reach Ataraxia is through a beautiful garden, legendary for its exquisite flowers, I've been told," Whitney continued. "I have heard the blossoms are in such vivid colors that it hurts your eyes just to take in their glory. It is guarded by the spirits of the Abyss, the evil beings behind the predatory world beyond the swamplands. They are beguiling and will use tricks to seduce you away from your mission of returning to Ataraxia."

"What kind of tricks?" Delilah asked in her sweet, slightly high-pitched voice.

"Oh, that I cannot tell you," Whitney said. "It depends on who reaches that garden. For these evil spirits look inside you to find your vulnerability and then trick you into defeating yourself with their wily deceptions. The only way I can imagine you escaping is if you could evade them in some way or travel through the garden without seeing them or listening to their voices."

"What is on the other side of the garden?" she asked. "How will I reach Ataraxia?"

"I don't really know, little one," Whitney said. "But I have heard that if you make it through the passage at the far end of the garden, you will know which way to go to get there."

Delilah took in all this information, trembling as she listened. Everything in her life so far had been a challenge. Now she was facing an even greater trial.

As Delilah struggled with these thoughts, Whitney's husband, Jude, who had been out foraging, returned and brought with him delicious white mushrooms, tender wheat kernels, clover, and grasses. That, along with the nuts and pumpkins and the berries that Gav and Seraphine had gathered for dessert, made for a delightful family dinner, which cheered up the lamb.

As they discussed Delilah's predicament, Whitney told Jude about the lamb's desire to return to Ataraxia to find her family.

"That's quite interesting," Jude said. "You know there's that little honey badger, Squeaker, who's been staying about a half mile away with Glowerth and his family for at least a year now, right?" he raised his eyebrow at Whitney. "Didn't they tell us he's been chattering about getting back to Ataraxia for a long time now?"

Whitney wrinkled her sizable, arched eyebrows at Jude in a way he knew meant he had said the wrong thing. As that look sunk in, Delilah raised her ears in excitement.

"Oh, dear, perhaps this is the answer to my dilemma," she blurted out with a mix of enthusiasm and a hint of trepidation. "Tomorrow, do you think you could direct me to this Squeaker?"

While Delilah was fearful of all the details about the journey to get back home, she had a brave heart and more courage than one would imagine in such a small being.

"We can take you there," Gavril and Seraphine shouted in unison. "We just saw him and Cedric last week when we all went cliff-sliding together," added Gav. This was a form of entertainment the younger Outliers had developed that involved "riding" down the most slippery of the shiny cliffsides—but only the ones that ended above grassy fields. Other spots were impossible because of the boulders at their base. Among the rules included no use of their wings. Most everyone used the giant leaves taken from the palm trees that fringed the ponds and streams in the nearby wetlands, their palm pads perfect for the trip downward.

"Can we, Mom? Can we?" the two shrieked, dancing around Whitney. "We promise to be careful!"

Whitney shrugged her shoulders in resignation. She didn't want to be the wet blanket to squelch the children's joy, and it would allow them to introduce Delilah to their friends.

"Okay," she said, "but after your playtime, I'll have an errand for you." Whitney had a hankering for the special purple clover that grew in the fields below Glowerth and Magda's home. Tying in that request with the kids' outing, she asked them to gather a generous bunch of clover and bring it home the next afternoon.

After dinner, while their children chatted with Delilah, Whitney spoke quietly, though with a stern tone, to Jude.

"What were you thinking?" she said. "You'll put ideas into the head of this wee lamb about getting back to Ataraxia! You know how many have tried that journey and failed! I'm fearful for her, Jude. When I spoke with her earlier today, I tried to make those swamplands sound as terrifying as possible to deter her. You make sure you tell her she is welcome to stay here with us as long as she wants."

Jude pulled Whitney over to his chest. He loved her dearly and hated when he was not in her good graces. She was everything he could have ever imagined in a partner for life. He often shook his head, wondering how he had managed to woo her to be his wife.

He'd come from a small family. His father had died when he was just a boy, and his mother had never had more children. It had just been the two of them. As a result, Jude had always dreamed of a big family. He beamed, thinking about their two sons and lovely little Seraphine.

As darkness enveloped the cliffside, the children retreated to their beds. Delilah lay in her grassy corner embracing the welcoming scent of the Outlier grasses that felt so soft and comfortable under her body.

She thought of Kibou, that silly bird, who was such a clownish character but fun to snuggle next to. And then of his unmerciful family who had sent her off unapologetically into the hands of Simon and to the Abyss. As she drifted off to sleep, Delilah wondered what they would be like, this unknown family she so longed to find.

Chapter 20

THE MATH CONTEST

Later in October in Lakeshores

Chairs clattered as the eighth-grade advanced math students ambled into Room 157, Mr. Lozano's classroom. He already had the chairs set up for two teams of three students each in his room and two teams of three students each in the extension space, which they would close off with the hinged divider they lugged out from the wall. Miss Weingarten, his teaching assistant, would be overseeing the teams competing in the extension room, and Mr. Lozano would stay in the main classroom. It was set up so the competing teams faced each other. They'd already chosen names for their teams. Allie's team was the Mathletes, Jenna's the Pi-thons.

Allie, Ben, and Sophia sat at one side of the room, with Stu, Jenna, and Lola seated opposite them. The other two teams were similarly seated opposite each other in Miss Weingarten's area. Mr. Lozano laid out the rules before the competition got underway.

He explained it would be a three-part contest, beginning with a team challenge, which would allow the team members to work together and turn in their solution; a point would go to the team with the quicker finish.

Then a series of individual questions would be presented to all six competitors, with a point awarded to the team for each problem that at least one team member got right. A quiz bowl would follow with three rounds. Each round would have sixteen questions asked in turns. If an answer was wrong, the other team could steal a chance to offer a correct answer.

"In the event of a tie, a tie-breaker question will determine who goes on," he concluded. "The winner will face off against Miss Weingarten's winning team. We will then have identified the team that will go on to compete in the regionals."

Stu leaned over to whisper to Lola, making a disparaging comment about Sophia's tunic top, which, with its decorative silver elephants fringing the bottom of the tunic and the sleeves, gave a glimpse into her Indian heritage. Stu was always prone to insult other kids' appearance—probably because he was slightly overweight and extremely self-conscious about his own looks.

Like others his age, he was struggling with acne. His parents were wealthy; his father, Jake Bradley, had inherited his dad's tech business, and his mother, Rita, a local real estate star, worked with many of the well-to-do families of Lakeshores on their home sales or purchases. As a result, Stu's parents were perennially preoccupied with their business affairs. Their son's common teen issues were generally ignored. A visit to the dermatologist should already have happened, but Rita and Jake were oblivious.

Mr. Lozano had his laptop screen projected onto a whiteboard, unveiling the question for both teams to begin solving. It was a quadratic equation about a car and a plane leaving the airport at the same time, with their respective speeds provided and the question being how long it would take before they were 164 miles apart.

The teams quickly focused. Ben had suggested to his team that each of the three of them start working it out on paper, showing their work to each other as they went through it to get a solution. Almost before he was halfway finished, Sophia showed them she'd solved it. It looked solid to Ben.

"Get your hand up, girlfriend," Allie blurted out.

Sophia's hand shot up as Jenna, sitting across from them, looked blankly at her, scowled, and shook her head in disbelief.

"The answer is forty-eight minutes," she said.

"I think we've got a real math star on our hands." Mr. Lozano smiled. "That's absolutely right, Sophia. Great start for the Mathletes. You've got one point."

Ben shot her a fist bump as the three celebrated their good start. Jenna snorted as the Pi-thons exchanged glances. "Okay, they beat us on this first one, but we'll whip their butts in the next round, right, Stu?"

Jenna mistakenly thought Stu was sharper than perhaps he really was, but regardless, she thought he was much cooler than that self-righteous Ben Lopez. This feeling stemmed from the fact that Ben had once stood up to Jenna for making a deprecating remark about Allie (she had said Allie was an opportunist who wheedled her way onto the newspaper staff where she didn't belong), and Jenna never forgot it. No one crossed Jenna without feeling the consequences somewhere along the line.

Mr. Lozano proceeded to the next stage. He had a student-helper monitoring who raised a hand first. These were shorter questions offered to all six students. By the time the round was over, the Pi-thons had picked up three points—two by Stu and one by Lola—and the Mathletes had three, with Allie, Ben, and Sophia all answering one correctly. The contest would be close: Mathletes 4, Pi-thons 3, going into the final round.

"All right, catch your breath," Mr. Lozano said with a laugh. "We're moving on to the final round, the quiz bowl!"

Stu squinted over at the Mathletes, trying to psyche them out with his stare. "You guys are goin' down," he scoffed.

"Yeah, right," Ben laughed. Allie looked at Ben, grinning. She loved his confidence, not to mention his great smile. She shook her head and told herself to focus on the moment at hand.

The math teacher peppered them with rapid-fire questions—some simple formulas they had learned, like factoring, prime numbers, volume, angle axioms, and quick word problems. The first two went to the Pi-thons, but on the third, Jenna rushed to give an answer, which was wrong.

"*Bzzt!*" Mr. Lozano barked out a noise indicating it was wrong. "Care to counter?" he asked the Mathletes. Before he got the words out of his mouth, Sophia gave the correct answer.

Lola and Stu exchanged annoyed looks meant for Jenna to see.

"Oh, c'mon. Gimme a break." She glared back.

But Mr. Lozano was already onto the next series of questions. Ben grabbed the next two in a row, then Stu got the next two. And on it went, back and forth, until Lozano wrapped up the quiz bowl with a final question.

"Thanks, Sophia, that's correct. Now, let's tally the results."

The result was anti-climactic because, during the quiz bowl, it was clear the Mathletes had chalked up more right answers than the Pi-thons.

"Mathletes: 31. Pi-thons: 24. Mathletes will be facing off with the winner from Miss Weingarten's teams to decide who will go to the regional competition later next month. And we'll have some after-school prep sessions to get ready for that—you can bet. Thank you, everyone, for your enthusiasm and best efforts," Mr. Lozano said. "You can work on your homework assignment for the rest of the period since there's just a few minutes left before your next class."

Mr. Lozano slid the extension room partition partway forward so he could slip over to find out how Miss Weingarten's teams had done.

Ben high-fived Allie and Sophia. Jenna glanced at them and rolled her eyes. She and Lola were already whispering about the cheer squad, while Stu shot an annoyed look at Ben. When the bell rang, the Pi-thons were first out the door. The victorious Mathletes, buoyed by their success, chattered together, basking for a moment in the success of their team effort before heading off in different directions down the hallway.

Chapter 21

Grace

Emerging from the crush of kids dashing for the cafeteria, Allie paused to look for Grace. Not seeing her, Allie went down the line, grabbing a few items for her lunch: a fruit cup, a salad, and a granola bar. She was a nibbler, so these would make do.

She glanced up and scanned the room, spotted Grace, and waved at her. She responded, motioning her to come over to her table.

Allie plopped down, nearly spilling her juice. "Hey. How's your day? Haven't seen you in a couple."

Grace smiled, her large, white teeth flashing a grin that Allie always found amazing. What she loved about Grace was that, in Allie's mind, she was incredibly pretty, but her friend seemed to have no recognition of it. Quite the opposite, she was quick to make jokes at her own expense about how tall she was, how skinny she was, and how much of a fish out of water she was at Lakeshores MS. Little did she know, that surprising lack of self-awareness was part of her beauty.

"I've been cramming all hours for a big test tomorrow in my history class. Didn't get to sleep last night 'til 1:30. I'm beat."

"Yuck, that's a drag," Allie agreed. Grace had four younger siblings. She got the impression that Grace's mom used her as a babysitter a lot of the time, having Grace pick up their clothes, fix snacks, and generally keep track of where they all were. Grace had told her she often couldn't start her homework until her three brothers and one sister were in bed because she had to supervise their evening routines. Once, when Allie invited her over to study with her at the Lees' house, Grace declined because her mom would be at work and she had to be home with the kids.

Grace was mixed race—her dad was Black and her mom white. She had told Allie once that she didn't usually sit at the table that some of the Black students frequented because she hated how people created categories, which they expected you to fit into. She said to Allie she tried to have friends who didn't necessarily fit in any of those boxes. Someone who is her own person, "Like you, Allie," she had said.

"You seem like you have a glow about you," Grace said. "What's up with that?" she asked, as she pushed her tray with fries to share in Allie's direction.

Allie looked down, blushing slightly, as she grabbed a fry and gobbled it up. "I think I have a big-time crush on Ben Lopez. We're on the math team together. He's smart and funny at the same time. And it doesn't hurt that he's super good-looking. That tapered fade is fire." Allie laughed at herself. It was the first time she was sharing with anyone her secret crush on Ben. "And he let me join the staff of *Aviso,* which means a lot to me."

"Ah-hah!" Grace laughed. "I knew there was something goin' on. You are too slick. Gotta give ya credit, girl; you've got good taste. But doesn't he hang out some with Lola Jeffries?"

"No way!" Allie scoffed. "They're in two different worlds." She perceived Lola as someone who would not hang out with a Latino guy, especially a semi-brilliant one, as she assessed Ben to be.

"Yeah, way," Grace retorted. "They were definitely an item, at least briefly. Ya know, opposites attract. But maybe that came and went. If so, Ben's even smarter than I thought."

"Interesting . . . that explains the eye darts Lola threw my way during math. But it's pretty clear there's nothing going on now." She made a mental note to somehow find out more about that. The noisy clang of the bell bumped Allie out of her brief reverie. "Oh geez, Gracie-girl, I gotta run."

"Oh, you don't get off that easy, Allie-Chun… more on this topic to come!" Only Grace could get away with her silly but affectionate nickname for Allie, who was fast becoming her best friend at the school. "I'll text you after last bell!"

"Sounds good!"

They giggled at each other as they headed out.

Chapter 22

AVISO

Allie had shifted her schedule after just a few weeks at school. Early in a new semester, Lakeshores allowed students up to two weeks to drop or add classes. She had originally signed up for journalism because she thought that meant she'd get to work on the school newspaper. After she learned that was not the case, she dropped it and switched to an art class. She felt that was her true calling.

Even when Allie had been a young girl, she displayed a special talent for drawing. She loved expressing herself through the vibrancy of colors, something her mom sighed and shook her head about when Allie was three years old and drew a picture of her family on the bathroom wall with her large-sized crayons. Thankfully, they had used washable paint on the walls.

After she had mustered the courage to talk to Ben Lopez about working on the newspaper, Allie was pleasantly surprised when he invited her to contribute to the artwork, either photos or cartoons, and said perhaps she could do an occasional writing assignment. He told her he already had enough reporters, but sometimes he liked to assign special projects. He had one in mind for the creative-minded Allie when he first approved of her joining the staff of *Aviso*.

But for this week, Ben was writing an editorial. The LMS cheer squad had become a controversial topic: the tryout policies, the selection process, the individuals on the squad . . . the conversation about it had spilled over onto social media where kids were venting their frustrations with the status quo, while others responded with blunt messages in support of the squad and the policies already in place, such as the unflattering one Lola had recently posted on Instagram.

His editorial was going to take aim at allowing conventional ideas and status quo policies to guide what the LMS cheer squad might become in the future. That day after school, Ben pulled Allie aside to describe his thoughts and see if she would be willing to develop an illustration that would complement his editorial theme.

"That's an incredible idea!" Allie said. "And so timely. They're still holding try-outs this week and next. Like you say, a lot of people are tweeting about it. I also see some horrible body shaming going on. Why can't our age support each other instead of tearing each other down? Anyway, there's a wide range of opinions, which means your editorial will get a lot of attention."

"Well, yeah. One of my goals as editor this year is to increase the readership of *Aviso*," Ben said. "Learning shouldn't be just in the classroom. And if we're not reading and learning about other points of view, how can we expect to be ready for high school, college, or life, for that matter?"

Allie nodded as she gazed at Ben's eyes, which sparkled with intensity as he spoke. Unfortunately, what she saw around her was people who loved to hide from facts. Kids her age were reflections of their parents' opinions, herself included. She knew she made choices and formed opinions based on stuff her mom and dad had taught her. But her dad had always told her to keep an open mind.

"Part of growing up," Dad had said, "is learning to form your own opinions. No one person has all the answers. The only pure truth is God's Truth, and you have to read the Bible to find out about that. But in the everyday world we live in, I read the newspaper, listen to the news, research topics online, and then try to make informed decisions based on the facts I can glean and on my faith, what I believe." She always loved her dad's openness and that he had never talked down to her.

Allie snapped back from her roving thoughts.

"Can't wait to read it when you have your draft," she said. "I'll start working on a couple ideas for the artwork. . . . I was talking to my mom the other day about this very topic, telling her about some of the trash talk I saw online. She said it's 'an opportunity' to demonstrate tolerance and grace."

Ben listened thoughtfully.

"Hmm . . . tolerance and grace. I might have to use that in my editorial." He turned toward his computer screen. Allie was already devising ideas for her cartoon. This was going to be a fun assignment.

Chapter 23

ART IMITATING LIFE

Meg stared out the window, a blank look on her face. She was struggling to craft a strong conclusion for the speech she was writing. Writer's block had hit, so she looked for a diversion to get her mind out of its funk. The house next to theirs was at least a hundred yards away, but she could see Mr. Hardin, their neighbor, climb out of his Jeep Wrangler. His English setter, Max, leaped to the ground as Hardin opened the back door.

SJ had been lobbying her for them to adopt a dog. "There's gazillions of wonderful doggies looking for a forever home," he told her as he paced around the kitchen one day. "We just need to find the right one for our family. Plus, it'd be good exercise. I would have a new job as a dog-walker." He had given her his expressionless stare, holding it there without blinking for ten full seconds, which meant he was super serious.

Periodically, she had been researching online, typing "best family dogs" into search engines to get ideas. She didn't want to rush into this because it would be a new family responsibility, and without a doubt, she already had enough responsibilities to handle in this new chapter of her life without Will.

But she had also discovered a small support group for single moms. One woman, Priscilla, had a daughter who was autistic, and she told Meg that getting a dog had helped Jett grow in so many ways, not to mention that the crazy antics of their border collie provided comic relief for the family.

As Meg read about the advantages of small versus large breeds, she heard Taylor tromp in with the kids behind her. It was Wednesday, the day Allie stayed after school to work on *Aviso* and SJ for the science club. On Wednesdays, Taylor, a young college student Meg had hired to help with transportation and errands, would pick them up—first SJ at Lake Bluff Elementary, then Allie at Lakeshores— bring them home, and help get some things ready for dinner while Meg worked.

"Hey, guys!" she yelled out to them.

"Hey, Mom!" Allie shouted back. "Goin' upstairs."

"Hey," Meg then overheard Allie say to SJ. "There's something I wanna tell you about." Meg briefly wondered what it was.

Allie had been waiting anxiously for the right opportunity to tell SJ about her adventure in Ataraxia. But SJ told her he couldn't talk then. He wanted to work on his science project alone. Allie could tell from the look he gave her that it wasn't the right time. She knew when he got focused on something, he did not want anyone pulling him away.

She tossed her book bag on the toy box in her room, disturbing the green frog pillow, one of the members of her stuffed animal collection she kept there, all lined up in a row. Her dad had made the toy box for her when she was a toddler and her mom had painted it. It was a treasure she would never part with.

She heard a loud *ping*. A text had arrived from Ben. They had exchanged contact information the day he asked her to join the *Aviso* staff. It was a link to the editorial he had drafted, so Allie pulled it up to read. Plus, she felt the excitement of getting a text from Ben in the first place. It was all so new.

> *Recently, the LMS cheer squad has become a controversial topic: the tryout policies, the selection process, and the individuals on the squad. The conversation about it has spilled over onto social media where kids are venting their frustrations with the status quo, while others are posting blunt, and often disrespectful, messages.*
>
> *We've all seen them on Twitter, Instagram, and elsewhere. Many messages support the current policies, which have been in place since the cheer squad was founded over 20 years ago. Others suggest it's time to think in a new way. According to the advisor to the cheer squad, these policies were originally established as guidelines to help get the cheer squad launched and*

*select members for it. The editorial staff of **Aviso** believes these policies have become outdated.*

Most LMS students recognize that the greater Lake Shores community has changed over time. As one reflection of those changes, our student body has become more diverse. Our students come from a variety of racial, ethnic, and religious backgrounds. Our ideas about music, dance, and who should serve on our cheer squad have also evolved.

We recommend that the LMS school leadership, working with the faculty advisor to the cheer squad and three or more students, develop updated guidelines that reflect a broader representation of the LMS student body and that the LMS Administration and student body alike develop those new guidelines with tolerance and grace. Such an approach will benefit everyone and result in a superior cheer squad.

Wow, she thought. *Ben even used my suggestion in the editorial's conclusion.* She smiled to herself.

Grabbing her sketch pad, Allie began putting some ideas on paper. As she reflected on the topic, an image rose in her head of the Guardians' Council in Ataraxia. It was as if she was looking through a foggy lens that mirrored her life in Lakeshores, despite their being in two different universes. There, she had seen the beauty of diverse members of the animal kingdom coming together with strength and unity to develop and protect their harmonious way of life. She thought of a split screen to support Ben's theme.

On the left side, she sketched five white sheep, all exactly the same, with no expressions on their faces. On the right side of the screen, she drew five of her Ataraxian friends: an owl with spectacles, a graceful gazelle, a stately tiger, a ram, and a sleek white dove. She chose colors that made the left screen look dull and static, while the animals at the right were depicted in vivid colors, with a school banner flying regally overhead. She thought about it for a moment and wondered whether her idea would work or not. She would refine her sketch and share it with Ben.

She couldn't wait to hear his reaction. Slowly, tiny step by tiny step, she was opening her mind and her heart to the possibilities for her in the town of Lakeshores. And it felt like Ben Lopez would be a part of that.

Dear Daddy,

I have a friend at school I like a lot. His name is Ben. The problem is, I'm always hiding inside what I really feel. I don't know why I act one way, all cool and self-assured, when I feel the opposite.

I have all these jumbles of thoughts running through my head that I'd like to say to Ben, but when I get ready to, nothing comes out. I really like him, but I keep all my true thoughts and feelings locked up inside.

I wish you were here to help me. You always had the best ideas about how to handle things. This seems like something hard I'm just going to have to work at. Thanks for listening,

Love,
Allie

Chapter 24

A Season of Change

Allie speed-walked to her locker while the first bell was ringing. As she grabbed the heavy math book she usually left at school, she heard a faint "hey" emanate from a few lockers away.

Turning, she was surprised to see Stu, Lola, and Jenna's friend.

"Hi, Stu," she said with a quizzical look. "Wassup?"

"Nuthin' much," he mumbled. Allie sensed he had more to say, but she was already late for her class. "You gonna watch the cheer squad tryouts after school today?" he said with a weird grin on his face. "I'm gonna go."

This didn't surprise Allie because Lola would be there, and she knew Stu liked hanging out with her and Jenna. But the look on his face perplexed her. Something between the cat that swallowed the canary and a snarky grin.

"Yeah, I am. I found out my friend, Grace, is gonna try out, so I decided to be there to lend my support. So . . . I'm kind of late for class. Sorry to run, but I'll see ya there then." Allie's voice faded as she rushed down the hall.

At lunch in the cafeteria the day before, Allie had been surprised when Grace told her she was going to try out for the cheer squad.

"Wow, I had no idea you were thinking about it," Allie said.

"Yeah, well, I've taken dance classes for a few years," Grace confessed, "so it would build on that and be a way to stay fit and active."

Allie nodded her head in understanding. "That makes sense. Plus, you look amazing. You would add class to the squad."

"Yeah, right." Grace rolled her eyes. But Allie could tell she appreciated her friend's compliment.

While they were talking, Grace's eyes were drawn to a boy heading across the cafeteria who towered over most of his classmates.

"Oh my, who is that?" she whispered to Allie. Her eyes followed where Grace was staring. A tall, Black, athletic-looking boy was setting down his tray at a table where several boys Allie recognized to be guys on the basketball team were motioning for him to join them.

"I dunno," Allie said. "Haven't seen him before. He must be a transfer, is my guess. But he is cute. I bet he ends up playing for the team with that height and build. All I can say is ya got good taste, girl."

They laughed as they chattered on. But as the two friends rose to head out of the cafeteria, Allie saw Grace glance at the boy's table just as he looked over her way. Their eyes connected for just a moment before Grace sauntered off to class.

Piles of the latest edition of *Aviso* were stacked in a bin at the main doors exiting the cafeteria. It was the issue in which the cheer squad editorial was published, along with Allie's cartoon, which appeared on the same page. Kids were grabbing it as they left. It quickly became the topic of conversation that afternoon. Reactions were split between supporters of the editorial's recommendation to make changes to the cheer squad selection process and critics who liked things the way they were.

Many of the latter group were friends of the existing cheer squad members, as well as kids who felt change was coming too fast to the Lakeshores community. They reflected the opinions they heard at home from their parents who saw, not just in Lakeshores, but in North Carolina in general, a steady stream of immigrants arriving from around the world, along with diverse groups migrating out to Lakeshores from nearby urban centers, such as Charlotte and Greensboro.

At the end of the day, the kids fled Lakeshores MS to head home. Allie had told her mom she would be staying after to watch the tryouts. She was on her way to the gym where they were being held. When she got there, several kids were already hanging out in the bleachers, while several teachers, including the advisor to the cheer squad, Mrs. Durwood, were seated at a table in the middle of the gym directly in front of the bleachers. They signaled for those in the bleachers to be quiet.

As the din subsided, one by one, the students trying out for a place on the squad came out from the locker room. Each had already been told a series of moves they were expected to demonstrate from simple leaps to cartwheels to handstands that transitioned to a forward roll. A catchy pop tune was playing, and each competitor finished with some requested dance motions described in the email instructions they had all received.

Allie saw Stu talking to Mrs. Durwood for a moment. She was pointing out how the mats were positioned on the central area of the floor—and how a couple of them were crooked. *Stu must have volunteered to help, Allie* thought. Why else would he be straightening out mats right before the tryouts? She saw Mrs. Durwood nodding her head and then motioning for Stu to get off the floor. He slid over to the side and sat on one of the lower bleachers to watch.

Grace appeared about a third of the way into the queue of participants. When she completed her first leap, Allie clapped noisily, continuing to whoop and cheer after each successful move her friend executed. She was impressed at how true to her name Grace was, moving with elegance and poise. *This should be a slam dunk,* Allie thought, mentally comparing all the students she had watched thus far in the tryouts.

"Thank you, Grace. Nice form," Mrs. Durwood said. "Next!" And just as quickly as Grace had bounded out, she slipped back into the locker room as the next girl strode out. The girls who were on the existing cheer squad had to try out again as part of the regular process each year. Twelve members made up the squad. Three past members were not returning to try out; two had left the district, and one had a health issue.

Allie watched a while longer while Grace was changing. Following two other girls, Lola appeared and completed the various moves. She was quite limber, finishing the athletics portion skillfully. But Allie thought her dance moves paled in comparison to Grace's. Her friend's stature and natural sense of rhythm gave her a clear edge.

About that time, Grace emerged from the locker room in black leggings and an oversized T-shirt. She had her huge mane of curly hair in tight cornrow braids against her head and continuing in neat rows down her scalp to her neck, where they cascaded down her back, crisscrossing with decorative colored ribbons. It had taken her auntie, who owned a hair salon, over six hours to do it.

Allie waved from the bleachers and waited. When Grace arrived, she asked her if she wanted to stay and watch some of the others, but Grace shook her head.

"I'm famished!" she said. "Let's walk down the street to that snack shop, O'Grady's."

Allie, whose stomach had been grumbling since the last period of school, jumped up. "Say no more! We are on the way." Allie sported a tunic top with yellow flowers on a violet background over light purple tights. Her black hair with its below-the-chin blunt cut complemented her slightly angular face, with its high cheekbones and perfectly shaped plump lips with a gently curved chin.

As they walked down the street, they heard a male voice shout after them.

"Hey, Allie, slow down!" She looked up to see Ben in the distance, waving as he jogged down the steps of the school. He headed in their direction looking sharp in a pair of chinos and a sky-blue T-shirt. His jet-black hair was slicked back in its usual ponytail.

She felt herself blush momentarily and then, recovering, she waved back.

"C'mon, join us, we're going to get a snack at O'Grady's," she said as Ben caught up with them.

"Cool. Glad I spotted you. I'm starved. Plus, I wanted to talk to you about the next edition of *Aviso*," he said.

"You know Grace, right?" Allie asked. Grace had told her she knew who Ben was but had never talked to him.

"Yeah, hi, Grace. 'Sup?"

"Not much," she said with a smile. "We just ditched the rest of the cheer squad tryouts to get a snack.

"Yeah, Grace already had her tryout, and she was awesome!" Allie said.

"Oh, that's great." Ben nodded. "Well, a new development . . . I heard back from the principal and Mrs. Durwood. They're sensitive to what we suggested in our editorial. They said it's too late this semester to initiate changes, but they support the ideas for the future, and they said they would keep the spirit of our hopes in mind, even as they make this semester's selections for the squad."

"Wow, Ben, that's amazing!" Allie blurted out. "I'm so impressed that Lakeshores is giving your editorial credence. You must feel so happy!"

By then, the trio had reached the snack shop, so they wandered in.

O'Gradys was an old throwback kind of place with rows of boxes displaying every type of candy bar imaginable. It also featured more recent, healthier items, such as granola bars, protein bars, packages of dried fruit, and a wide variety of nuts. Run by the O'Grady family for over fifty years, the shop also had a small grill and soda fountain. Three small tables took up the back of the room where kids often hung out.

Today, they were monopolized by guys who had just finished intramural sports, both track and basketball. Grace did a double-take as she noticed the new boy she had admired from a distance in the cafeteria.

"Ben," she whispered, "do you know who that tall guy at the middle table is? The one with the 76ers cap on backward?"

"Oh, yeah, he's new. They call him Dak. I think it's short for Daksonius. His family moved here from Philadelphia. He just started classes here this week; he's in my earth science class."

As they finished browsing through the second aisle, Ben waved at the new boy, and said "Hey, man, how's it goin'?" Dak looked up and raised an eyebrow.

"Yeah, man. Okay, I guess." He glanced at the three of them.

"Yeah, so Dak, these are my friends, Allie and Grace."

"Hey," Grace said.

"Hey, Dak," Allie said. "Ben said you just moved here. So you're a 76ers fan? Sorry, but I'm a Wizards fan," She laughed and continued, "So we're not gonna be rooting for the same teams."

Grace was too tongue-tied to say anything despite Allie kicking her foot. She just flashed her beautiful smile. But Dak's friends had pulled him back into their conversation, so he waved goodbye and turned back to his table.

Ben, Allie, and Grace finished picking out their snacks and headed outside. Allie told them that Taylor was going to be picking her up shortly. It was Wednesday, and she would have already picked up SJ before they had to head home. She would have liked to stay and talk longer with her friends, but Grace had already heard from her mom, who was going to pick her up soon so she could help prepare dinner and watch her younger siblings.

"Let's talk tomorrow about the content for the next issue of the newspaper," Ben said to Allie as she devoured her Mounds bar. "We have the same lunch period. I'll look for you there."

"Sure, that sounds good," Allie said. "Looking forward to hearing what you have in mind." Inside, Allie was cheering. It seemed that not only did Ben want to talk with her about *Aviso*, but maybe there was a spark going on between them. She restrained herself from skipping up to Taylor's VW when she saw her easing to the curb with SJ in the back seat.

"Bye, Ben. Bye, Gracie-girl," she said as she waved and climbed into the car, greeting SJ with an extra big smile.

As Taylor drove them home, SJ told Allie that he was going to submit his fluoride-ion battery project in the upcoming regional science fair. He said his teacher had urged him to enter because she felt he had a shot at placing in it "because your concept is so advanced," he mimicked. So far, SJ had to rely greatly on existing research combined with his calculations to determine the potential of more available fluoride as a replacement material for lithium-ion batteries. SJ theorized that this idea could lead to more affordable batteries for, among other uses, electric-powered vehicles.

"So impressive, dude," Allie told her brother. "Can't wait to see where this leads. You're gonna be famous one day, for sure."

He glanced at his sister, expressionless, but his rapid blinking told her he was excited by her praise. Then, a slight smile appeared on his lips.

When they arrived home, Allie ran upstairs to dump her stuff in her room. Her phone pinged.

"Already heard from the judges! I'm in the final round for a spot on the cheer squad," Grace's text read.

"That's fantastic!" Allie texted back, with a thumbs-up symbol. "When is it?"

"Friday . . . two days from now."

"Great! Will tell my mom. I have to be there!"

"Awesome."

Allie threw on some sweats and ran downstairs. Her mom had asked her to rake up some of the fall leaves that were now covering their lawn. It was heading for November. The orange and crimson leaves on two huge maples, one on each side of the yard, had begun falling, resulting in a multi-colored carpet that covered the lawn. The early evening air was crisp, fragrant from damp leaves and the smell of chicken roasting on an outdoor grill somewhere on their street. SJ emerged and skipped down the front steps to help with the leaves.

Chapter 25

Ben

Maria spoon-fed baby Wilfred as his older siblings gobbled up the plates of *huevos rotos* she had prepared for their breakfast. Her oldest, Ben, was busy pulling clothes out of the dryer and sorting them into piles for Manuel, age ten, Sophia and Santiago, eight-year-old twins, Nico, four, and little Wilfred. Watching her oldest out of one eye, Maria shook her head. What would she do without Benjamin, the apple of her eye?

Already four inches taller than his mom, Ben helped keep her world in order. When the internet went down, Ben fixed it. When the kids needed rounding up from the neighbor's house, that was Ben's job. If she needed help moving furniture or fixing a broken lamp, Ben was there—and always with a smile, an upbeat comment, or a laugh.

Not only did he help her manage the mundane but demanding details of the busy household, he did it with style. Full of energy, Ben was constantly on the move while carrying on conversations with his mom and siblings at the same time. His dark brown eyes sparkled with a touch of mirth as he teased his mom about her endless diets. The toll of six kids had done a number on her waistline, so she was always trying a new diet to "get back her girlish figure," she joked.

It wasn't that her husband, Javier, wasn't helpful. But he worked construction, which meant long hours, leaving at daylight and often returning late in the evening. She loved Javier and respected his hard work to support the family, but it was Ben on whom she often relied.

She worked as a maid at a motel about eight miles away from their house, which enabled her to manage her schedule and family logistics. Despite both Maria and Javier working, there never seemed to be enough money. The pandemic the country had struggled through had subsided, but the inflated prices of everything remained. Gas, food, utilities, shoes for growing kids . . . living paycheck to pay-check was the norm.

Maria's older sister, Bella, had just moved in with the family. She had suffered an injury to her hip in a car accident a few years ago, leaving her dependent on a cane. But she helped watch the younger children during the day when Maria worked and in the evenings when Ben had homework.

The household was crowded. Ben shared a room with Manuel; the twins had bunk beds in the room with Nico, and the baby's crib was in Javier and Maria's bedroom. Javier and Ben had partitioned the sunporch at the back of the house to create a small bedroom for Bella when she had made the move up from Texas to join them. Bella had told Maria that her world now revolved around her nieces and nephews, which made her feel needed, a contributing member of the family.

It was Friday, the last day of the school week. Ben selected his favorite oversized white T-shirt over relaxed-fit, dark gray jeans. He had been thinking about it for a while: At lunch today, he was going to ask Allie if she'd go to the December dance with him.

He liked Allie a lot. But with her reserved manner, he couldn't tell if she felt the same way he did. He knew she liked working with him on *Aviso*, but she didn't easily reveal her feelings past that relationship. He figured he'd take the direct approach and find out.

"C'mon, Manuel! Ready to go? Make sure the twins are ready to walk with you to the bus stop," he called out. Manuel, Sophia, and Santo all rode the same bus to their elementary school. His mom dropped off Nico at a preschool near their home while Bella watched Wilfred. During his mom's lunch break, she picked up the two from preschool and dropped them back home with Bella.

The twins were already out the front door as Manuel trotted after them to catch the bus. Ben swung by the kitchen to give his mom a goodbye hug. It was part of their morning routine.

"Wish me well, Mom," he said. "I'm asking my friend Allie to the December dance today."

"Oh!" She smiled. "How could she refuse such a handsome young man? You better tell me about it this evening."

"I hafta work tonight. I'll let you know if you're still up when I get home." Few of his friends knew, but Ben had a part-time job off the books at a local bodega. He spent his time in the back of the store, preparing food orders, cleaning up, and stocking the shelves when customers were few. It was a way to help the family out a little, plus it gave Ben a little spending money so he didn't have to ask his dad for any. He barely saw his dad some weeks because of the long hours he put in at the construction site. The last thing Ben wanted to do was ask his dad for an allowance when he knew his parents were just squeaking by.

As soon as he was off the bus, Ben scurried up the steps to the main entrance of the middle school. He fist-bumped Jaxson, a guy from his English Literature class, while heading for his locker to grab a textbook. Lakeshores MS had only three levels: a basement, the main level, and the second floor. It stretched out in endlessly long hallways, making an elongated rectangle. Rushing between bells to classes could often take the full time allotted to get to the next class because of the long wings.

Students were midway through their morning classes when the bells blared throughout the school signaling a fire drill. The school had been alerted at the beginning of the week that there would be a fire drill, so no one was overly surprised. Every classroom had an exit plan that had been laid out the first week of school. For the most part, everyone left the building in an orderly fashion.

Outside, a steady din of conversation rose from the congregated students. Allie and her math class, which had been in session, had filed out to the sidewalk in front of the north wing of the school. She was chatting with Sophia when she noticed Stu whispering intensely to Lola. Trying to pick up on their conversation, she only caught a couple of phrases—something about "slip by to get things ready," and toward the end of the conversation, "see you after . . ." followed by a giggle from Lola and a wink from Stu. She wondered what that was about before she turned her full attention back to her conversation with Sophia.

Lunchtime rolled around and Allie headed to the cafeteria. As she got in the line for a tray, she spotted Grace already ahead of her making her selections. They had a system now where whoever got through the line first would grab a table somewhere near the center of the room. They had developed a small cadre of "lunch buddies" who sat with them: Often Ben, sometimes Sophia and Matt Kendall, who was a reporter for Aviso, and Emma Hughes, who carpooled with Grace since she lived down the street and their moms were friends.

"Hi, Gracie!" Allie arrived and set her tray down, unloading a salad, ice water, and her usual crispy fries with lots of ketchup. "Are ya nervous about today?"

"Nope," Grace lied. Allie couldn't tell, but Grace had stomach flutters and felt if she acknowledged them, it would make them a reality. Instead, Grace switched the topic. "You won't believe this, but I was chatting with a friend of Dak's, and he told me that Dak is gonna invite me to the December dance! I'm blissed out. But I'm trying to keep my spirits calm since this is just what his friend told me."

Since their brief meeting at O'Grady's, Allie and Grace had discovered that Dak lived in Grace's neighborhood and rode her bus in the morning to school. Grace had already told Allie she had struck up a conversation with him on the bus, discovering he was a little shy at first. But with the ice broken, he opened up about his hopes to get on the basketball team and had her laughing at his lame jokes that were mostly at his own expense. She was pleased to find that behind his attractive exterior, Dak had a kind heart.

"Get out!" Allie grinned. "You have to let me know what happens." Allie had told herself she had no particular interest in attending the dance—mainly because social events were not really her thing. But deep down, beneath the trained-to-be-stoic exterior, she felt a twinge of emotion. Not jealousy of Grace, but a faint desire to be part of this new community she had been thrust into.

At that moment, Ben walked up, lunch tray in his hands. "May I join you?" he asked. "I don't want to interrupt if there's important 'girl talk' going on," he teased.

"Sure thing! C'mon, grab a seat," Grace said while Allie smiled, nodding her head. Ben sat down next to Allie and across the table from Grace. Over Grace's shoulder, Allie could see Lola, Stu, Jenna, and another boy she didn't recognize, eating together. Lola's eyes met Ben's as she glanced his way, gave an ingenuous wave, and returned to an intense conversation they were having. Something about the expression on her face bothered Allie. *I'll bet they're up to something,* she thought to herself.

"For the final round of tryouts this afternoon," Grace was telling Allie, "they gave us a routine to do that includes some more demanding moves than the first round. In part of it, I need to do a flip from a handstand, go into a split, do some dance moves, and then do a backbend into a flip to end it. I've practiced it in the gym after PE a couple times and last night in my yard. I feel pretty much ready," she said.

"Oh, I'm excited for you," Allie clapped. "I'll be there again to cheer you on. Ben, are you gonna stop by to see the cheer team tryouts?"

"Sorry, I don't think I can make it. I want to work after school on the layout for the next issue of the paper. But if I finish in time, I'll come by." As Ben finished up his mac and cheese, Dak walked by. He glanced at the table and paused as if to say something, but then hesitated. Allie saw Grace had spotted the hesitation; she jumped up and announced she was finished and grabbed her lunch tray to drop off at the cafeteria exit.

"Oh, hi, Dak!" she said as she left the table. "Wanna walk with me while I drop off my tray?"

"Sure, headed that way myself," he said. As they walked away together, Ben glanced at Allie. She turned her head toward him and gave him a quizzical look.

"'Sup? You look like you're pondering something. Anything I can help with?" she asked.

"Well, yeah, maybe." Ben, who was not usually at a loss for words, felt uncertain. "I-I . . . wondered whether you might want to go with me to the December dance?" The words spilled out quickly, and then he just stared at her.

Allie's green eyes, which had been squinting at Ben's face suddenly widened, then narrowed as they were tugged closed by the broad smile on her mouth.

"Yeah . . . I mean, yes . . . definitely! That'd be super fun!"

Ben breathed a sigh of relief. Allie's reaction had been swift and sincere, which gave him a lift after he had worked hard to summon up the courage to ask her. To reward himself, he went back to get seconds of his mac and cheese. *Glad to get through that one*, he thought.

Little did he know, Allie was both happy and nervous about the invite. She was excited to know that Ben felt the same connection for her as she felt for him. But it also made her feel more self-conscious. The first thing that came to her mind was that she must talk to Grace as soon as possible about this new development. She needed to sort out her feelings, and she had to talk to Grace about what she would wear to the dance! That is, if indeed Dak had invited her.

After Ben finished his seconds, the two picked up their trays and walked together to the counter to drop them off, both sensing a world of possibilities ahead.

As Ben and Allie passed by her, Lola followed them with her eyes, displaying a slight knit in her eyebrow as they left the cafeteria.

Chapter 26

STU

Stu had always struggled with insecurities. He was the middle child between an over-achieving older brother and a spoiled younger sister, who was beautiful and unfortunately knew it. This was not surprising since her parents had told her this frequently while showering her with gifts and lavishing praise as the baby of the family.

Unlike his brother Rich, who was naturally athletic, Stu, three years younger, was more awkward, hadn't shed his baby fat by thirteen, and preferred playing video games in his room to throwing a football—or playing any team sport, for that matter. Because his family was financially well-to-do, they could afford a palatial home in the most desirable neighborhood in Lakeshores and a full-time nanny to help care for their home and the kids.

Feeling ignored at home, Stu actively sought approval from his classmates at school. He had a long shock of dishwater blond hair that he'd periodically flip to the side by pitching his head until it had become part of his moniker—the head jerk to flip the hair off his face.

The acne he suffered from, along with the pudginess, heightened his insecurities. Thus, when two girls he viewed as attractive, Lola and Jenna, began chatting with him in math class, Stu went out of his way to be funny, even if it meant being a bit of a clown at times.

He became a purveyor of information—or disinformation—about other kids to ingratiate himself more with new friends, such as these two girls. It didn't occur to Stu that this role as a gossip might one day backfire. Nevertheless, the girls seemed to lap up his gossipy tidbits, which spurred Stu to take on a more snotty and belligerent tone.

One day, it was about a boy in their class wearing clothes that looked like hand-me-downs; another day, it was making fun of the slightly overweight girls trying out for the cheer team. Based on the laughs he got from several classmates in response to his running commentaries, including Lola and Jenna, Stu felt he had found a social niche. People liked him; they laughed at his jokes and seemed to appreciate his snide observations.

Along with this evolving persona came a disturbing development. Stu had observed a growing dislike by Lola and Jenna for Allie, then for Grace, who Lola described as the "tall skinny friend of Allie's who's trying out for the cheer team." To further seal their friendship, he decided to volunteer to assist Mrs. Durwood after school with setup for the cheer team tryouts. For the first round, he had helped with positioning the mats, putting one of the partitions in place for the gym, and sweeping up afterward.

His ulterior motive for doing this was an evil plot to sabotage Grace's tryout, something he had cooked up in the course of several gossip sessions with Lola and Jenna. Knowing that Grace was listed as the last participant in the order outlined for the final round of the tryouts, Stu aimed to apply some oil on the mat before Grace's routine. This was the secret the three friends had been snickering about when Allie saw them together. It was a cruel trick to perpetrate, about which Stu seemed to have no qualms.

The last bell rang as classes dismissed at Lakeshores MS. Kids peeled out of the building as buses in one row and the parents' carpool in another loop, waited outside. Grace headed to the girls' locker room next to the gym to change into a leotard and shorts for her routine.

Allie went to the gym bleachers, found a good spot a few rows up where she'd have a great view, and settled in. She pulled out her sketchbook and began working on a new idea for a watercolor she wanted to paint of the gazelle, Aurora, whom she had admired in Ataraxia.

Unbeknownst to Allie, Stu was positioning himself for the malicious prank he was planning. He had nabbed a small bottle of olive oil from the pantry at home, which he now had in his book bag.

As Allie sketched and Mrs. Durwood looked on, Stu shifted the mats to align them properly, after which he walked along with a rag, leaning over occasionally to wipe the mat as if cleaning any dust or moisture from the surface. He repeated this numerous times—first at the mat closest to the locker room, then at the midway point of the mat, and last, further up on the third large mat where the participants would be finishing their routines.

Allie glanced up and watched Stu, but seeing Mrs. Durwood standing by approvingly, she fell for his routine of cleaning spots on the mat.

Finally, the tryouts got underway. Each participant had a routine to demonstrate that included dance moves, leaps, jumps, and several required floor exercises. Eighteen students were in the final round, each trying out for the twelve spots on the cheer squad. They could choose individual music to go with their routine.

Allie thought that out of the first half, five of the nine showed real talent; the other four either couldn't complete the routine or fell during one or more of the moves they were supposed to execute. Particularly challenging were the final moves, which included executing three forward handsprings followed by two back handsprings, a forward walkover, and concluding with a final handspring and somersault. Those who were able to complete the routine without falls and who demonstrated poise and grace would most likely earn those coveted spots on the squad.

Mrs. Durwood announced a brief break while scores for the first group were tallied. Back in the locker room, the nine who waited for the next round to begin were chatting nervously between stretches to stay limber. Allie saw Stu walk over with his rag, wiping off what were apparently wet spots on the mat.

A loud buzzer heralded the start of the second half of the tryouts. Allie felt nervous for her friend. She knew it was important to Grace because as much as she tried to act low-key about it, Allie could tell Grace really hoped to make the squad. Well, as far as Allie was concerned, it would be a huge mistake if she wasn't on the squad because she was not only athletically talented, but she was also beautiful, inside and out.

Lola came out first, performing her routine to a Billie Eilish song. She moved well and included some unique dance moves intertwined with the required floor exercises. Her smart bob haircut set off her pretty features while she danced, flipped, and smiled through to her final somersault. Allie figured she was probably a shoo-in. Stu clapped noisily and whistled his support.

She was followed by two participants who both flubbed their floor routines badly, but the next three got through their routines smoothly without any falls. In her head, Allie scored nine she thought were probably in the mix. Only three more to go, and the last would be Grace.

Allie's stomach had knotted. She wondered how Grace would do with the pressure of coming last. She said a prayer for her while she popped a piece of bubble gum into her mouth. Whenever Allie felt nervous, she opted for chewing gum.

The next-to-last performer came out strong. She had an extra kick in her jumps and did her routine to a song with a fast beat. After she finished, Allie noticed Stu back out wiping a couple of spots on the third mat where the last girl had finished her routine. Then he slipped back to his spot on the bleacher.

Grace stepped out with her big smile as a jazzy Gershwin tune began to play. She glided effortlessly through her dance moves and then advanced into the floor exercises. Allie thought her front handsprings were amazing, and they were followed by flawless back handsprings.

Then, as Grace completed her routine with the final handspring, Allie heard a gasp as Grace went to the mat, her hand slipping. Adjusting, she tried doing an aerial walkover, then falling into the closing somersault, which she successfully completed. She raised her arms high and smiled. Then, as she turned to leave the mat, her foot slipped again. She twisted her ankle as she slid off the mat and came down at an awkward angle onto the floor with a loud *thwack*.

"Ahhh!" Grace cried out with pain etched in her voice.

Allie was down on the floor and alongside her friend in a flash. "Gracie, oh my, are you OK?" she blurted out. By then, Mrs. Durwood was there beside Grace as well. The advisor reached down on the edge of the mat, where she spotted some type of sheen. Rubbing her fingers together, she murmured that it felt oily.

"Stu! Get a wet rag over here right away!" she barked. Stu dutifully arrived, wet rag in hand, and wiped the mat profusely everywhere. No one yet suspected it was as much a move to cover his tracks as it was to respond to the PE teacher's order.

"Grace, how is your ankle feeling?" she asked as she leaned over to help Grace stand up and test the ankle.

"Well, nothing's broken," Grace said, "but it really hurts. It's probably a sprain." It was red and already swelling.

"Sit here," the teacher soothed as she pushed forward her chair for Grace to sit down. "We've got ice in the locker room fridge. Let's ice it down right away to minimize swelling."

She picked up the bullhorn to dismiss everyone. "Thanks to each and every one of you for your participation today. Your routines were amazing. I will post the names of the new cheer team members outside the gym on Monday morning. You're dismissed!" she shouted.

As Grace sat, Mrs. Durwood zipped off to the locker room to get the ice, but before leaving, she cast a dagger-eyed look at Stu, who was now sitting on the bleachers with a blank expression on his face. Allie wondered if she suspected malfeasance, but for now, the advisor was focusing on treating Grace's injury.

"I can't believe that happened!" Allie said, shaking her head.

"I think it was done on purpose," Grace said. "There was something slippery on the mat right where I landed at the end of my routine. It wasn't there during the first round on Wednesday. Did anyone else slip on it?" Having been in the locker room during the previous routines, Grace had not been able to see if someone else might have experienced the same issue.

"I was watching from the very start, every participant," Allie said. "There was no sign of anyone else having a problem or sliding on the mat during their routines." Something clicked in Allie's mind. "But I did see Stu helping Mrs. Durwood by mopping spots on the mat that were wet, I guess. Now I'm wondering if he did more. Maybe he secretly rubbed something to make it slippery!"

While the two friends were talking, Stu silently escaped with his backpack and its nefarious contents. If there was no proof of what happened, there was no way they could tie him to Grace's fall. The girls didn't know that he was still hoping his efforts would pay off.

They would all find out on Monday when the selections were posted.

In the meantime, Mrs. Durwood arrived with the ice pack. She wrapped it around Grace's ankle, which she elevated on another chair she had brought with her.

"Let's give it fifteen minutes before you try to walk on it," she said. "Is someone waiting to pick you up?"

"Nope. I told my mom I'd text her when tryouts were over. So it's fine. And I'm kind of shaking, so I'd like to give the ice pack and myself a few minutes here without moving."

Mrs. Durwood went about cleaning up, putting away her paperwork, and packing up her bag while Grace and Allie talked.

Allie learned that Dak had, in fact, found Grace just before she went to get ready for the tryouts and had asked her to the dance. Grace's brown eyes lit up as she told Allie about what he said when he asked her, including that he was happy Ben had introduced them that day at O'Grady's.

Allie laughed at that since Dak had not said much then, but clearly, her amazing friend had not escaped his attention. Then Grace told Allie the basketball coach already had Dak signed on as a forward for the Lakeshores MS team, which Dak said made him super happy. Talking about things took Grace's mind off her sore ankle.

The fifteen minutes had passed, so Grace took off the ice pack and stood up, gingerly putting some weight on her foot. She winced.

"Here, lean on me while you get started, and let's see if you can make it out front. Then you can call your mom. I'll stay with you 'til she gets here," Allie said.

Leaning on Allie's shoulder as she started to work her way forward, Grace could put more weight on her left leg and hobble along. The friends made their way to the front steps of the school and sat while Grace texted her mom.

Apparently, she was just leaving the attorney's office, where she worked as a paralegal. It would take her twenty minutes to get there. Allie called her mom to let her know about the delay, sharing the entire story on the phone.

"I'll be there in about twenty minutes so you can wait with her," Allie's mom said. "And tell Grace I'm praying for her to have a speedy recovery!" *I'm so lucky to have such an understanding mom*, Allie thought as she turned to Grace.

"My mom's glad I'm staying with you 'til your mom arrives, and she said to tell you she's praying for you to have a speedy recovery. And I am too," Allie added. But her green eyes registered her concern as she looked at Grace.

"Wow, tell your mom thanks," Grace said. "Y'know, your friendship means so much to me, Allie. I feel like a lot of things are looking up right now. You've a big part of that. Now, hopefully, I can work through this sprain to get back in action soon."

The conversation turned to the dance, what they would wear, who they thought might go with whom, and whether the two of them and their dates might go together. As they chattered away, a horn honked, signaling that Grace's mom had arrived. In their white SUV sat her two brothers in the back seat, whom their mom had picked up on the way from afternoon daycare.

Allie helped Grace as she made her way over to the car, carrying her backpack for her. She waited while Grace got settled into the front passenger seat next to her mom, who waved to Allie, thanking her for waiting with Grace.

"I see my mom pulling up now," Allie yelled. "Let me know how your ankle's doin' later!"

"Will do, Allie-Chun," she yelled back.

Allie ran over to the Volvo and jumped into the front seat. Her mom waited for her to buckle up. "Where's SJ?" Allie asked.

"He's at home making a batch of chocolate chip cookies with Taylor to celebrate winning first place in his category at the science fair!"

"Oh, how exciting! I'm so happy for him." Allie squealed with delight for her little brother. "Can't wait to tell him."

The car seemed to lilt home, chugging along happily as mother and daughter shared in the family's joys of the day. Allie talked nonstop, recounting for her mom her invitation to the dance from Ben, her growing friendship with Grace, and the scary event at the close of Grace's floor routine.

"There was slick stuff on the mat that messed up the final moment of her routine. I think Stu could have done something to try to sabotage Grace's tryout," Allie said, with a tinge of anger in her voice. "But I'm not sure. I'm just gonna watch and wait to see how things play out. Sometimes people have a hard time hiding their guilt. Most of all, I hope Grace's injury heals quickly! And I hope that despite her slip, Mrs. Durwood will still select Grace for the cheer team. Her routine was awesome!"

But she knew they wouldn't know until Monday.

Once they parked, Allie raced in to give SJ a fist-bump, a high-five, and cheer for his science fair award. He turned around and searched the tray he'd just taken out of the oven, then handed Allie the biggest cookie. He had a serious look on his face, conveying that today was a truly big day for him.

As soon as she went upstairs, Allie got a short text from Grace, telling her the ankle was feeling slightly better. She had it propped up on a pillow in the family room while she braided her sister's hair and had taken Ibuprofen, which was helping. Her mom had decided she didn't need to go to the doctor unless it felt worse tomorrow. The swelling was down, which was a good sign.

"So relieved!" Allie texted her back. "Rest up!" she wrote, posting a heart alongside her message.

Dear Daddy,

This is so terrible, but someone tried to cause my friend Grace to get hurt while she did her cheer tryout routine. I think it was this boy, Stu, who might have done it. It's terrible because even though it ended up just being an ankle sprain, it could have been much worse! She could have broken her ankle or fallen on her head or something else.

I think you sent an angel to watch over Gracie because she said she's doing a lot better. I'm SO relieved.

Even though he didn't get caught, Stu will have this on his conscience. I think hurtful things we do, even if we don't face consequences right away, will haunt us in some way later in our life.

Thanks for listening,

Love,

Allie

Chapter 27

Squeaker

Morning, at the home of the Outliers of the Abyss

"C'mon, let's get going!" Seraphine shouted. She was waiting for Delilah and Gavril to finish breakfast so they could leave for their friends Cedric and Squeaker's home.

The honey badger was small for his breed but had an oversized personality and the hubris to match.

A year earlier, Squeaker's mother, Daphne, had been banished by Malvelnia for her mistake of eating a particularly tasty small rat snake she had found lingering near a log she often checked under for just such a treat. Unfortunately, the father of this rat snake was a popular figure in Malvelnia who had assisted the Heralders on several spy missions to obtain information about Ataraxians.

A gray langur up in the trees happened to observe the entire thing, reporting it to the Malvelnian leaders. In a matter of days, Simon apprehended her. He put herbs from a particular root—which caused temporary paralysis when it was consumed—all over the honeycombs in a honeybee hive that Daphne frequented.

"Good morning, Daphne! What a beautiful day we have!" Simon bellowed once he spotted her. "I just had a delightful morning treat: some delicious honey in the honeybee hive over in that hollow tree stump," he said, pointing to the spot where he had inserted the paralytic herbs.

"Oh, thanks for the tip, Simon," Daphne said, squinting upward at Simon, who was perched on a branch in a large oak tree. He retreated further upward, nearly out of sight, then swung to a higher branch where he was camouflaged by clumps of small branches covered with leaves.

Daphne looked toward the beehive. She didn't trust Simon, but her love for honey outweighed her suspicion as she wandered in the direction of the hollowed stump. Honey badgers, after all, got their name from their love of that sweet golden substance, one of their favorite foods. Sure enough, once she got closer, she could see the honeybee hive was quite large with an abundance of honeycomb. Perfect for a morning treat.

Simon hadn't noticed, but with her was a small juvenile honey badger. She carried him in her mouth to get closer to the hive, then dropped him beside her while she stuck her long snout into the hive and chomped down noisily on the honeycomb, chewing and slurping the delicious honey inside the prisms of beeswax.

Soon, however, Daphne felt strange. She went to lie down next to her son, grabbing him in her mouth for safety, but suddenly found herself unable to move. In a matter of seconds, Simon swooped down to grab the honey badger. He knew the effect of the herbs was temporary, so he needed to move swiftly to send her down into the Abyss; without drugging her, Simon would not have been able to subdue Daphne. He would assuredly lose a bout with a creature known for its success in fights.

It was then he noticed the smaller badger in her mouth, but she had such a strong grip on him that Simon left him there as he carried Daphne to the edge of the cavernous hole. He walked her down the precariously narrow path far enough to drop her onto the bigger ledge further down. From that ledge, there was no path back to the top. The only path was the narrow one that spiraled down, the one Delilah would navigate one day in the future.

The little badger squeaked for his mother to get up. Daphne still lay on her side, but she was starting to stir and able to turn her head and lick her son's fur and then his face.

"I can hardly move," she whispered. "But if I keep wiggling and trying to get up, maybe the circulation will return, and I'll be able to see where I am." So for the next half an hour, Daphne wiggled and stretched and wriggled some more until she could feel all her limbs moving. The effect of the herbs was wearing off.

She righted herself, keeping her son behind her against the cliff wall. It was dark and shadowy, but she saw the narrow path leading down from the ledge. Carefully, Daphne, keeping her son always on the inside, began the descent.

"Keep walking; keep going," she told herself as they continued through the terrifying and dangerous place in which they found themselves. "That Simon is evil. He knew I would eat that honey . . . and then something happened to me. But I have to protect you, my son, no matter what."

An hour later, they were halfway through their descent, unaware of what lay ahead or where this dangerously thin path led. It was then Daphne heard a faint buzzing in the distance, a muffled sound. *But it is definitely buzzing,* she thought. She hastened her pace, nudging her son onward. The noise grew louder and louder until it was a deafening buzz that engulfed Daphne's ears.

"Hurry! Keep going and hurry!" she shrieked to her son. "Don't stop; keep going, whatever you do. Don't stop or look back."

At that moment, Daphne looked up as a squad of giant hornets as big as crows crowded over her, grabbing at her with their legs. Two stung her. She shrieked as they lifted her from the path, flying upward with her grasped in their hairy legs. Vainly, she bit at them.

Honey badgers are known for their sharp teeth, able to tear through the tough skin of snakes, and she was able to grab onto several legs clutching her, but the sheer power of the gigantic bees was too much for her. They were joined by more, which repeatedly stung her. The last thing Daphne saw as she succumbed to the venom and was flown upward was a small black and gray dot of movement down the path as her son disappeared from her sight.

Squeaker, as he later came to be known, had continued creeping downward along the narrow path. His small size and dark, muted colors served to hide him from marauders. Preoccupied with their prey, the nasty hornets never noticed Daphne's son.

He could hardly breathe from fear and feeling upset as he crept forward. Just as he was about to take another step, Squeaker felt something tickle his nose. He froze, standing motionless in his tracks. He tried to see what it was and realized not only was it tickling his nose, but it was sticky too. *But what is it?*

He brought up the claw of one of his toes to swipe the sticky thread off his nose. It was then he realized it was a thin strand of a gigantic spiderweb that engulfed the path. He glanced sideways to see out of the corner of his eye a gigantic spider at least five times his size. His eyes bulged; he stopped breathing as sweat dripped down his forehead.

He did not realize, however, that having just consumed a hearty lunch, the old queen spider was sleeping. Since she was not moving, Squeaker started breathing again, concluding that the spider hadn't seen him.

As he surveyed her web, he noticed a hole in need of repair near the bottom of where the web connected to the wall of the steep cliff. Squeaker stared at the hole. It was small, but so was he. If he raised up on his hind legs, he could leap through the hole, so long as he didn't let his hind feet catch on the fine strands and wake the gigantic spider from her slumber. Mustering his courage, Squeaker went up on his hind legs and leaped through the hole. Success!

Aargh! he thought to himself. *I'm not free of this web yet.* He faced another hurdle, a second intricately woven wall faced him. In this case, however, he saw that if he flattened his body like a pancake, perhaps he could slide underneath unnoticed. Squeaker stretched out his body to make it as wide and flat as he could, while at the same time, he slid his body gently forward.

Every muscle in his body tensed. He almost caught a thread with his butt as he evaded the web, but noticing the danger, he forced his tail down into the dirt path, just clearing beneath.

Dripping with sweat, Squeaker peered backward. Not a sign of movement from the queen. Darkness had filled the dark void around him, leaving Squeaker with no sense of his surroundings. He took one step at a time, unclear of where he was in his descent that had now spanned several hours.

He reached what appeared to be the bottom of the gorge. In the dim light of early evening, he saw pools of water dotted with small grassy islands. He heard water splashing down on rocks in the distance, but around him, the air was quiet, still. Squeaker nosed here and there along the water's edge, sniffing and searching.

Where is my mom? he wondered. (He had convinced himself she had escaped from those horrible hornets.) *And where are the other honey badgers, the ones by our home?* Perplexed, he wandered further along the pool until he reached a clearing. It was the first moment he saw other signs of life.

Squeaker spied several small creatures. They were Outliers, fairies heading home after a day of play. Squeaker followed them from a distance. They were chirping, sounding happy, and he was tired, hungry, and losing strength. As the group laughed, teasing each other as they trotted along, Gavril, who was bringing up the rear, noticed the little badger trudging along behind them.

"Wait, guys, hold up," he said. "There's a little guy behind us who might need some help."

As Gavril leaned over to talk to the little honey badger, all the baby badger could do was squeak back at the fairy child.

"Oh my, we've got a squeaker here," Gavril chuckled. But he saw that the badger was small, quite tiny even, and seemed plum out of energy. A taller boy, Cedric, walked over and scooped Squeaker up in his arms, nestling him close to his chest.

"Squeaker it is," Cedric said. "I've been wanting a little friend to brighten up our household." Cedric had no siblings and his parents, Glowerth and Magda, were serious types, albeit extremely proud of their son and wonderfully supportive of him.

For his part, Cedric, being the only son, faithfully worked to help his father with gathering food and keeping their family safe. The biggest threats to safety were occasional attacks by creatures of the swampland when the Outliers were scavenging for food. For that reason, Cedric helped his dad on such journeys by acting as a sentry, or on occasion, switching roles and gathering roots, berries, and greens, while his dad served as the lookout.

The friends continued home to the cliffs that evening, agreeing that Cedric should take Squeaker home.

That night, the honey badger whimpered in the makeshift nest that Magda had put together for him. He missed his mom, and everyone here was so different. Not different in a bad way, simply different from any creatures he had ever known before in his short life.

As the days turned to weeks, Squeaker recovered his strength each day as Magda fed him the sweet lingonberries that grew nearby and the blueberries and tasty wild lily bulbs that Glowerth had discovered on the banks of the pools.

Squeaker's fun-loving personality emerged, along with his gusto for whatever he undertook. Whether helping the family forage for food or standing watch for snakes, Squeaker was skillful and unafraid to take on any new task.

The family had discovered soon after he arrived that their newest family member had a taste for snakes, the most unwelcome creatures of the Abyss. The fairies feared them and steadfastly avoided them. But with Squeaker, they could now be more relaxed about that threat.

Likewise, whenever he and Cedric went cliff-sliding, Squeaker took the lead, squeaking and screeching at the top of his lungs as he sailed lickety-split down on his palm pad.

That particular morning, Cedric and Squeaker were getting ready to go to a nearby orchard when they heard voices outside. Peering out, Cedric saw three figures approaching.

Delilah arrived first, a few steps ahead of Gavril and Seraphine. She stopped abruptly and waited for them, suddenly shy at the prospect of meeting Squeaker.

"Yo, Cedric," Gavril called out. "C'mon out!"

Cedric rushed down from the recessed area of the cave that was his home to greet his friends.

"Oh, wow!" He smiled. "Great to see you guys. But me and Squeaker, we can't play right now. Mom asked us to pick apples today before we can do anything else. Squeaks and I were just getting ready to leave in a few."

Delilah looked up shyly as Squeaker stepped out into the sun.

"Oh, this is Delilah," Gavril said, introducing the lamb to the badger.

"Hi," Squeaker said. "Do you guys wanna go with us to the apple trees?"

"Sure thing," the three answered in unison. They headed off, bringing with them some bags made from twisted vines in which they could bring home the apples. The orchard was about a mile from their home. On the way, Delilah took the chance to talk to Squeaker about how she had arrived here and her desire to get back to Ataraxia.

"Oh, wow!" Squeaker said. "I've got the same idea. But I've heard it is a fierce journey to try to return home. I'm not afraid, though," he said with a tough edge to his voice. "I can battle snakes and other kinds of slimy creatures. You would need someone to go with you since you're just a small creature. But I'm not really clear on the route to get to where we want to go."

"Whitney told me about it," Delilah said. "I would have to pass first through the swamplands, which is treacherous. On the other side of that and along the banks of the swamps are the grassy lands, where she said many snakes live, including Abaddon, king of the Abyss. While some of his minions sleep, others wait for innocent victims to attack. Further on, there's a garden filled with exquisite flowers; but dangerous spirits inhabit the garden that I would have to evade while trying to find the exit at the far side of the garden. If I were able to reach that place, she told me I would be able to see my way home to Ataraxia."

Squeaker weighed the information Delilah shared. He knew it would be better not to attempt such a trip on his own. But with a lamb? And a girl at that. He kept his thoughts to himself as they reached the orchard and began pulling plump, luscious red apples from the lower branches of the tree.

Delilah ran alongside Gavril and Seraphine. She had Seraphine drape the bag over her back with the edge looped around her neck. That way, as the Outlier children picked apples, they could drop them into the bag. The five of them paused to snack on the apples, Squeaker devouring three in the time it took for each of them to eat one.

All the while, the badger thought about his conversation with Delilah. She was plucky, and clearly a good partner at the current task. Perhaps she was just the positive, helpful cohort he would need to achieve his quest to return home.

It was an instinctive drive within him to return to his pack. Of course, he did not realize that his mother had met her death, so he held out hope of seeing her again. But also, the small colony of honey badgers, including passing glimpses of his father who had been out gathering food most of the time after his birth, were images he retained. Returning home was the only thing that made sense to him. And he decided, on the spot, he would make the trip with Delilah.

"What do you think about making that trip together?" Squeaker asked Delilah, while Gavril and his sister were fluttering near the top of the tree to select a few choice pieces of fruit. "After all, you would need someone tougher than you to watch out for those devious snakes or other creepy reptiles. I am tougher than the creatures I've gotten to know among the Outliers," he bragged. "It'd be much safer for you to travel with me than by yourself."

Delilah was nodding, even before he finished his sentence.

"Let's do it," she squealed. "Right away. No time to waste. Truthfully, that's why I came along today with Gav and Seraphine," she admitted. "Their dad said he had heard you wanted to get back to Ataraxia. From that minute on, I was so hopeful about meeting you and seeing whether you might want to attempt this difficult journey together."

Squeaker tilted his head back, staring knowingly at the lamb.

Of course, he thought. *She knew she needed someone tough and brave to go with her.* He gave her a confident wink as Gavril and Seraphine rejoined them. They divided the apples into two bags so Delilah wouldn't have to carry too heavy a load and headed back home. They wanted to allow enough time for some serious cliff-sliding.

Once they had dropped off the apples, they joined a group of Outlier young-sters who were already out on the cliffs, shrieking and hollering as they careened down the surface, which had been rubbed smooth by endless lines of kids astride their green fronds and racing downhill.

Squeaker rushed to reach the launching point first, ahead of his friends. He grabbed a palm pad from the pile discarded by others who had already quit for the day.

Squeaker was a show-off. Whenever he went sliding with Cedric, he always had to beat him down the cliffside. Today was no exception. But today, he had a new audience to impress: Delilah.

Laughing, Cedric and Gavril pushed and jostled each other, trying to be next behind Squeaker, while Delilah and Seraphine sauntered over, giggling at the spec-tacle of the three trying to beat each other to the launch. After reaching the bottom, it was a hike on a narrow path cut into the cliffside to get back to the top, part of the rigor of the sport.

After half a dozen screech-worthy rides down, Gav and Seraphine told Cedric and Squeaker they had to run the clover errand for their mom. The field was not too far, and they wanted to do it before it got too late. Before parting ways, Squeaker took Delilah aside. "What do you think about leaving tomorrow?" he asked.

"I'm ready if you are," she said. "I'll talk with the family this evening. I need to let them know. They've been incredibly kind to me."

It was a feeling that Squeaker shared. The Outliers was a special community that overflowed with hospitality for the rare visitor who arrived. It was a vestige of the spirit that had shaped the community many generations earlier—stragglers who came together with others for mutual survival.

Discovering these ancient cave dwellings greatly enhanced their survival by becoming a haven that Outliers were pleased to share when a visitor did survive the descent into the Abyss.

But those who had ventured into the swamplands had not returned. Tales about the journey that Whitney had shared with Delilah were based on stories that had been passed around over the years. No one ever seemed sure whether they were fact or fiction. Tomorrow, Delilah and Squeaker were determined to find out.

Chapter 28

MAKING CHOICES

Monday morning at Lakeshores MS

The bus pulled up to Lakeshores MS on the early side of the morning bell. As soon as her feet hit the ground, Allie scooted off toward the end of the school building to where the gymnasium was located. As she got closer, she saw Stu and Lola heading in the same direction. The three converged at the same moment at the doors of the gym where Mrs. Durwood had already posted the list of the new cheer squad team members' names in oversized black letters.

Allie scanned the list from the side because Stu and Lola were hogging the space directly in front of the doors. She stood her ground, waiting for her two class-mates to move so she could get a better look. She also noticed Lola's name about halfway down the list, as well as the name of one of the Latino girls whom Lola had made fun of in her Instagram post.

"Congrats," Allie said, turning to Lola.

"Oh, yeah, thanks," she said, winking self-assuredly. "I'm glad my routine went so well on Friday. Too bad about your friend twisting her ankle at the end."

Allie shifted closer to the list as Stu and Lola turned away. Her eyes drifted down the list, almost missing it. But the last name on the list was Grace!

"Fantastic! Looks like whoever tried to sabotage Grace's routine totally failed, and whoever it was should be ashamed of himself," Allie said, shooting a penetrating look at Stu. He glanced back at her but immediately cast his eyes downward. Allie thought, *Even though Stu hasn't been caught, he will have to live with what he's done.*

Stu and Lola shook their heads as they walked away. "Can't imagine how *she* got on the list," Lola said as they departed.

"Agreed," Stu sniped. "What was Durwood thinking?" As their voices faded in the distance, Allie could have sworn she heard Lola say, "Next time, you gotta get it right."

Allie turned back to survey the list of names. Suddenly, she heard breathing over her left shoulder.

"Wow! I made it!" Grace shouted. "You must be my good luck charm, Allie." Grace grinned, hugging her pal.

"No, you made it on that list because you're talented!" Allie said. "I'm so happy for you. And wow—you're walking without crutches!"

"Yeah, I just have this ankle wrap," Grace said, looking down. "The swelling was gone by yesterday. It still throbs a little, but my mom said the ankle wrap should help. I'm just thankful it wasn't more serious."

"Let's get going," Allie said. "I'll see how you're doing when we get to lunch." The two friends chatted as they headed off to class.

In math class, Mr. Lozano talked about math regionals, which were coming up the following week. They were going to be held in Charlotte.

The Mathletes had won the faceoff with the team from Miss Weingarten's class, earning the spot to compete for Lakeshores against other middle schools in their region. He asked Allie, Ben, and Sophia to stay after class, then proceeded to hand a pop quiz to everyone.

The quiz took up most of the class period. Each person sat in place with the quiz turned over until every student had finished. In the back of the room, Jenna stole glances at Lola's answers the couple of times Mr. Lozano turned away. Allie knew the two friends had a silent pact to help each other when circumstances permitted, such as furtively sharing answers when they could pull it off. That was one reason, she guessed, that when they shared a class, they always tried to sit at desks next to each other.

As the last student turned over her test and put her pencil down, the bell rang. Allie, Ben, and Sophia hung back for a moment so Mr. Lozano could speak to them. He handed them permission forms, which they needed to have their parents sign, as well as directions to Highland Middle School in Charlotte where the competition would take place the following Saturday.

"If you have any difficulty with getting there, let me know," he said. "Parents usually drive their kids to these events. But if that's a problem, please tell me, and we'll figure it out."

The teammates then headed off for their next classes.

"Allie, I'll see you at lunch," Ben said. "I gotta run to get to my next class. It's way over on the other side of the building."

Allie and Sophia were walking to the next class together, which fortunately was just down the hall—a few classrooms away. Sophia, who was a quiet girl, told Allie she hoped she could contribute to the team's performance.

"Oh man, Sophia, you're such a math nerd," Allie said with a laugh. "You'll be the one that helps us win."

"I wish I felt as sure about that as you do," Sophia said sheepishly. It was the first time Allie recognized that part of the reason for Sophia's quietness might be her insecurity.

"Maybe we could get together and do some math drills," Allie suggested. "I bet Mr. Lozano might help us too. We could review and do sample challenge-type questions. I'll talk to him today, if I can, and ask him if he could arrange something after school."

"That would be great," Sophia said. "I could definitely use the practice. And maybe it would make me feel more comfortable about competing. It makes me so nervous to even think about it. My parents are already counting on us to win this competition, and it totally stresses me out."

As they talked more, Sophia confided that she had even thought about a way to ease her anxiety by taking some pills her mom had in her bathroom cabinet for tension. Her mother suffered from an anxiety disorder and had a prescription from the doctor for it.

"Sometimes," she told Allie, "with all the jerks here who say such mean things to me, I just wonder if life is worth it. I'm different, I get it, and different means *misfit*—at least that's what it feels like the way some kids treat me."

Allie knew what Sophia was talking about. Because of her Indian background, Sophia looked and sounded different from many typical Lakeshores students.

Her English, which she'd learned during her childhood in Chennai, had a strong accent, which, when she talked quickly, made her difficult to understand. Her face was dark brown—not uncommon for people from her hometown in southern India. Her long nose and sharp chin resulted in Stu giving her the nickname— behind her back, of course—of Sophia the Vermin (her last name was Verma).

In his inimitable fashion, Stu loved to come up with nicknames to both laugh at and put down classmates. In Sophia's case, Allie had discovered her nickname in the girl's bathroom, where it was scrawled on the back of a stall door in round, swirly cursive letters, "Sophia the Vermin loves cheese."

"Sometimes, I think it would be easier to just take a whole fistful of those pills and escape all of this," she said, holding up both hands to indicate Lakeshores MS, its brood of insecure adolescents, and life in general.

Allie froze. The conversation had only lasted a few minutes between classes, but she was freaked out by what Sophia was saying. She had alluded to taking her own life! This was mind-shattering. But she knew she had to say something.

"No way, Sophia. That would *not* be easier, and it would be such a terrible mistake! You are special," Allie blurted out. "God made you uniquely and perfectly. We have to talk later but don't think about that for another moment. You are an awesome friend, and I don't want anything to happen to you."

There was no more time to talk as the bell rang and the teacher for their English class closed the door.

Chapter 29

A Person of Substance

B en was in the process of editing articles for the next edition of *Aviso*. One was by Matt, a sports reporter who had written about the fall/winter sports teams, including one on the basketball team that Ben was now reviewing. Another was about school resources available to kids at Lakeshores.

Mental health issues were receiving more coverage among the mainstream news media, and Ben wanted *Aviso* to report on the help available for anyone who was suffering from those types of health issues.

Past generations had tucked mental health into a private vault, not to be openly discussed. When he talked with his mom about it, she said when she grew up, if someone in your family suffered from a mental illness, you had to keep your lips sealed. It was considered embarrassing.

And if it got recorded in your health records, you could be denied certain jobs and be stigmatized in other ways. As a result, his mom said, no one talked about it. But she told Ben that writing an article about mental health issues and the kinds of help available was a good thing to do.

"Times have changed," she said as she fixed a pot of black beans and rice. "Kids today are facing tough pressures at a younger age than we did. Letting them know they can get help, even at school, is a good thing for your classmates to learn. Not everyone has a close-knit family like ours with a built-in support system."

Ben agreed. A number of his classmates were living in single-parent households, having experienced their parents' divorce and the angry fights before they split up.

Many openly discussed having depression, taking anti-depressants, or being the victims of bullying or harassment.

"I live in a single-parent household," Allie told Ben when they first discussed the article he was planning. "But not by choice or even divorce. My dad died from cancer when I was eight years old. My mom is a widow who doesn't seem interested in remarrying, probably because my dad was such a wonderful guy," she mused. "Hard to find anyone who could measure up, for sure."

Ben had taken in all that information and concluded that was why his friend seemed older and more mature than other girls her age. Maybe she'd been forced to take on more responsibilities in her family at a young age.

There was nothing frivolous about Allie Lee. Rather, Ben saw Allie as a person of substance, a thinker, more inclined to listen and hold her tongue than spill what was on her mind. It was taking a while to really get to know Allie, but her friendship was worth it. In his mind, Al—as he called her—was one-of-a-kind and didn't seem to mind it, unlike many classmates who did everything to fit in with everyone else.

Chapter 30

SOPHIA'S ESCAPE

When the lunch bell rang that day, Allie hurried down to the cafeteria. She could hardly wait to talk to Grace about everything. And of course, she'd get to talk to Ben, and hopefully, Sophia would join them too. She needed to talk more with Sophia, but it would probably be better to do that one-on-one.

"Gracie-girl, happy to see you!" Allie called out as she neared the table Grace had snagged.

"Me too, Allie-Chun! It's a super day today, even if I do have a test coming up this afternoon in earth science—yuk. Dak walked me here, but he has to go hang with his b-ball buddies," Grace said, leaning her head sideways. Allie followed the direction her head was aiming and saw Dak and three other tall dudes chowing down on hamburgers.

"Oh, I'm so excited for you about making the cheer squad!" Allie grinned. "You are going to be the star of the team with all those moves you got, girl."

Grace chuckled. "Well, the good news is, I spoke with Mrs. Durwood about the ankle. She said I should attend the practices, but until my doctor gives me the green light, she won't expect me to participate. It's already feeling a lot better, so I figure I should be ready to start some of the routine, lower-impact stuff in another week or so."

"That's terrific, Gracie. Matt told me there won't be a basketball game until after Thanksgiving, so hopefully, you'll be in action by then. I know you wouldn't want to miss one of Dak's games, right?"

"Yeah, no way."

As Matt and Ben arrived, the girls were busy making plans to go shopping together over the weekend for dresses to wear to the dance.

"Glad I don't have to worry about that stuff," Ben laughed. He had a light blue collared polo shirt, which complemented his tan skin and dark brown eyes. Allie thought he looked particularly handsome. She felt her face flush as she looked into his eyes.

"Oh," she remembered, "I saw Mr. Lozano in the hall and chatted with him about a practice session. He said if we wanted to stay after on Wednesday to do some prep for the regionals, he'd be available. Does that work for you?"

Ben nodded. He had to work on Tuesday and Thursday that week at the bodega, but Wednesday was open. "We'll have to ask Sophia if that works for her," Ben said. "But I haven't seen her yet at lunch, have you?"

"Nope, and I've been watching for her," Allie said. "Haven't spotted her yet." The lunch group got to giggling as they tried tossing grapes to see who could catch it with their mouth in midair. It was a Monday, and no one felt like being serious.

Sophia never made it to the cafeteria. She had gone to the school nurse, complaining of a migraine. The nurse took her temperature and had her lie down on the couch in her office for fifteen minutes. But because Sophia still felt terrible, the nurse contacted her mom to see if she could pick her up from school. No success. Her mom was in the middle of a presentation at work. But Sophia's dad was available, and within twenty minutes, he was there at the school's main office signing out Sophia.

"So sorry you are feeling bad, Soph," her dad said as she settled in the passenger seat of the family's Pathfinder. "When we get home, I want you to take a Tylenol and get in bed. I have to go back to the office, but your mom said she'll come home a little early so you won't be home by yourself for too long."

Sophia nodded, leaning back as she rolled her seat into a reclining position and closed her eyes. Once they pulled into the driveway, she slid out of the seat and walked through the garage door, which her dad had raised.

"See you this evening," he called out. "Feel better soon."

Sophia stopped in the kitchen to pat Louie, the family's calico cat.

"Hi, sweet boy," she whispered.

She padded upstairs, having left her shoes at the doorstep. Sophia's headache was a pain that started in her head and traveled down to her heart, where it stirred up a storm of unhappiness and hopelessness. She glanced in the mirror in her parents' large bathroom. Staring back was an image she had come to dislike.

"You are just plain ugly," she said to the girl in the mirror. "You should just get it over with." Tears welled in her eyes, splashing down from her dark lashes to the marble countertop. She glanced up at the medicine cabinet to the left of the double vanity.

Her mother had her own cabinet; her father's was the one on the far side of the second sink. Scanning the shelf, her eyes found the familiar anxiety meds her mom took.

Sophia grabbed the bottle along with some sleeping pills sitting on the bottom shelf. She turned the faucet to fill the blue cup that sat by her mom's toothbrush, then threw a handful of pills down her throat followed by a huge swig of water. It tasted bitter.

She followed that with about a dozen sleeping pills, then headed to her bedroom and closed the door behind her. She put on her favorite PJs covered with Hello Kitty images, threw back the bedspread, and sank into the cool, lavender sheets.

Closing her eyes, Sophia went to a familiar fantasy, imagining herself walking hand-in-hand with a boy who gazed at her admiringly. Her violet sari floated behind her as they strode toward the dance floor. She was gliding effortlessly with her handsome partner as she fell into a deep, deep sleep.

Chapter 31

THE GOLDEN RULE

Over at Lake Bluff Elementary, SJ and Russell were in a break-out group the school offered for kids on the spectrum who needed practice developing social skills with other kids and adults. It was a new, experimental program, and thus far, parents were pleased with this learning opportunity the school offered.

When Meg enrolled SJ at the school, she was delighted to find out about the program and made sure SJ was registered for it. It met three times a week, part of SJ's weekly class schedule mix, allowing him to remain in his regular classroom activities yet receive this specialized training during the week as well. The goal was for students to feel like they were just like any other students at Lake Bluff, but who just happened to also participate in this social skills module.

SJ was glad that when the teacher for their social skills class asked them to work with a partner, he could team up with Russ, his friend. They were working on an exercise about bullying.

Miss Cosgrove, the teacher, put up a series of pictures on an easel at the front of the classroom depicting children acting like bullies as they made fun of other kids, calling them names or even threatening to hit them.

"I don't like this at all," Russ said to SJ. "It reminds me of what happened to us that day in the locker room. It makes me want to go home." Russ, who was a redhead, had a lot of freckles that already made his face pink. But as he spoke to SJ, SJ could see Russ's face get a shade redder.

"I know—you're right, Russ," SJ said. "That's because those guys who did that are bullies, just like they're talking about in these pictures. But going home isn't going to solve the problem. We're friends. So we can look out for each other. Another thing is talking to a teacher or someone in charge, like when that happened to us, I went and talked to Coach Lemmel."

SJ stared at Russ's face. "You've gotta know I've got your back," he told Russ. "I know you told me that growing up, kids made fun of you." Russ was an only child, so this was something new—to have a friend to whom he could turn, someone who was reliable.

"My dad always told me to just follow the Golden Rule," SJ told Russ. "Treat other people the way you would like to be treated. That's from the Bible."

"Really?" Russ raised a questioning eyebrow. "I never heard about that one before."

"Yeah. My dad showed me. He always told me I have a really good memory with numbers. It's in the book of Matthew in the New Testament, Chapter 7, verse 12, in Jesus's most famous speech, the Sermon on the Mount."

Russ sat quietly, seeming to mull that over for a minute.

"Yeah," he finally said. "The world would be a lot better place if people actually followed that rule."

SJ nodded. He thought about the kids at Lake Bluff who had mistreated him and how they tried to bully him and Russ for no good reason except to exert their power over them.

"You're right, Russ," SJ said. "The universe would be a better place if everyone followed the Golden Rule."

Chapter 32

HONORING WILL

W hen Allie and SJ got home from school that evening, Meg had something special planned. It was November 12, their dad's birthday, and
the family was going to dedicate a tulip magnolia tree, one of the
most beautiful flowering trees grown in North Carolina, in his memory.

Meg had hired a landscaper to install the tree in their front yard. She had
him put a low curved stone wall behind where the tree was planted to set it apart
from the other areas in the yard. Now she was standing admiring it, a cap turned
backward on her head to hold in her wiry curls. She had on faded blue jeans and
a sleeveless blue and white blouse that revealed her toned arms—the byproduct of
her early three-mile runs before the day even started. And over lunch, she would
often work out with weights as part of her fitness routine.

They had finished their dinner of spaghetti, garlic bread, and salad, which was
their usual Monday evening fare. Meg could be pretty darn predictable: spaghetti
on Mondays, chicken on Tuesdays, leftovers on Wednesdays, breakfast for dinner
on Thursdays, and pizza night Fridays. Sometimes she varied it but not by much.
It was less to think about and the kids seemed fine with it.

"We'll say a prayer and then light these candles," Meg told the kids. "Daddy
would be so proud of you guys—how you've worked hard to adjust here, and what
great helpers you have been for me."

Meg handed each of them a candle, and then, holding her burning candle
wick next to theirs, set the children's alight. Evening crept in, bringing its gray and
mauve cloak that now settled over the solemn assembly. The features of their faces,

at first barely discernable, gradually became clearer in the heightened glow of the candlelight.

Holding hands with Allie and SJ as the sun set, Meg lifted up a prayer. "Thank you, Heavenly Father, for our beloved husband and father, Will. You blessed us with his presence and chose to take him home to Your kingdom. We dedicate this precious tree in his memory, remembering as the Psalmist wrote, 'That a person is like a tree, planted by streams of water, which yields its fruit in season and whose leaf does not wither—whatever they do prospers.'

"We pray this tree grows strong and tall, giving praise to You, Lord, as it reaches its limbs to the heavens. And that its leaves never fade and its flowers fill our yard with sweet fragrance each year as we breathe in its hope and hold dear Will close to our hearts."

Meg peeked at Allie, who was keeping her head down as her eyes brimmed over for a moment with tears, quickly brushing them off with the side of her hand. She loved her kids' hearts.

The evening grew darker as clouds moved in. The wind rustled the leaves of the newly planted magnolia tree, and it sounded to Meg as if Will was whispering in her ear: *I'm here, I love you, I'll see you again one day.*

Chapter 33

SOPHIA

As the school bus pulled up to Lakeshores MS, Allie saw Ben, Matt, and Grace on the front stairs of the school; they were sitting on the cement steps and talking. She hurried over, hoping to have a chance to chat before the bell rang for classes. Grace looked up with a disturbed expression.

"'Sup?" Allie asked.

"Terrible news," Ben said. "Matt lives on the same street as Sophia, and this morning there was an ambulance at her house and a sheriff's car. His dad went by to see what was going on and heard that they took Sophia to the hospital. She's in a coma! That's all we know right now."

Allie's face turned white. She sat down, speechless at the news. *Sophia in a coma? How terrible!* She immediately thought of what Sophia had said to her the day before. Could Allie have done something more to help? She just hadn't imagined that Sophia was serious about what she had said. But maybe it was something else that had sent the girl to the hospital.

When Allie reached math class, she was overwhelmed by a wave of sorrow when she saw Sophia's empty chair. Mr. Lozano arrived and, after shutting the door behind him, he said he had an announcement about Sophia Verma.

"Sophia was taken to Stanbridge Hospital by ambulance early this morning, where she is in a coma. Her parents informed the school about it," he told the class. "We don't really know anything else at this time, but please keep Sophia and her family in your thoughts during this difficult time."

"Oh," he added, "in light of these developments, we'll send our alternate team from Miss Weingarten's class to the math regionals this weekend." Allie realized that even their confident, upbeat math teacher was taken aback by this sad development.

Mr. Lozano then directed everyone to page 143 in their math textbooks to do some practice algebraic equations.

"While you're doing that, I'll finish grading some papers from my other class."

For that period and beyond, Allie couldn't focus on the schoolwork in any of her classes. At lunch, Matt told them that when his dad went by the Verma's house, her dad had spoken to him for a moment and told him Sophia had been asleep when her mom came home from work, and not wanting to disturb her, just let her stay in bed.

However, when she wasn't up early to get ready for school, they realized something was wrong. They couldn't wake her, so they called 911. The paramedics put her on oxygen and got her to the hospital. So far, they didn't know whether she was conscious yet or not.

After Matt left to get to the library over his lunch break, Allie told Ben what Sophia had said to her the day before and how guilty she felt for not doing something.

"You didn't have any time to do anything, Al," he said. "And it was such a brief exchange. It's not your fault. But what she told you, it highlights how destructive the taunts or insults that our classmates unleash on others can be. It's a red flag for us to do something."

"Like what?" Allie said. "It seems like a big problem."

"I dunno," he said. "But I want to write something about it in *Aviso*. Not about Sophia, of course. I wouldn't invade her or her family's privacy like that. But about changing how we think, how we act toward each other. And with all the pressures that we face with school and grades, the added burden of feeling shamed can push someone over the edge."

"Yeah, you're right," Allie said. "Maybe we could start a club . . . or a group or a movement at Lakeshores MS with the theme that every one of us deserves a safe space, a way to feel secure, even during the pressures and pitfalls of social media, gossip, and bullying. After all, I don't think anyone really wants to be linked to that kind of behavior, right? So maybe there's a way we create a place and a group that kids want to be part of?"

"Brilliant! I love that idea," Ben agreed. "Maybe we could propose setting aside a room that we could make into a hangout."

"That's a great idea. We could try to find some comfy furniture and post useful information about resources for kids who are hurting, like what's available from our school but also information about getting help, like for stress, problems with alcohol or drugs, or other mental health issues."

"Yeah, and we could form a group to help decorate and think about how to make it come together," he said.

"Oh," Allie said, "I'm psyched! It makes me feel like something good will come out of Sophia's situation. Speaking of which, I need to get going. I want to make sure to get home on time today so maybe I can call her family and see if I can find out how she is doing."

"Okay, text me later and let me know what you learn," Ben said. "Have a good rest of your day. We'll talk more about this idea soon."

The two friends dumped their food trays off and headed in different directions.

Later that day after she got home from school, Allie told her mom about everything that had happened with Sophia. She also told her mom she wanted to see if she could visit Sophia at the hospital.

"Well, this is probably a difficult time for her family. Why don't you let me call her home and ask whether that would be possible or not," her mom said while she looked up their number.

Allie watched as her mom called and Sophia's mother answered the phone. Allie was unsure whether Mrs. Verma would approve of her wanting to visit, but she was pleased, once her mom got off the phone, to find out Sophia's mom thought it was a good idea. Sophia was still in a coma, but the doctors had suggested that family or friends be there and talk to her. They felt it would be positive stimuli that could be helpful.

Allie's mom got the address and room number and told Sophia's mom that Sophia and their family were in their prayers. She said Allie would come by the hospital Friday after school to visit.

When she got home from school that Friday, Allie selected a book she could take to read to Sophia. Then she and her mom left for the hospital. Her mom told her she'd wait in the reception area while Allie went to Sophia's room.

The light in the room was slightly dimmed. Sophia's dark hair lay feathered across the pillow, making her face look chalky pale in contrast; her dark lashes lay still over her closed eyes. There was a needle with IV fluids being pumped into the girl's body to keep her hydrated and nourished. She was no longer on breathing support, something the doctors had considered a positive development in Sophia's hoped-for recovery.

Sophia's dad sat in a chair, looking tired, but when he saw Allie, his eyes brightened. "It is so lovely to have you come by to visit with Sophia," he said, his voice cracking. "Please take my chair. I'm going to go get a cup of coffee and take a little break. Thank you . . . thank you for coming."

Allie smiled politely, shook Mr. Verma's hand, and obediently replaced him in the chair. She watched as he stepped into the nearby elevator and headed down to the basement level where the cafeteria was located. She turned back to gaze at her friend who looked very small lying tucked under the sheets. Allie could see her breathing, but otherwise, she saw no signs of stirring.

"Sophia, I am so sorry that I didn't get to talk to you more that day you told me how sad you were feeling. I wish I could have told you more about how amazing you are and that kids are dumb and mean, and we just have to stick together and ignore them. But I'm telling you here and now that you have to get better. You are special, and I want to be your friend and get to know you better. So you have to recover from this coma . . . please, Sophia."

Allie continued talking, chattering about her family, about school, and about anything cheery she could think of. Then she remembered her book. It was a collection of Psalms, the beautiful poems written by King David, a man who, according to the Bible, God Himself called "a man after My own heart." She began with the 23rd Psalm from the New International Version.

"The Lord is my shepherd," she began reading, "I lack nothing. He makes me lie down in green pastures . . ." She continued reading the familiar and comforting words. Next, she chose Psalm 77, concluding with verses 13 and 14, even raising her voice for emphasis: "Your ways, God, are holy. What god is as great as our God? You are the God who performs miracles; You display Your power among the people!" Allie felt a tear form in the corner of her eye as she called out to God.

"That's right, You are a God of miracles, and we need a miracle for my friend, Sophia. Wake her up, Lord, and show her how much You love her and how much her family loves her."

As she finished her prayer, Allie felt someone's presence in the room. Mr. Verma had returned. Allie rose from the chair. Then, standing close to the bed, she took Sophia's hand in hers for a moment before stepping softly away, nodding to Mr. Verma as she left.

Chapter 34

THE SWAMPLANDS

Delilah departs for the Swamplands

It was still dark outside when Delilah awakened the next morning. Her heart fluttered with excitement the moment she opened her eyes, anticipating the day ahead. She had offered glowing words of thanks to Whitney and Jude that past evening after she, Gav, and Seraphine had arrived home with a bag filled with fragrant, purple-flowered clover. Whitney tried to convince the lamb to consider staying with them longer. Even knowing she had a companion for the trip, Delilah saw her shudder at the thought of her and Squeaker heading off through the Swamplands.

Delilah didn't know Whitney had chosen not to share the story of her uncle, who many years ago had ventured into the edge of the Swamplands, searching for his son (her cousin) who had gone missing there. It was a gruesome piece of family history.

Whitney's cousin, Jalen, had been playing with two friends along the fringes of the Swamplands, an area forbidden for the fairy children to play. He noticed a funny-looking chartreuse-colored frog hopping across a large broken tree trunk lying in the gray-green waters. It had large red eyes and orange toes. His companions were busy wrestling with their pet prairie dog, which they had found as a baby and tamed. Jalen hopped up on the trunk, skittering after the brightly festooned frog. That was the last he was seen. When his two friends turned around, Jalen was nowhere in sight.

"Jalen! Yo, Jalen, stop it. Quite hiding and show us where you are!" they had shouted. Silence. They searched, becoming increasingly frantic because they knew they would already be in trouble for playing in the forbidden territory. After nearly an hour, the two friends flitted home to report Jalen's disappearance to their parents.

After the boys' punishments (they were grounded for the next two weeks) came the agonizing part: going to tell Jalen's father what had happened. Tall and robust for an Outlier, Lomar's body visibly slumped when he was told the news. Recovering from the immediate blow, he insisted on hearing a detailed description of exactly where Jalen's friends had seen him last. He told his wife he would be back later, once he found Jalen.

It was early afternoon by the time Lomar began his search, peering painstakingly at every inch of the murky swamp banks in the area the boys had described.

He saw three different fallen trees that lay limbless in the water, but only one was the size that matched what they had reported. Lomar stepped up onto the trunk and stared at slimy grasses that clung to the bark. As he walked along it, he noticed a sandy patch further off to the right where a monstrous, black boa constrictor at least seven feet long, lay on its side. It appeared lifeless. In truth, it was basking in a deep sleep.

Suddenly, Lomar's eyes zeroed in on a horrifying sight. In the middle of the snake's body was the outline of a small form about the size of his son. Then, as if to confirm it, he saw a bulky area protruding near the thinner skin of the snake's underbelly, the clear silhouette of a pair of wings crushed within its innards.

Lomar froze, all color draining from his face. As he stared, paralyzed with grief, a small chartreuse frog with bright red eyes and orange toes hopped atop the snake's leathery skin. Then the frog hopped from the motionless snake's body onto a lily pad. It was unaware of the sinister role it had played in Jalen's fate.

Chapter 35

Day of Departure

Squeaker was sad at daybreak to bid farewell to Cedric and his foster family of many months. Although he had a bit of an ego, Squeaker was a fun-loving creature. He had brought jokes, pranks, and laughter to the household. During that time, he had doubled the size of his tiny frame and filled it out. He had also grown in confidence and pride.

Instead of feeling insecure about or self-conscious of his differences from the Outliers, he felt he was stronger and tougher than most of them. Without a doubt, he was more solidly muscular, something he lorded over Cedric, Gavril, Seraphine, and now, little Delilah. He felt a newfound purpose as he headed to his friends' house. He would protect Delilah as they faced this new adventure together.

Delilah watched as Whitney packed a small sack of berries, clover, seeds, and nuts for the lamb to take with her. She took turns giving Gav and Seraphine farewell hugs before waving goodbye.

Lilac and orange streaks were just peeking over the horizon as the incongruous pair, lamb and badger, sauntered off together, picking their way down the narrow path from what had been their temporary cliffside dwellings. Delilah glanced back at the now pearlescent pink rising up behind her. She figured it was the last time she would see the crystalline reflection of first morning sunrays on that starkly beautiful cliffside. But she was ready for whatever lay ahead.

Chapter 36

Return to Ataraxia

October morning in Lakeshores

S J and Allie walked out the front door and down the flagstone path that Aunt Agatha had installed eighteen years ago. Worn and cracked in a few places, it was still an elegant walkway in its gray-blue and tan hues. As they trudged down the sidewalk together, Allie tried to sum up her crazy experience of Ataraxia, but a jumble of words poured out.

"SJ, I'm going to . . . going to tell you something. Something that you cannot repeat to anyone," she started, her eyes as riveting as the tone of her voice.

"I've been waiting to tell you, but last week . . . there were animals of all kinds, and they were talking! I made friends with a sheep family and took care of a little injured vulture named Kibou!" The words tumbled out as she tried, in the distance of a couple street blocks, to explain the strange events that had transpired and which, she felt, would change her forever.

"What I'm trying to say is I traveled to an entirely different world!"

SJ looked at her skeptically. Allie could tell by the way he rolled his eyes that he thought she was teasing him with her improbable tale.

"Are you feeling all right, sis?" he said. "This doesn't make sense. You're teasing me, right? You've been in your bed every morning. I've walked with you to the bus every day . . . when did all this happen, and how did you get to this other *universe*?"

"It was through that huge painting in my room," she said, "the one Aunt Agatha hung in there years ago, the one that I liked so much when I first saw it. It has magical powers! I'm dead serious! It was the other night—when I was trying to get to sleep—when I heard a voice calling me. First, I thought maybe it was you calling from your room. I could not figure out where it was coming from. Then I realized it was the sheep! The one in the distance in that painting was calling me. I know it sounds insane, SJ, but you gotta believe me. . . . But don't speak to anyone about it."

They were almost to the corner where SJ had to wait for his bus. Allie could tell he still doubted her story.

Then SJ's bus rounded the corner, heading their way.

"Okay. I won't say a word to anyone," he agreed. "But tonight, I wanna hear more about it. It's hard for me to even imagine how this could happen, so you'll have to explain. And show me."

"Absolutely," Allie said. "After dinner, we'll go upstairs to *do homework*." Allie signaled quotation marks with her fingers as she said *do homework*. "Mom's in the middle of a big speech she has to finish this week, so I know after dinner, she'll go back to working on that. It'll be the perfect time. I've been wanting to tell you, dude, but you've been so busy with your science project and other stuff."

SJ boarded the bus after it pulled up and the door opened. Allie watched him as he settled into the seat next to his nerdy friend, Russell. She could see SJ twirling his hair nervously. He glanced out the window as Allie waved goodbye.

That evening, a Friday, was one of the most beautiful early October nights Lakeshores had experienced in years. The air turned crisp as a cool front moved in, bringing the first hint of autumn weather. After dinner, their mom asked the kids to put out the recycling bin at the curb for the Saturday morning pickup.

While outside, Allie said, "Tonight's a good night to show you what we talked about. C'mon up to my room." The two shut the garage door and headed up to Allie's room. As they shut the bedroom door, SJ glanced up at the painting that Allie had told him was the entryway to this weird world.

Her eyes followed his. She froze for a moment. The painting had changed. Instead of seeing two large sheep and a lamb on the hillside, now there were only one larger and one smaller sheep, which she recognized as Molly. And alongside her was Luke.

"Oh my," she blurted out to SJ. "The painting is different. There's a big sheep, that's Molly. And her son, Luke. But no sign of Graham. Something must be going on there! We have to find out . . . see if we can help!"

As she pushed her old toy box in front of the painting, Allie explained to SJ how she had first entered what she now knew to be Ataraxia, how she had heard a voice calling her, telling her to step into their world. Afterward, she said, she had looked up that word online—*Ataraxia*—and saw it was a Greek word meaning "a state of calm serenity." That made sense as she reflected on the unified and peace-seeking nature of its residents.

"Molly, Luke!" she whispered fiercely as she peered at them for any sign of movement. She saw a stirring, climbed atop the toy box while grabbing SJ's hand, and lunged her right foot forward. Again, the strange sense of a suction pulled her forward through the cool Jell-O. She felt for SJ's hand. *Yep, still locked in mine . . . * and then with a *plop*, they were knocked forward into the beautiful, lush green pasture in which she had arrived before.

"Hey, Allie!" Luke yelled. "How ya doin'? And who's this you've brought along with you?"

"Hey, Luke! Hi, Molly! This is my brother, SJ. Sometimes our mom calls him Speedy 'cuz he's super-fast."

Molly smiled at Allie. "Oh, it's so lovely to see you again, Allie. And now your brother too. What a pleasant surprise. And on such a beautiful day. It's so nice to meet you, SJ."

SJ glanced around the meadow and spotted a funny-looking bird on a large, patterned cloth. The bird fluttered and flipped in kind of a somersault with a dash of humor. "Who the heck is that?"

"That's Kibou," Allie said.

"I'm happy to see you again, Allie. My wing is getting better, but it still hurts when I try to fly. So I'm enjoying the day here in the meadow."

SJ stood with his mouth open as the conversation unfolded. Allie knew it must still be a shock for him to hear the sheep, and now this small vulture, talking.

Molly straightened up her neck from the clover treat she'd been enjoying. "We should probably head back home now," she told the group. "I'm concerned that I haven't heard yet from Graham about the Council's meeting at Malvelnia. He

should be home. We need to check back. If he's not there, I'm going to send you over, Luke, to find Aurora to see what's happened."

The gazelle, Aurora, lived in a forest glen near their family. As one of the councilmembers, she would have heard by now what had come out of the meeting Graham, Zion, and Solomon had attended. Molly hoped maybe Graham would even be home by now. She was feeling more tired than usual, lately, so she wanted some time back home to rest.

As they headed back, Aurora came leaping down the path, soaring to a stop at their feet.

"Molly!" she said. "I've just had word from the Council. Graham, Zion, and Solomon are being held as prisoners by Wendigo! They've broken their word about our leaders meeting safely with them."

Molly gasped. "Oh, dear, no!" she exclaimed. "Are they OK? How will we get them released? Is there a plan?"

"As far as we know, yes, they are all right. The Council had already agreed on a plan, but now, given these dire circumstances, we have amended it. We are moving up our timeline, and we will begin . . ." Aurora paused. Only then did she seem to notice that Allie was loosely carrying the scarf that held Kibou. Seeing the small vulture's face, she cut off her words in mid-sentence.

"Who is that?" she asked, startled by the black feathers.

"It's the injured young vulture we found on our journey to the meeting," Luke said. "He's doing better, but he can't fly yet."

"I see," Aurora said. "Walk ahead with me, Molly, so I can fill you in."

Aurora and Molly rushed on ahead, creating a distance between themselves and Luke, SJ, Allie, and Kibou. As they walked, the gazelle shared the details of the plan to strike in the dead of night to release their leaders from the rocky enclave where they were being held. Molly shed tears, worrying about her dear Graham but holding onto hope for his safe return.

Aurora leaped away, her mission accomplished. She had shared the news with Molly. Once they reached the small grove where they lived, Molly found a grassy spot to rest her weary body. SJ sat down on a rock near her.

"Who is Wendigo?" he asked.

"He's the ruler of Malvelnia," Molly said. "King Wendigo. He's evil! His most recent decree was to begin counting and branding every citizen of Ataraxia. Horrible creature! And now he has captured my poor, dear Graham."

"Well, Mrs. Molly, you should know that Kibou says that one is his dad—that Wendigo guy," SJ said.

Molly raised her head with eyes wide.

Chapter 37

KIBOU'S WHEREABOUTS

As Queen Eris headed into the royal compound, Estrelle was near the entranceway as she arrived.

"Mom, Kibou is missing," Estrelle said. "I haven't seen him since yesterday. He said he was going to be practicing some dive bombing moves out near the monkey caves," she said, rolling her eyes.

While Kibou had only been flying for a few weeks, he loved to show off and zoom down toward the ground at fast speeds, both to impress his friends and prepare for the future when he would be expected to forage for his own carrion instead of relying on his parents to bring it to him.

"You're supposed to keep your eye on him, Estrelle!" Eris squawked. She looked nervously at the gnarled trees nearby, scanning the branches for her son. Then she scanned the horizon, half expecting she'd spot him.

"I do," Estrelle pouted. "It's not my fault that he has a mind of his own."

"Your father is not going to be pleased about this. There's a lot going on right now between our kingdom and the Ataraxians; we need to find Kibou and make sure he's all right," she said firmly. Eris soared to the top of the tallest banyan tree and scanned the land and air for Simon.

"That worthless Simon is never here when you need him," she fumed out loud.

Meanwhile, in Ataraxia, Allie saw that Kibou was recovering from his injured wing. It was sore when he fluttered it, but he told her it felt much better than when he had first slammed into that pesky tree branch. But he wasn't able to fly home yet because when he started to ascend, a pain still rippled through his wing.

It might take a few more days before it was healed adequately for the long flight. It had taken him a good part of the previous morning to reach the monkey caves when he flew there from his home, so he knew it would take him even longer when he was ready to venture home.

When Allie had decided she needed to head back to her world the first time, she had placed the back sack around Luke's neck so he could more easily carry Kibou as he and his mom headed back to their home. They told Allie that Kibou, who was a fun-loving character, was livening up the sheep family's life. He liked to put on shows for them to pass the time.

"Kibou, Kibou, Kibou is a smash for you!" he sang as he made some smooth flutter steps to the right and then the left. "Kibou, Kibou, Kibou brings lots of fun for you."

Luke laughed at the crazy bird. Even though his parents didn't like to speak of the vultures, Luke thought Kibou was a terrific addition to the household. And he told Allie he wished he could stay.

"I told my mom, 'C'mon, Mom, can't Kibou stay and live with us?'" Luke said to Allie. "He's so much fun. And he seems super comfortable with us."

"There's no way a vulture is going to live in this household," his mom had told Luke with a huff. "When your father gets home, we must find out what the Heralders have told him about getting this vulture boy back to his family."

Little did Allie and Molly know at that time, but a massive search was underway by Kibou's parents to find their son since Devon, the recipient of Graham's message about the injured vulture, had never reached Malvelnia. In his exuberance over a newfound friend to play with in the mango grove, Devon had completely forgotten about the message he was supposed to deliver.

The capture of the Ataraxian leaders was an impetuous move on the part of Wendigo. He hoped the extreme action would intimidate the Ataraxian Councilmembers and exert psychological terror over their citizens.

Instead, it was inciting an angry reaction. The councilmembers had hastily gathered at the amphitheater as soon as they heard the news of the capture and imprisonment of Solomon, Graham, and Zion.

"We need to be focused," shouted Lucius over the din of loud chattering. "I need your attention, now! We met previously and agreed on a battle strategy should we need to launch it," he said. "Malvelnia has taken unprecedented and unprovoked action.

"After the Days of Fear, our kingdoms had agreed that whenever a meeting was required between leaders of Malvelnia and Ataraxia, we would never take advantage. We would respect the importance of a peaceful exchange without harm coming to any of the participants. In this way, we would be able to keep open lines of communication.

"But Moriah has reported the calamitous news that our leaders, who went with honest intentions, have been detained by King Wendigo. According to our intelligence, Diego and his henchman have Solomon, Graham, and Zion imprisoned on Mt. Kukulkan!"

"Oh my, it can't be!" Ellie cried out. "How horrible. Do we know if they've been harmed?"

"From what Moriah and her team saw, they are not hurt," Lucius responded. "But this unconscionable move by Wendigo requires us to launch our battle plan . . . with a slight change to the start time."

He looked around furtively to make sure no spy was in the vicinity. Drawing the councilmembers closer to him, he whispered, "As we agreed, our approach will be to catch them by surprise at night. However, given the new circumstances, we will begin our stealth attack at the far side of Mt Kukulkan.

"Lilly, we will need your toughest, battle-seasoned honey badgers as we believe a cadre of snakes could be assisting Diego's group.

"Katy, we will need your fiercest bears to take on Diego and his crew, along with a strong contingent of tigers. I will be speaking to Zion's older son, Ethan, about that. I know he will jump at the chance to help in the effort to free his father.

"Aurora, you will help create a diversion to draw away Diego's guards."

Lucius continued to review the plan. While one group, as laid out, would need to strike first to free their leaders, the original plan entailed a stealth attack at the east side of Mt Kukulkan in the middle of the night. Over the years, the population of Ataraxia had grown monumentally because of the temperate climate, and they had a wide array of vegetation, including fields of grasses and clover and fruit trees of all types, with an abundant water supply.

Now, as they faced the challenge of a battle, their numbers were significant. The Council would deploy over a thousand honey badgers to attack the snakes, beginning alongside the banks of the Indigna River and driving them back into the grasslands closest to Mt. Kukulkan.

Orion would follow with hundreds of skunks, assembled and ready to spray and temporarily blind any snakes or monkeys who tried to interfere, while the hyenas would guard the monkey caves.

These attacks would open the central approach to Malvelnia where the wolves, led by Jake, a second cadre of tigers, and Helen's fiercest foxes would confront any crocodiles, snakes, or vultures who tried to prevent them from attacking head-on.

A central battalion of oxen would lead the way to frighten any vultures who might try to counterattack. In the past, the vultures had always been fearful of oxen because of their sheer size and sharp horns.

While this meeting was going on, the royal household in Malvelnia was in a panic. Wendigo had learned the news that his son was missing.

"How can this be possible?" he shouted. "He's always stayed relatively close to home, even while he's been learning to fly. Estrelle! You were supposed to be keeping an eye on him. When did you see him last?"

Estrelle cowered from Wendigo as he stomped toward her. "We had breakfast together yesterday, and Kibou was here with me," she said. "But then he was fluttering around here and there, and I was busy. I didn't notice until later that he was nowhere to be found. I didn't say anything to Mom because I was sure he'd turn up. You know Kibou." She rolled her eyes. "He's always joking and playing games. I figured he was just trying to tease and hide from me."

Wendigo was livid. "So he's been missing since yesterday? He could be anywhere! And here we are, in a disagreement with Ataraxia, and I'm going to need to send Simon and maybe my brother to form a search party for Kibou.

"A fine state of affairs, Estrelle!" he screeched. "No thanks to your self-centered behavior." With that, he turned away from his daughter and flew off to find Simon. Eris fluttered over to calm her daughter and then hurried after Wendigo.

In less than half an hour, Simon had been located.

"Look, Simon, I need you to get a team of Heralders working double-time to find out what's happened to Kibou!" Wendigo instructed. "As soon as you have any word, let me know. I can send my brother, Ashok, but I hate to bother him," he said. "You know, he can be moody, right, Simon?"

He gave Simon a penetrating stare. Simon shivered. He knew what Wendigo was getting at. The last time Simon had fallen down on a job for Wendigo, Ashok had swooped in to finish up but not without leaving the jagged scar still etched into Simon's grizzled visage as punishment.

"I'm sure that won't be necessary, Your Highness," Simon blurted out. "I'm on it. I'll have an answer for you swiftly. I promise we'll find him and get him home safely."

With that, Simon loped off.

His first stop was at the edge of the grasslands, a rocky area where many of the Heralders lived.

"I need your help—quickly!" shouted Simon, spotting several monkeys on the rocks. "Wendigo's son is missing. He's just a young one, just got his wings going, so to speak, and now he's disappeared. I'll be in big trouble if we can't find him and let the royal family know he's safe."

Several large reddish-brown monkeys, part of the team Simon often worked with, climbed down the rocks to where Simon was standing. Off to the other direction, two gray chimpanzees swung over from a nearby tree limb.

"We're ready to help you, Simon. Tell us more about this young royal so we can put together a proper search."

"He's still pretty small; he's got his black wing feathers but still has lots of whitish fuzz around his head and body. His name's Kibou."

Nearby, Devon, the chimp who had received the message from Graham, was watching his father speak with Simon. When he heard the name "Kibou," his eyes bugged out. He started jumping up and down in excitement, yelling to his dad, "I know . . . I know about him."

All eyes turned to Devon.

"What do you know, son?" asked his father quietly.

"You know the sheep, the family of Graham, the big ram?" Devon said. "He spoke to me. He told me that a young vulture had injured his wing, but that he would be OK. They took him with them in a scarf. They were carrying him with them!"

In his enthusiasm, Devon forgot to mention that Graham had said they would keep him safe until someone was able to take Kibou home.

"Slow down, Devon," Simon said, sternly. "Where and when was this?"

"It was on the main path from the meadows," he said, "but they were all walking toward their meeting place. It was a good while ago—I can't remember exactly when, but it was Graham and his family and a strange-looking creature with black hair who was with them."

Simon knew this must have been two days ago because the Council had met yesterday, which led to Graham, Zion, and Solomon's visit with Wendigo.

"No time to lose," Simon said. "I'll head to Graham's home to retrieve Kibou."

Of course, Simon knew Graham would not be there. He figured his task would be easier with the ram imprisoned atop Mt. Kukulkan.

As Simon swung from tree to tree toward Graham and Molly's home, he fretted. Simon was a worrier—no surprise. Over the years as a Heralder, he had been careful to attune his messages to his prime recipients, the leaders of Malvelnia.

He avoided passing on news of events in Ataraxia that might ruffle the feathers of Wendigo, Diego, and the others who ruled. After all, Simon had risen in importance and influence over the years for his brand of self-serving loyalty.

Once, when others among his simian clan, including several strident chimps, had complained about his sly, fraternizing approach to their communications role among the kingdoms, Simon had nipped that in the bud. Diablo, a particularly malevolent python, and several of his henchmen had silently invaded two of the chimpanzees' tree nests, using their razor-sharp teeth to subdue everyone, and their strength to then suffocate them, including their wives and two children.

An agreement existed in Malvelnia whereby the monkey habitat was off limits to snakes, given the recognized communications role of Heralders, who served all members of the communities. Clearly, Simon, who held a protected status because of his close relationship with the Malvelnian royals, had been behind this incursion. As word spread of the tragedy, the dissidents heeded the gruesome warning. Further criticism of Simon had been squelched.

At Molly and Graham's house, Luke saw Simon approaching and notified her.

"Allie! Please hurry and take Kibou down by the brook. There are some tall grasses there where I'd like you and your brother to play for a while with Kibou. Please, right away!" she urged them. The rapid blink of her eyes and the urgency of her voice propelled Allie forward.

Before Molly could say another word, Allie and SJ, with Kibou still nestled in the knapsack, hurried eastward toward the brook. With SJ in the lead, he motioned Allie to follow him to where he had noticed the gigantic grasses and reeds alongside the brook earlier. Kibou, unaware of Simon's approach, was enjoying the sweeping motion of the knapsack, which had lulled him to sleep.

Swinging down to the ground, Simon approached Graham's grove. His family had staked this out long ago as their resting place. Simon saw the plump ewe resting in a corner.

"Hello, dear Molly," Simon said in a sugary voice. "I have had news that you might have an unwelcome visitor here, a young vulture. I'm happy to tell you I'm here to take him off your hands."

Molly gazed at Simon, her wide eyes beautiful, even as they flashed with anger.

"Don't call me 'dear,' Simon, and no, the vulture you speak of is not here. Tell Wendigo he will see him upon the safe return of Graham and his fellow leaders, who have been unjustly imprisoned, a violation of the laws our kingdoms agreed to years ago."

"But I've been told that Graham himself said the youngster was OK," Simon blustered. "What have you done with him?"

"That's none of your business, Simon. Return and take my message to Malvelnia. That's your role, after all, isn't it?"

In their kingdoms' laws, the Heralders had been given the special status of messengers but with the unspoken understanding that they would remain neutral, merely acting as messengers, not arbiters of truth.

"Yes, yes, of course, Molly," Simon said. "OK, I see he is not here. But is he in the hands of one of the other members of the Council? I'd like to be clear when I relay your message."

"Yes, you may tell them that," Molly said. "He's not here, and as you know, neither is my Graham! If Malvelnia expects Kibou's return, you must release Graham and the other councilmembers—unharmed."

With that, Molly stood firmly, staring at Simon until he turned and left.

As he grappled up a huge hawthorn tree nearby, he surveyed the area, including the meadows beyond Graham's home.

He gazed intently at the path, at the lush clover fields where acres of wheat rippled in the breezes that swept over Ataraxia. His eyes continued to the brook, but the huge rushes were not moving alongside the bubbling waters.

What he didn't yet know was that wisely, Allie had sensed what was at risk. She had found a particularly comfortable mossy indentation along the water that dipped below the eye line of the rushes and had settled the three of them there.

Simon turned and rushed on. He was heading to the amphitheater to see if Kibou was being held there, or in any of the other haunts of the usual suspects in Ataraxia. But his quick surveillance yielded nothing. There was nothing to do but to return with the message for Wendigo.

He pondered Molly's brazen message. She had the upper hand for the moment. He wondered whether Wendigo would agree to the exchange she had proposed. And he fretted as he made his journey to Mt. Kukulkan, shivering at the threat the king had alluded to that might befall him, the one that involved Wendigo's mercenary brother.

The sun sank lower on the horizon, casting plum, orange, and lilac rays across the heavens. Rushing toward his destination, Simon's anxiety level rose, and as he would discover, rightly so.

Chapter 38

MOLLY

Molly's heart pounded inside her chest. Never had she spoken so boldly to anyone in her life, particularly not to a creature of power, such as Simon. She always depended on Graham to speak out for her and defend his family. But now, she recognized it was a family crisis, and she must protect her family at all costs.

The round ewe had been happily awaiting Graham's return. She could tell the signs clearly now, that they would be expanding their family. But suddenly, that news had been superseded by fear for Graham's well-being.

Her conversation with Simon had taken great gumption on her part; she hoped justice would prevail, that Wendigo would see the logic, and that his love for his son would convince him to make the exchange. But Molly, with her honest and forthright nature, knew little of the character of Wendigo.

As a lamb, she had frolicked carefree in the meadows, a tender-hearted young-ster known by the other creatures in Ataraxia as "sweet Molly." One of the other lambs she played with years before, gently butting heads as they kicked up their heels, was Graham.

He had been born a little earlier than Molly, so being a bit larger and older, and he became protective of his friend. He told Molly he thought she was quite adorable, with her wide-set eyes and long black eyelashes.

Graham wanted to be a strong figure like his father, who was widely respected among not just their kind, but many others in the kingdom. But he had a stutter that made him feel timid. Molly did not care at all about his stutter, which he had told her helped him feel more relaxed and confident. Over time, Molly noticed his stutter had begun to subside somewhat.

As they got to know each other better, Molly told him, "You don't need to bother about that. You are strong and brave like your dad. You will be a leader; I'm sure of it."

While Molly buoyed his confidence, Graham remained humble. It was a quality that contributed to his respected reputation as he developed into a stately ram. By the time a year had passed, Molly and Graham were inseparable. They realized they were partners who would never do each other harm, only good.

Despite his slight stutter, Graham was soon seen as a natural choice to become a member of the leadership Council that presided over Ataraxia. With Molly at his side, Graham seemed even more attractive to others. That view of Graham and Molly had not changed. If anything, they had become an even more important part of the lives of Ataraxians.

Several minutes after Simon left, Kibou awoke from his nap and stuck his beak out of the knapsack.

"Where are we going now?"

"We're going back to see my mom in a little bit, but we're going to get a drink of water here," Luke told the plucky vulture. With that, he pushed Kibou playfully with his nose, at which Kibou fluttered backward, caught his balance, and burst into a cackling laugh.

"You're too much, Luke! We've gotten to be rather good mates, haven't we? Y'know, I had another lamb friend named Delilah, but my mom sent her away with that big orangutan, Simon. I was so sad about that. She was sweet and kind . . . like a sister. Not like my real sister, Estrelle. She's a pain in the tail feathers. But Delilah wanted to find her real family. She looked like you, Luke, not with dark feathers like me. She was beautiful, soft, white, and fuzzy. Her side made a wonderful pillow at night."

Allie and SJ's eyes zeroed in on Luke's face, for the young ram had jerked his head upward the moment he heard Kibou mention the name *Delilah*.

Luke knew that was the name his mom and dad had given to his little sister, but he was told she had died! He was never to speak that name in the house, his dad had told him, because it was too painful for his mom to hear.

"C'mon Kibou, let's go up to the house," Luke said. "The visitor is gone, and you have to tell my mom about this lamb. Even though I never met her, my mom had a baby lamb, which they named Delilah. But she didn't survive, or so we thought. I never got to meet her. It's probably a coincidence, but I'd like you to tell her about your friend right away."

After getting a quick drink at the brook, the foursome headed back to the grove where Molly was resting.

"Mom! Mom!" Luke shouted as they arrived.

"What Luke?" she answered. "Is there something wrong?"

"No, but you have to hear about something Kibou was telling us. Right away!"

Kibou waddled over and looked up at Molly's wide eyes, which were now set in a quizzical expression.

"OK, you probably wonder how I get along so well with you and Luke," Kibou began. "You see, I have an adopted sister, a lamb, who was brought to us when she was just a wee baby. Me too—I was just a new fledgling.

"That baby lamb was weak at first, but she was so sweet. We snuggled and warmed each other at night as we went to sleep. We laughed and played together like brother and sister. We were just the best of friends. But when I was talking to her one day, she told me we weren't the same and that she wanted to find her real family. That made my mother and my older sister angry, so they sent her off—banished her to that scary place, the Abyss. And I cried."

Molly listened and then said, "But who is this lamb? There are other families of sheep like us. Perhaps it is one of theirs?"

"Kibou said this lamb was named Delilah," Luke said.

Molly's eyes widened. "No, it can't be possible," she said. "My Delilah didn't survive. Simon took her body away. How did this Delilah come to be part of your family?" Molly asked Kibou.

"Simon brought her. She was sick when she arrived. But we warmed each other up," Kibou said fondly. "And as the weeks went by, she got stronger. . . . I miss her."

Molly shivered as she listened to Kibou's story. *Was it possible*, she wondered, *could my baby be alive? Oh, dear. Even if it is our Delilah, she was banished to the Abyss!* Tears pooled in the corners of her eyes, splashing down on the ground. *How could that be?*

Kibou looked down, sorry he had told the story.

"It's Estrelle, my sister. She's mean. And she has a way of getting my mother to go along with her," Kibou confessed. "I'm sorry I've made you sad."

Molly locked the conversation in her heart. While it was a gruesome tale, it gave her one tiny fragment of hope that Delilah might still be alive. But she pushed that down deep in her consciousness because the reality was that no creature was known to have ever returned to Ataraxia from the Abyss.

"Molly!" Allie said. "We need to let others know that you have an important visitor here."

"Yes, of course, Allie. Of course, you're right. Do you think you and SJ could run on and find Aurora again to share this information? She stays in an area of the woods nearby. Do you think you can find her, dears?"

"And while you do that, I will take Kibou with me to a secret place that only Graham and I know about. I think that would be a wise thing to do."

"Yes, sure, Molly. We'll run and do that right away," Allie said as she placed Kibou in the back sack and hung it around Molly's neck.

Allie pointed to a grassy path that led further east, toward a distant tree line. "It's that way," she told her brother. SJ took off on the path, leaping over the small rocks and tree limbs along the way, as Allie raced close behind. As they neared the woods, Allie could already see a shadowy form moving through the woods.

"Aurora," she called out. "Is that you?"

"Yes, I'm Aurora. Who is calling out my name?" a musical voice responded.

"Aurora, it's Allie and my brother, SJ."

The shadowy figure reached a clearing where now Allie could see it was Aurora. She drew closer to the gazelle. "We came to tell you about something important," Allie said, speaking in a raised whisper. "Molly said we should tell you because of Malvelnia's threat to your kingdom. It's that Kibou, the injured young vulture they've been caring for, is King Wendigo's son!"

Aurora gasped. "We must let the Council know as soon as possible. This information could be incredibly valuable since our diplomatic approach to finding a peaceful solution to Malvelnia's demands has been rejected."

Allie thought for a moment. "Maybe since we are different—not Ataraxians—we could act as messengers? Do you think we could help in that way? Take word of Kibou's safety and the desire of Ataraxia for a peaceful solution to this conflict?" Allie said.

Aurora nodded. "Yes, perhaps. Let's see what others might say." Gazing at the two, Aurora said, "Hop on my back. We're going to the Council to discuss this right away." Aurora knelt down as Allie and SJ hopped onto her back, then she raised back up on her hooves and vaulted toward the edge of the amphitheater, the place where all councilmembers knew to go if there was the need for an immediate meeting.

SJ wrapped his arms around Allie's waist, and Allie held the gazelle's long neck as the children marveled at the speed of her graceful strides. She leaped forward on her willowy, long legs, her eyes darting around her for any sign of intruders as they dashed to their destination.

Allie breathed in the smells of the wild lilies, the damp leaves, and the moss; honeysuckle branches hanging from trees brushed her cheek. Holding fast to Aurora's neck, she thought she had never felt more a part of God's creation, the distinctions between humans, animals, and plants blending into one harmonious, natural ecology. Allie knew, going forward, she would never see the world in the same way again.

Chapter 39

THE PLOT THICKENS

While Simon was scurrying back to Mt. Kukulkan, the evening was creeping in.

On the other side, unaware of Molly's ultimatum sent via Simon to Malvelnia, a rescue party had already departed for its mission: to safely bring home Solomon, Zion, and Graham.

A small cotillion of mockingbirds had been dispatched earlier to find observation points near the rocky enclave where the three were being held. The goal was to obtain details of their imprisonment from different vantage points and share these with the rescue party at a point agreed upon in advance and one that would give them valuable intel before they scaled the wall of the plateau.

The far side of Mt. Kukulkan, where the party was headed, was hilly country, ruggedly beautiful, with its abundance of purple heather, Jericho trees, sage bushes, small evergreens, and cascades of wildflowers spilling over the hillside. At a certain spot known for an outcrop of boulders that looked like the face of a lion and accessible by a path trampled by creatures of all sizes over the years, the rescue party had agreed to pause and wait to hear from the mockingbirds.

Beyond the path that circled the plateau, the cliffs rose dramatically. The final stage of the rescue would require them to scale the side of the plateau—not an easy task, but given the roughness that provided traction and a substantial number of rocky ledges, it would be possible for the group to do. Once accomplished, the rescue party waited for the mockingbirds to arrive.

As agreed upon, the rescue party comprised Ethan, Zion's son, who was joined by two of the fiercest tigers he could enlist in short order: Katy, one of the largest Kodiaks in Ataraxia, along with her brother, Jason; and Lilly, who brought with her six honey badgers, three of whom were known for the great number of snakes they had slain during their lives.

The winged messengers reported that the cave where their three leaders were imprisoned was guarded by Diablo himself, along with three crocodiles who had been assigned to this duty by Diego. They also spotted anywhere from six to nine snakes camouflaged in the rocks. Unfortunately, they could not guarantee there were no more.

"Thank you for this valuable information," Ethan said. "Because we have the challenge of Diablo, I'm going to volunteer to take him on. Also, Lilly, if you think you can handle the smaller snakes with three of your crew, I'd like at least three others to help in subduing Diablo.

"I'll ask you badgers to zero in on Diablo's torso while I go after his head and jaws. But I assure you, this will be a tough fight. The best thing in our favor is that at night, hopefully with the temperature colder than tonight, the snakes will be sluggish. Diablo and the other snakes should be slow to react.

"Katy, you will be in charge of the crocs," Ethan continued. "You and Justin have a lot of power in your size. I think you will be able to attack those crocodiles and keep them off balance. Plus, I'm going to ask our mockingbird friends to go and alert Aurora while we're scaling the cliff to create a diversion that will hopefully draw at least one or more of the crocodiles away from their duty at the rocks."

After learning of the rescue efforts and dropping Allie and SJ off, Aurora and seven swift gazelles had moved stealthily from the west, through the grasslands, and then up a secondary path that took them atop the less steep side of the plateau. They were making their way as silently as possible toward the rocky enclave, even as the rescue party on the eastern side of Malvelnia was starting to scale the cliffside.

Already, they knew their role was to create a diversion that might draw guards away from the cave. The mockingbirds had to search as they flew, looking for the party to update them. Once they spotted Aurora's group, they swooped down and landed on some sapling birch trees. They waited for Aurora to approach, whispering that Katy, Lilly, and Ethan were already scaling the cliff.

After learning the status of the plan, the gazelles moved on, quietly approaching the rocks but then waited at a slight distance until the mockingbirds called. That would be the sign that the rescue party was poised to attack.

This particular night favored the rescue party. The moon was ensconced in clouds, muting the light it might have normally cast on the group nearing the top of the cliff. They moved slowly to make their ascent as noiseless as possible. Bringing up the rear were Katy and Justin, with Ethan leading the way.

Once atop the plateau, Ethan watched for the mockingbirds. They flew overhead high above the rocks. The lead bird swept downward, saw Ethan nodding his head, and immediately raced up again and over toward the gazelles.

A minute later, Aurora's herd leaped closer to the rocks. Diablo raised his head. Though his vision was weak at night, he felt the vibrations of their hoofs in his huge, scaled body.

Diablo stretched out over fifteen feet in length, his body thick, his head and jaws savage. He alerted the crocodiles to the sound. Faster than Diego, Phinehas, the crocodile whom Diego had appointed as the lead, raced out from the rocky enclave after the gazelles. He was surprisingly fast, given his relatively short legs. The herd ran tantalizingly close, drawing him further out at the very moment Ethan and the honey badgers leaped on Diablo.

As they soared by, Phinehas snapped at the last gazelle in the herd, his teeth nipping its rear leg. That momentary taste of blood was enough to absorb his attention; oblivious to the fight ensuing behind him, he scurried after the herd of gazelles.

Katy threw her weight on one of the crocodiles, while Justin tackled the other. The honey badger brigade was teasing and then taking out the snake guards posted among the rocks.

The mockingbirds had been accurate in their estimate of six to nine for the number of snakes . . . three of the larger snakes had already been attacked and killed by the badgers; three snakes were waiting to strike, and two more had slithered away to watch from deeper inside the rocks. They avoided honey badgers whenever possible because of their formidable reputation among the community of snakes. Their sharp teeth were known to cut through any hide, no matter how tough and armor-like it might be.

Ethan jumped on Diablo, positioning his body atop the python right behind the juncture where his head and gigantic jaws ended. Initially, he had sunk his teeth in and, now, was desperately trying to hold on.

Loyal to their assignment, the three honey badgers were using their sharp teeth to bite into Diablo's torso, repeatedly striking, seeking to tire him and penetrate his thick skin, disabling him.

Diablo hissed violently as he whipped his head back and forth, throwing Ethan off and turning to strike at the tiger's throat.

As he stuck his fangs into Ethan's neck, a huge, clawed paw struck his jaw with the momentum that all 1500 pounds of a Kodiak bear could deliver. Justin had already beaten off his crocodile, rendering it immobile, and had turned just in time to see Ethan's plight.

The blow threw Diablo backward, causing him to lie writhing in pain. Ethan, despite the blood at his throat, leaped back atop Diablo's back, biting again at the base of his head. By now, the extent of the injuries the honey badgers had inflicted to Diablo's torso paralyzed his movement. With a decisively deep bite, Ethan ended the life of one of Malvelnia's most evil leaders.

Pausing, Ethan realized they were near victory. Rushing to the cave, he entered, while two of the guard pythons were finished off by the badgers. He gnawed through the layers of vines holding his father, then Solomon and Graham.

Even as this was happening, Phinehas, who had been too slow to catch the last gazelle, had rushed back to the skirmish underway. Seeing that Diablo had been overpowered, Phinehas headed straight for Katy, flipping his tail, while he approached to slap any others who might follow him.

He roared as he clapped his jaws shut on Katy's leg, trying to roll her backward. She was unable to respond with her leg held firmly in his teeth.

In one stride, Justin took hold of the base of Phinehas's jaws and with his tremendous power, forced them open, releasing his sister. Angry from her injury, Katy clawed at Phinehas's face, momentarily blinding him.

That allowed Justin to deliver a blow, knocking the huge croc on his back at the moment Ethan, who had freed the captives, leaped over and sunk his teeth deep into his neck. It was a death hold, as Ethan forced his teeth deeper into his throat until blood flowed heavily, pooling on the ground, and Phinehas stopped stirring.

Success! The rescue party looked around the rocks. No more snakes emerged. If any were still present within the rocks, they had retreated out of sight. They had effectively taken out the three crocodiles, including the fiercest, Phinehas, while killing one of the most feared python predators in Malvelnia—Diablo.

Solomon was weak from a lack of water. The group waited while he repeatedly filled his beak from the very pool where previously the crocodiles had slept.

Zion nuzzled Ethan's head, licking his neck where he had been wounded. Ethan felt the sting from his wound but knew it would heal. He was proud to have helped to secure his father's freedom.

Once restored, Solomon told the group he would fly back to Ataraxia to advise the other councilmembers of the successful rescue and signal the launch of their battle plan.

"Godspeed, old friend," Zion said. "We'll plan to circumvent the plateau on our return. But I hope to join in the fray later, once I'm briefed upon our return."

"Thank you, dear friends, for your c-c-c-courage and bravery," Graham said. "But I know these creatures will discover our absence quickly, so we must move swiftly." The most vulnerable of the group, Graham did not want to put others in danger. He knew he must make a rapid escape before their captors arrived.

"Yes, brother," Zion said, using the familiar term in a show of solidarity. "Ethan will lead the way down, but we must take the more difficult way on the steeper side of the cliff. Do you think you can manage that?"

"I'm ready. I will try my b-b-best," he responded, mustering up as much positivity in his voice as he could.

While Graham had never scaled the steeper back side of Mt. Kukulkan, he had heard it was extremely treacherous for his kind. He remembered his father telling him about a trip he once had made by that route many years ago and that the key to his successful descent down the cliff was by way of the ledges on the cliffside. Thus, as the Ataraxians made their way down the cliff, Graham kept his eyes glued on each ledge he could reach.

Halfway down, Ethan saw Graham stumble as the ledge on which he stood crumbled on one side. The tiger watched as Graham, despite a moment of panic, leaped to the next ledge, securing his footing so he could pause and catch his breath. This was no easy descent, but Ethan knew that Graham's love for Molly and Luke back home would urge him forward.

"You can do this. You've got this," Ethan called up to his friend.

Finally, Ethan realized they were almost to the base of the cliff. Looking up, he saw Graham still a ways back, apparently stuck on a ledge, unable to see that a bigger ledge was directly below, after which a short jump would return him to the narrow path that led the rest of the way to safety.

Ethan ran back and urged Graham onto the ledge below. Ethan saw Graham nod his head as he leaned his neck over the edge and spotted the much larger ledge right below. The trick would be to land on the right spot and not overshoot it. In a deft move, the ram jumped down, using his back legs to kick against the cliff wall and propel himself onto the ledge.

His front legs landed solidly, but his back legs weren't on the ledge yet. Rocks flew as he struggled to pull himself up onto the ledge. Ethan could almost hear Graham's heart beating hard as his hoofs clawed the rock wall.

Then . . . safety! Ethan watched as Graham landed firmly with all four hoofs finally stable on the ledge leading to the path.

Seeing his friend had made it, Ethan turned back to the path with a sigh of relief. Despite the darkness, Ethan could see the path ahead, a welcome sight as the pair continued toward safety.

Chapter 40

THE BATTLE

While Graham, Ethan, and members of the rescue party continued eastward to Ataraxia, Solomon flew swiftly and directly to speak with Moriah, informing her to get the stealth attack underway. The element of surprise was especially important, so Moriah would need to spread the word straightaway to the others leading the attack. She alerted the winged messengers, who spread the news with urgency.

Almost immediately, Albert had assembled his corps of hyenas, which numbered in the hundreds, around all the known Heralder habitats—primarily the monkey caves as well as several fruit groves.

A secondary cotillion of skunks joined the hyenas outside the caves. They would be ready to attack and intimidate them, whether orangutans, mandrills, lemurs, chimps, or any other species, to prevent them from taking tactical information to Malvelnia. The skunks' spray was a great complement to the ferocity of the hyenas, making the combined force formidable.

Observing they had not yet been detected, Albert signaled his forces to move in closer.

Heading toward the Idigna River region populated by Wendigo's frontline of crocodiles and vipers were the honey badgers led by Lilly, several hundred leopards, and Lucius, who brought up the rear with a string of oxen spread as far as the eye could see. Lucius had enlisted the largest males among the oxen, those who sported gigantic horns and sharp hooves, making them effective warriors against tough-hided reptiles.

Meanwhile, Orion was already creeping up the more easily navigated edge of Mt. Kukulkan with two-hundred fifty skunks. They would work to blind the anticipated attack by the vultures and any others of Wendigo's army.

Following them were packs of wolves, led by Jake, and tigers ready to take on whoever came their way. Before leaving for his mission to Malvelnia, Zion had urged all his tiger combatants to be ready for battle, regardless of the time of his return.

As all of this was unfolding, Simon had reached Wendigo.

"I'm pleased to inform you that Master Kibou is alive and being cared for," Simon began. "But the Ataraxians will not reveal his exact whereabouts until Graham and the councilmembers you have taken hostage are safely returned . . ." Simon's voice trailed off, knowing Wendigo would be furious. He stepped back as if expecting a physical blow.

"Outrageous!" Wendigo screamed, slapping the monkey's face with his wing. "Absolutely not. You mean you could not convince those inferior creatures to cooperate? I'm disappointed, Simon—extremely disappointed in you."

King Wendigo imposed his full size on Simon as he pushed forward, glaring into his face. "You are not giving me all the details. Who did you speak to about this?"

"Well, I spoke first to the Heralders, then to Molly, Graham's partner," he told the king. "I was surprised that she already knew about the hostages," Simon confessed.

"You mean you cow-towed to a sheep?" he scoffed. "I will take care of this immediately through other means. You are dismissed."

And with that, Wendigo turned away from Simon. The orangutan stood frozen for a moment, knowing he had fallen short of the king's expectations, for which he knew he would have to pay in the future.

Wendigo promptly put out a call for his brother Ashok to help him.

"The priority is to get my son home safely," he told his brother.

Ashok nodded in agreement. "So you've got the ram, Graham, captive?" he asked.

"Yes, and two others of the Council. They came to discuss my edict, but their refusal to obey it landed them in our holding cell."

But as he spoke, Eris arrived, seething. "Your prisoners have escaped! And Diablo is dead!" she shrieked.

King Wendigo shook his head in disbelief, visibly shaken.

"This is war! The Ataraxians have brought it on themselves! Eris, alert Diego. We need him to assemble his warriors."

"I will signal the serpent army. They may be without Diablo, but Gavin will happily lead that ruthless battalion in his absence. And I will launch my vulture regiments before those treacherous councilmembers make it back home."

Gavin, Diablo's cousin, was a ferocious, one-eyed python.

"Ashok, we must wait for this initial battalion to advance before we pursue retrieving Kibou."

But as Wendigo spoke these words, the honey badgers were already advancing a solid front into the Indigna River region. Snakes who had been prowling for food in the grasslands were shocked by the line of honey badgers approaching them.

The small mammals' aggressive reputation caused the snakes to hastily retreat to the river. For a honey badger, a small to medium-sized snake is easy prey. But they would have more to contend with once they reached the Indigna, where some of the largest snakes slithered, including boas, pythons, and humongous anacondas, some weighing as much as five hundred pounds.

As the badgers advanced, the hyenas and skunks, as called for in their battle plan, surrounded the monkey habitats. Given the monkeys' role as messengers, it was essential to keep their movements under control.

The Council had agreed their goal was to contain the enemy, impress Malvelnia with the power of their forces, and squelch Wendigo's attempt to force Ataraxia into submitting to his edict. They hoped to do this with a minimum of bloodshed, although they knew lives would be lost. As Jake, Orion, and Lucius made their way up Mt. Kukulkan, a fierce battle was underway.

Orion was the first to spot the army of vultures as a black-feathered cloud descended from above, dive-bombing them.

"First volley," shouted the skunk as the line split three deep, the front row aiming and squirting their horrible blinding torrent at the vultures as they arrived. Screeching ensued as the vultures flew back, some falling, temporarily blinded by the spray.

"Second round," Orion shouted, as the next line of skunks turned bottoms up to spray their winged enemies. Again, the vultures were overcome by the powerful nature of the skunks' chemical weapon, many retreating and others unable to navigate without their sight.

Taking advantage of the vultures who were temporarily incapacitated, Lucius and his oxen followed, clearing the path forward by leaning down and tossing the vultures with their huge, horn-bedecked heads, throwing some vultures as much as forty feet—just like tossing a feather pillow. Even as they did this, Orion launched a third line of skunks to unleash their sulfuric substance, but this time, it was on the crocodiles arriving at the battle scene, led by Diego.

"Helen, you focus on the vultures!" yelled Lilly, who had left a large squad of honey badgers at the west side of the river while continuing up the mountainside with another huge squadron.

"We will assist Lucius and Jake's teams in attacking those hinge-mouthed reptiles," she shouted. Even as Lilly barked out orders, another wave of vultures swooped in, several striking creatures with their razor-sharp talons.

Angered by a gash they cut across his shoulder, a large, silver fox leaped and grabbed the vulture in its teeth, shaking it violently back and forth. It fell to the side as the fox turned to take on another vulture.

Jake and his front-line pack of wolves saw the crocs coming and worked their strategy, trying to roll each one over to attack their underbellies. With their snouts and teeth, they pounced on a mid-size crocodile, successfully rolling it over. A particularly fierce she-wolf leaped on his belly, ripping through the skin with her teeth. Soon, others joined in before the now helpless reptile could try to right itself.

The pack shifted to take on a pair of smaller crocodiles snapping aggressively at the wolves, injuring one in the leg. Zion and Ethan had now joined the battle, along with a streak of tigers.

A Siberian tiger named Silas, seeing the fight in progress against the crocodiles, jumped atop one, clawing at its face, and then grabbed its side in his teeth enough to throw it in the air, flipping it over. Its feet flailing in the air, another crocodile met its fate.

But as the battle ensued, the vultures inflicted damage. Several foxes lay on their sides, having been severely slashed; as they lay wounded, Gavin headed over to finish them off.

Near the monkey caves and the fruit groves, the hyenas were effectively keeping the monkeys at bay. Several baboons threw apples at the hyenas, trying to draw them away from their posts. But so far, they were holding fast to their positions.

Solomon, who had hastily returned after his escape from Mt. Kukulkan, went to the meeting place at the Amphitheater. There, he had been briefed by Moriah on all that had transpired in his absence, including the departure of the various regiments to their battle positions.

As they talked, Aurora arrived and stood alongside her previous precious passengers, Allie and SJ. While Solomon was assessing the battle and their positions, Aurora shared with him the important update regarding Wendigo's son.

"I'm sure Molly has taken Kibou into hiding. You know, she has told me before that she and Graham have a secret place that no one knows about."

Aurora was right. After the successful rescue from the caves and his return, Graham hurried home to check on his family. When he arrived and didn't find Molly, he knew where to go. Once he found them, Molly told him about the visit from Simon, which had left her rattled and upset.

Knowing that Kibou was the king's son, Graham insisted that Molly and the young vulture stay in hiding. Only he and Molly knew about the secret place they had discovered together when Graham was courting her.

It was an underground cave tucked under a grassy hillside, a natural indentation that had been hollowed out further by a hibernating bear. As teenagers, they would hide there and talk for hours, often oblivious to their parents' calling, which had landed them in trouble more than once. Now, as adults, it was the perfect place for Molly to hide with the royal child.

Aurora shared Molly's message, that she had met with Simon and had sent word to King Wendigo about his son. While Solomon pondered the situation, Allie stepped forward.

"Mr. Solomon," she said, "my brother and I are from another place. We don't look like any of your citizens of Ataraxia, which could work in our favor. We think perhaps we could go to speak with the king and try to barter with him.

"We could offer the safe return of his son, Kibou," Allie said, "for a peaceful end to this war and renunciation of this unfathomable edict! What do you think?"

SJ nodded his head in agreement with his sister, eyes sparkling and a look of readiness on his face.

The graying owl paused to consider Allie's proposal.

"You and your brother are brave to offer your help to our kingdom," he responded slowly. "But you would be putting yourself in grave danger. I cannot ask you to do that. The king is a sly fellow; depending on his mood, he might act agreeable and then turn around and harm you. Trust me, having just gone through imprisonment requiring others to put their lives on the line to rescue us, I am not ready to ask you to do this."

"Aw, c'mon," SJ said. "You can tell us the best way to reach Wendigo. And Allie can be very persuasive."

Allie looked up, surprised but thankful for her brother's vote of confidence. "SJ is right; we can do this. We want to do this, and we must. After all, the king wants his son returned safely. That is a huge piece of leverage. Perhaps this is why God brought us into your world, to help you achieve the justice you deserve." As she spoke, Allie remembered her mom's prayer and thought perhaps this was how she might bring the Light and the justice her mom had called out to God for.

Solomon peered at the two children. Although humans were foreign beings to him, he recognized these were still youngsters developing, not even full-grown ones. *Where did this bravery inside them come from?*

They did not appear to have any natural armor like the armadillos had. Nor did they have talons, like the vultures, or horns like the oxen. No, the children had something that emanated from within. Perhaps it was this personage called "God," whom Allie had just mentioned.

"If you play this role of messenger, for which our citizens would be eternally grateful, you must assure Wendigo that Kibou is hidden and safe and sound," Solomon said. "You can tell them Ataraxia proposes he calls back his warriors, and we will do likewise and ask him to cancel his edict.

"We would like him to meet us at a neutral location. At that time, we will return Kibou safely to him. Then all of us can return to a peaceful co-existence. I think, given what is at stake for him, he will comply," the owl said, a glint of hope emanating from his voice.

"Where is the neutral location you are thinking of?" Allie asked.

Solomon looked at Aurora with a penetrating glance. She nodded her head as if reading his mind. "The Waterfalls?" she asked.

"Right, just what I was thinking," Solomon replied. "It is the same place we met before when we all agreed to the end of the Days of Fear. In front of the Waterfalls . . . on three sides, it is flat and open. The rock cliff behind is also a safe backdrop for such a meeting. Just tell him the Council proposes we all meet at the Waterfalls so we can all bring this chapter to a peaceful conclusion."

Allie and SJ looked at each other. They knew that hasty delivery of the message to King Wendigo was essential. So did Solomon. Already, he knew, lives were being lost. The stealth attack had been a good strategy, but it was now early morning, and the battle dragged on. It wasn't sustainable.

"You must take this with you," Solomon said, holding out an olive branch. "Our kingdom has used this as a symbol of peace before. It is a story from long ago that an olive branch survived the great floods that covered our land. Wendigo will know what it means when you hold it above your head as you approach the royal home. If you are successful in your quest, and as you leave Malvelnia, look upward for Moriah. She will be there, out of sight. Once you let her know your result, she will relay to me the news. Let us hope for the best."

Allie took the olive branch and thanked Solomon.

He told the children the safest way for their journey would be to swing out to the north side of the grasslands and approach Mt. Kukulkan from that side. "There's a narrow path you can take, which will be more shielded from the dangerous skirmishes going on at present," he warned. "But be on guard! That area is not free from slithering marauders of one sort or another. You must be quiet and be careful."

With that send-off, Allie and SJ began their fateful trip. Everyone held hope in their hearts that they might be successful in persuading the mercurial king to do the right thing. But who could know? As Allie and SJ's mom often told them, "You do the best you can do. And that is all that you can do. The rest is in God's hands."

Chapter 41

INTO THE SWAMP

As Delilah and Squeaker reached the edge of the swamplands, the sun was emerging, burning off the mist, which reluctantly loosened its hazy fingers from around the cattails. Delilah was happy to see Squeaker take the lead, picking his way carefully and quietly.

Colorful water striders gracefully skimmed the surface of the water; a nearby bullfrog surfaced to eat a couple of the bugs. A handsome pair of gray herons flew overhead. Turtles lined a tree limb that hung down, grazing the top of the water. Their heads barely peeking out from their shells, they eyed the strangers entering their domain. As Delilah followed after Squeaker, she overheard them comment on the two friends.

"What do they think they're doing?" said one with a green and yellow mottled shell.

"Obviously, they don't know," said the other, shaking her head. "They must not have heard of Abaddon, or they would not be tiptoeing in this direction." Delilah took in their comments. Of course, she had heard about the frightful python from Whitney. She shivered and scampered ahead to catch up with Squeaker.

A dragonfly flitted overhead, buzzing past Delilah's ear, its blue-green wings reflecting glints of sunlight. Scanning the swamp waters, she could see tree limbs and a few rocks were sticking above the murky water's surface.

The pair paused to plot a quick route, noticing that about a half mile ahead, there was a dry-looking sandy mound that might make for a momentary resting point. Delilah continued obediently behind the honey badger, placing her hooves exactly where she saw Squeaker walking. Once, she lost her footing on a slippery patch of slimy grass that covered the tree limb's surface, but she recovered by lurching forward to reclaim a safer, drier portion for her limb.

Squeaker looked back. "You good?" he asked.

"Of course. I'm right behind you," she said, with the most confident-sounding voice she could muster.

"Great. If you glance ahead in a little bit, we'll reach that sandy mound in the distance, and we can pause there to catch our breath."

Peering ahead, Delilah saw the spot. She breathed a sigh of relief. Picking their way precariously through the swamp was painstaking and required so much intense focus, they thought a safe spot to rest a moment was a good idea.

Squeaker continued to advance warily. Delilah saw his eyes dart left and right, searching for any signs of danger. As the pair neared the sandy spot, Squeaker stepped ashore first and turned to wait for Delilah, who was a few yards behind him. To his horror, out of the corner of his eye, he saw the ridged back of an alligator suddenly surface several feet away from the lamb.

"Hurry, Delilah!" he screamed. "Run!"

Delilah scrambled forward, her legs bobbing as she struggled to reach solid ground.

Seeing the gator rise up as if to grab at Delilah with its huge jaws, Squeaker had to create a distraction. Leaping, he landed on the back of the armored beast and, using his sharp teeth, bit into its head near its eyes. The alligator shook its tail violently, trying to shake off the badger, but without success. Squeaker was not letting go.

Then began violent efforts by the alligator to get Squeaker off its back so it could attack *him* with its powerful jaws. It swooshed forward into the swampy waters and rolled its body in the water, veering away from the sandy spot where Delilah was now trying her best to hide from view.

There were a few bushes on the tiny island. One had especially huge leaves, which allowed her to visually shield herself from view. There, she watched, holding her breath, wishing with every cell in her body that Squeaker would survive the awful battle.

As the alligator rolled, Squeaker let go, grabbing instead at the softer underside of the creature, sinking his teeth into its throat, and drawing blood. It made a screeching sound, shaking its head violently. Unable to hold on, Squeaker fell off, disappearing into the water. With blood escaping from its wound, the injured alligator slunk away, retreating before its strength dissipated.

Delilah held her breath, scanning the water's surface for her friend. Then she saw Squeaker push his head above the water's surface, gasping for air. The scrappy badger was winded and exhausted, but other than that, he was not hurt. He paddled onto the sand, throwing himself down to recover.

The lamb, still hidden by the bushes, saw Squeaker open his eyes and twirl, searching for a sign of his companion. She imagined he thought another creature must have stolen her away!

"Thank you, thank you!" her voice whispered loudly from the bushes.

Startled, Squeaker realized it was Delilah's voice. He trotted over. There, safely settled on the sand and out of sight, was the sweet lamb.

"Oh, my goodness! For a second, I thought some other nefarious creature had stolen you away," he said. "We are safe, for the moment. Let me creep into those bushes with you, and we'll stay here and rest a while."

"You were amazing, Squeaker," she said. "When I saw that alligator zooming toward me, my heart nearly burst. It was all I could do to get myself off that log and onto the sand," she bleated. "I would now be in its stomach, without a doubt, if it weren't for you. I owe you my life, dear friend."

The two, lamb and badger, huddled together while they quietly reflected on their morning. By now, they had successfully ventured nearly a mile into the swamplands. Squinting into the distance, all they could see was the same terrain: swamp waters, craggy trees with shaggy, moss-laden branches, and pieces of tree limbs scattered across the water.

"Ya know," Squeaker said, "staring into the distance, I believe I see at least a couple more of these sandbars. Maybe we can try to find them as we continue ahead, kind of like way stations where we can rest. Because we really need to clear this swamp water before it gets dark." It was still morning, but the skirmish with the alligator had slowed them down.

Delilah imagined what it would be like if they were stranded in the swamp by nightfall. Even the thought of it frightened her. If one alligator had surfaced and attacked them in the daylight, what creatures and how many might band together under the protection of the dark? She shuddered as her mind's eye imagined the swamp creatures surrounding them.

"You're right, Squeaker—absolutely! We need to keep moving. One thing Whitney told me is that once you get through the swampland, you reach the tall grasses. I think we are more vulnerable in these murky waters. At least on dry land, we can find a safe place to rest for the night."

She also remembered, however, Whitney warning her that snakes inhabited the region of the tall grasses, which were ruled by Abaddon, the mammoth-sized python. She decided she would not mention this to Squeaker just yet.

Chapter 42

THE PROPOSAL

"SJ, I'm trying to keep up, but you're too fast for me," Allie called out as SJ trotted ahead of her.

"Don't worry, sis. You'll catch up. I have to pause here for a bathroom break anyway," he said.

They were about a third of the way into their journey. It was still early morning, but it would be midday before they reached Wendigo's royal headquarters. They were in the midst of what was known as the grasslands, a gorgeous swath of land covered with tall buffalo grass and milkweed. Sunflowers swayed in the breeze, their yellow faces cheering on the children as they hurried toward their destination. The path grew steeper; shrubs and evergreens rose ahead of them, signaling a different ecology. As they left the grasslands behind, SJ felt a sharp sting on his leg.

"Ouch!" he exclaimed. "I was just bitten, and I think it was by a snake," he said. Just as Solomon had warned, a snake who lived under a large rock along the path had viewed SJ as an unwelcome intruder, struck his leg, and bit him. Fortunately, it did not inflict venom.

The kids paused while Allie looked at her brother's leg. It was red, but there was no sign of serious swelling. "As soon as we find water, a stream or pool or something, we need to clean that. Otherwise, it doesn't look too bad. How d'you feel?" Allie felt his forehead and concluded it felt normal.

"Aw, I'll be fine. Let's just keep going," he said.

Soon the two were emerging from the brush onto the plateau itself. They could see Wendigo's home looming in the distance. No one could miss it, with the flowering trees and bushes that framed the front entry and the gigantic banyan trees surrounding it that gave such a distinctive look to the palace.

They could also see signs of an ongoing battle to the south. Vultures hovered above; sounds in the distance reverberated across the distance—snorts and screeches and the thump of bodies slamming against each other. Allie and SJ rushed ahead.

"Don't look over there, SJ. Just keep going; keep going forward. We should be able to get to the palace soon," Allie said.

SJ, who was feeling some pain in his leg, didn't mention it to his sister. He knew they were on an important mission, a crucial one for these new and special friends.

True to Solomon's words, the sun was at its highest point in the sky by the time they arrived at the Malvelnian king's palace.

King Wendigo peered into the distance, watching as a pair of strangers approached. As they neared the entryway, the girl pulled out an olive branch, holding it high above her head. Even with the battle, Wendigo had two huge vultures, their heads red and hairless, serving as sentries while he watched from a platform of branches and twigs high above the ground.

From this vantage point, he could observe the numerous skirmishes underway at several battle locations. But all the while, he glanced back at the strange-looking pair approaching his palace.

He wondered what type of creatures these were, moving swiftly and steadily upright on two feet. Odd as they looked, he noticed right away the olive branch the girl creature held aloft. *It must be the doings of Solomon,* he thought. *Why else would these creatures be familiar with the tradition of this signal for a peaceful mission?*

Wendigo's sentries fluttered alongside the two children.

"We'd like to speak with the king," Allie told them, mustering up her most authoritative-sounding voice. "Is he here?"

Inside, she was quaking. The large, black vultures with their hairless heads and unfriendly expressions made her stomach churn. Tension always went to her stomach whenever she faced formidable challenges.

"Move this way," they squawked. "Right this way now. We've had our eyes on you both for quite a while."

The sentries ushered the pair into a large room, which Allie and SJ soon realized was the hollowed-out trunk of a monstrous banyan tree. At the end of the room stood King Wendigo—tall, with mottled brown and gray feathers and a white hairless head from which shone his beady eyes.

A ruffled plume of white feathers rested at his neck as befitted royalty but made his featherless head look small in contrast to his humongous five-foot-tall body. Perched on a large branch that rose parallel to the ground across the far end of the room, he spread out his wings to their full ten-foot span and ruffled his wing feathers.

His intent was successful; Allie gasped, huddling close to her brother, intimidated not only by the size of the king but also by his frightening talons that glistened in the light.

"What are you here for?" Wendigo's voice boomed forth. "Are you friend or foe?"

"My brother and I are here to share news from Ataraxia with you," Allie said. "That's why I've brought the olive branch, to clearly show we mean no harm. Rather, we'd like to be of help, both to you and to the friends we've made in the other kingdom."

Wendigo raised an eyebrow at the girl with an air of disbelief. *Why*, he thought, *would this unattractive creature, with that funny thatch of hair on her head, be interested in helping me?* He shook his head back and forth to register his disdain.

"It's true, King Wendigo!" SJ chimed in, pacing in a small circle as he spoke. "We have news of your son, Kibou, who is a funny guy, by the way. He makes us laugh so much. He is fine, no worries . . ." SJ's voice trailed off. Wendigo was not the least bit amused by his comments.

"The members of the Council," Allie jumped in, "want you to know that Kibou is safe. He has been under diligent care and protection. But the creatures of Ataraxia want the battle to stop. They are also asking you to withdraw your edict. Citizens are frightened. They believe your decree will lead to control over them, perhaps even injury.

"We don't think that is your intent. If you will consider their request, they want a return to peace, and they promise the safe return of your son." Allie's words spilled out as she rushed to say everything swiftly but clearly and then gauge the king's reaction.

Wendigo squinted his eyes as he stared at the two standing before him. "I must give you credit," he said, "for being willing to come here, knowing that our kingdoms are battling. No one is safe during such times. I appreciate your bringing news about my son." Wendigo forced the civil response out of his beak. In truth, he was livid about the situation, but he did not want to do anything to provoke actions that could bring harm to Kibou.

"However, I will reply by presenting a challenge to the two of you. I will send a message back to Ataraxia through you, but only one of you will go. The other will stay here in Malvelnia to ensure a favorable result. You may relay to the Council that I am considering their request to vacate my order. However, I need to give that further consideration," Wendigo lied. He had no intention of changing his mind. But until Kibou was back home, he would pretend as if he might acquiesce to their demands.

"King Wendigo," Allie said. "I must tell you that the Council is being truthful. I was there when Kibou was first found. His wing was injured, and he told us all about it! He had been practicing his flying, doing some dive-bombing tricks, when he accidentally hit a tree branch and hurt his wing. We gave him food and water and took care of him because he was unable to fly. I know he will be happy to return home. But you need to know that we are being truthful! The Council said to propose a peaceful meeting at the Waterfalls. Please . . . this will be a way for Kibou to return safely home and the kingdoms to find a peaceful solution."

Though distrustful by nature, the king still listened. He felt doubt in his heart, but this pair did not seem to have a particular agenda, so to speak, and Kibou had certainly been trying out his wings just about the time he disappeared.

Perhaps all would transpire as these two described. But to ensure that happened, he had already decided they would have to choose one of them to deliver his message back to the Council. By keeping one of the children at his palace, he would have insurance that Kibou would be returned safely, as promised.

"You must decide which one stays and which one goes," Wendigo cackled. "Whoever goes tells those Council stooges when my warriors see a flock of white doves flying above the Indigna River, we will sound the call to end the battle. Then, by my signal, they will see my forces move back. We will then proceed to the Waterfalls for Kibou's safe return. I will guarantee safe passage out of Malvelnia for the one of you who stays behind. And for the time being, we will put a hold on enforcing my census," Wendigo said. "My brother Ashok will be my representative at the Waterfalls. And my wife, Eris, of course. She has been heartsick since our son's disappearance."

The king stared at Allie. He could tell she did not trust him, but he figured his strategy of splitting up the two would keep the control in his court.

"Allie, you have to let me go," SJ stated firmly, his eyes blinking. "Here's a chance for my speed to pay off. I'll just go back to Ataraxia the way we came but at double speed. I'll report all the details, the doves, pulling back on the fighting, the hold on the edict, and agreeing to meet at the Waterfalls."

Allie's eyes widened. Her little brother had listened well. And yes, she knew he was by far the faster of the two of them. "SJ, that's great; that sounds perfect," she said. "Don't worry about me. The king won't try anything with the high stakes of the safe return of his son. But do hurry!"

With that, Allie reported to King Wendigo that her brother would be leaving to carry the king's message back, while Allie would stay behind.

SJ looked at Allie, and in a rare moment that shocked his sister, SJ hugged her. He looked down quickly to shield his show of emotion, a tear in his eye, as the sentries slid to either side of Allie and ushered her back to a corner of the room.

Feeling emotionally and physically drained from all that had taken place that day, Allie sat down on a pile of moss and twigs as she watched the form of her brother disappear in the distance.

She did not notice the dark shadow in the far corner of the room. The king's brother had taken in the exchange between SJ and Allie. Still seething over the escape of the Ataraxian leaders he despised, Ashok concocted a plan of his own, which he was about to execute.

Chapter 43

A Surprise

Squeaker picked up the pace as they ventured further into the marshy waters. Fortunately, the swamp was peppered with rocks and enough broken tree limbs to provide a route to that sandy mound in the distance. It was nearing midday as the sun rose higher above them.

Stepping onto a large rock, Squeaker turned and smiled as Delilah caught up. She stepped onto the rock, but its damp mossy surface didn't offer much footing. She slipped into the water but was able to hurl her front legs up on a nearby rotten tree trunk, pulling herself up with all four feet on the soft wood.

She nodded at Squeaker, affirming she was fine and ready to keep moving. In this manner, they picked their way across the waters. At one point, seven snakes swirled nearby. They appeared to be water moccasins, but apparently seeing no aggression on the part of the lamb or badger, they slithered on their way without pausing, leaving only faint ripples behind them, which quickly vanished.

As they neared the sandy mound, Squeaker noticed it was an unusual color, different from their previous stops, with no plants growing on it. He stepped onto the dry ground as Delilah followed right behind him. They both sat down to rest.

Suddenly, the ground beneath them began to sway. Startled, Squeaker glanced down. As he did, he saw the mound rise as the water's surface fell below them.

"Ah-h-h-ck!" screeched Squeaker. "What's going on?"

"We're not on a sandy mound," Delilah bleated. "We're on someone's back!"

Sure enough, the two had mistaken the back of a hippopotamus for a sandy rest stop. Squeaker braced, keeping his body low on the creature's back, while the monstrous hippo slowly turned its head to the side to examine the strange pair seated on her back.

"You're disturbing my rest," the hippo said. "What are you two doing in this swamp? I've never seen you before, and I usually spend part of each day right here by the cattails. Whatever are you doing here?"

Squeaker was surprised to hear the hippo speaking to them, especially in such a calm tone. He cleared his voice, mustering a response.

"Oh dear, Mrs. Hippo. We did not realize we were on your back! My friend and I are trying to make our way through the swamp to reach the dryer grassland on the other side. We are trying to pick our path carefully because earlier we ran into a not-very-friendly alligator. We just want to pass through here safely."

"No problem, my dears," she said. "If you'd like, both of you can ride on my back to the far side of the swamp. I was just getting ready to end my nap and head over that way."

Squeaker looked at Delilah, eyebrows raised in surprise. After their encounter with the alligator, he was not expecting this huge creature to be so friendly, much less offer them a ride across the swamp.

"We are delighted to accept your generous offer," Squeaker said, happily swishing his tail back and forth. "My name's Squeaker, and this is Delilah. Is there anything we can do in return to show our appreciation?"

"I'm Daisy," the enormous hippo said. "Yes, there's one thing you could do. I've had a terrible toothache for nearly a week. It is extremely painful! Do you think one of you could look inside my mouth to see if there's any way to stop this dreadful pain?"

"Sure," he said, glancing quickly at Delilah to see if she agreed. "Once we get across the swamp, let us look inside your mouth, and we'll see if we can help you."

"Yes," Delilah said. "We'll do our best. You are being so kind to bring us to dry land. Thank you, thank you!" She kicked her back heels to show her appreciation for Daisy's kind gesture.

Daisy slid forward into the murky swamp, making sure to keep enough of her body above the water so that Delilah and Squeaker could stay aloft. Within an hour, they reached their destination.

Daisy waddled onto the grassy bank. Leaning forward gently, she lowered her head and front legs to let the two youngsters slide off her back and onto the ground. Then, as promised, they asked Daisy to open her mouth so they could try to determine the cause of her toothache.

"OK," she said. "It's the third tooth over from the center on the bottom of my mouth," she told them before opening her huge jaws.

They could see right away why Daisy had a toothache. The gums around the troublemaking tooth were red and inflamed. The tooth itself looked brown and had a line through the center of it where it appeared the tooth had fractured, allowing infection to form.

The badger and lamb agreed, they needed to figure out a way to pull out that infected tooth. But how? The size of the tooth was huge. Daisy was already in a lot of pain, so how could they possibly get rid of it?

Then Squeaker had an idea. What if they could tie a vine tightly around that tooth and the other end to a tree trunk? All they would have to figure out was a way to get Daisy to jerk her head backward, away from the tree. It would hurt a lot, but if it was done swiftly, it should work.

Squeaker explained the idea to Daisy.

"That sounds really painful," she whimpered. "But I don't think I can bear this pain much longer. Let's give it a try," she agreed. At the thought of it, her breathing had sped up.

Squeaker proceeded to search along the edge of the swamp for a vine or vines long enough to use for their procedure. Delilah saw a long green vine hanging on a black willow tree. Together she and Squeaker pulled it down, the entire length reaching more than thirty feet. Squeaker ran and tied one end tightly around Daisy's fractured tooth, while Delilah held the other end in her teeth and wound it around the willow several times.

"How are we going to find a way to get Daisy to jerk her head with enough force to actually pull out that infected tooth?" Delilah said. Squeaker lifted his paws up and shrugged.

Even as he did that, a tiny bog lemming, slightly larger than a field mouse, ran under Daisy's stomach as it nervously darted toward its home. Daisy, who hated mice and was horribly fearful of them let out a blood-curdling screech.

Caught off guard by the lemming's sudden appearance, Daisy lost her balance and crashed onto her side. The immense weight of her body and her fall away from the tree caused a huge jerk on the vine. Out popped the tooth in a dramatic moment, root and all.

Poor Daisy moaned, but the offending tooth was gone. Delilah ran to her.

"Oh! You poor thing," she said. "When I stayed with Whitney over at the cliff dwellings, she kept a yellow flower, the calendula, with other herbs and fine sand for treating cuts and infections. She was so sweet to put some in my bag with the berries, roots, and other snacks that she gave me before we left. Let me put some on that sore mouth," she said.

Before Daisy could object, Delilah pulled out the yellow dried flower and poured out the herbs and sand, added some water to make a paste, and then placed the mixture on the empty hole in Daisy's jaw. Daisy whimpered again, but then Squeaker and Delilah heard an "Ahhh" emerge from Daisy's mouth. The potion had already begun to provide its soothing and healing effect. In a few days, they hoped the hippo would find the toothache had disappeared.

"Thank you!" Daisy said to the youngsters. "It is a wonderful coincidence that we ran into each other today."

"I think it was definitely meant to be!" Squeaker said emphatically. "We are so thankful to have met you, Daisy. But before we go, can you tell us anything about these grasslands and how to get to the beautiful garden we've heard about?"

"We both want to return to our homes, which are in Ataraxia. But we don't know how. We've been told we have to pass through a garden filled with the most beautiful flowers we will ever see, of every size and color. Daisy, do you know how we can get there?"

The hippo stared at the pair: the badger with a bit of swagger and the gentle-voiced lamb.

"I'm afraid you have a challenging path ahead of you," she said, shaking her head with concern. "I know the garden you speak of. And what you have heard is correct. But from what I have heard, it is also a place of deceptions.

"There's a spirit that inhabits the garden. It will welcome you, make you feel joy and comfort, and then it will entice you to stay," Daisy warned. "I've never heard of any creature who has traveled beyond the garden, so I don't know how you will find the path to return to Ataraxia. That is all I can tell you about that.

"But before that, you must make your way across the grasslands. If you look far ahead toward the horizon, you can see a green hill that rises above this flat land where we stand. I think it must be a half-day journey. That is where you can enter the garden.

"I will warn you now that this grassy area is inhabited by some serpent creatures that I avoid," the hippo continued. "Most are not a threat to me, but there is one who rules this area and who preys on smaller animals, squeezes the life out of them to consume them. It is Abaddon!" Her eyes squinted as she spit out his name. "He is said to be the largest python here in our world. He ventures near the swamps too. But you must keep your eyes and ears open. He is a master of stealth. If he attacks and gets wrapped around you, it will be only moments that you'll have left to survive."

Squeaker glanced at Delilah. He could see the fear register on her face.

But despite trembling slightly, she turned to him with an unflinching expression of resolve. "We both want to get home. I know the journey is dangerous, but I do want to continue, Squeaker. Are you with me?"

Squeaker searched her face for a moment, then blurted out, "We're a team, aren't we? C'mon, I'm with you all the way. We'll be basking in those fragrant flowers before you know it!" With that, he flicked his tail back and forth to impress Delilah with his confidence.

She didn't know that, inwardly, he used the moment to bolster his determination. He was sure the lamb would never make it by herself. She needed him, which made him feel important, necessary. He shook his furry shoulders with pride.

"I have to head back to my family now," Daisy said as she bade the pair farewell. "I am so thankful our paths crossed. My mouth still hurts a little but nothing compared to the terrible pain I was experiencing before. Thank you both and best wishes for a safe journey."

Daisy rumbled back into the swamp waters. Soon, she was gliding through the water, heading toward a pool of deeper waters.

The two friends' eyes followed Daisy as she disappeared into the distance. Then they turned back to view their destination, the heavily treed hill Daisy had pointed out to them as the location of the garden.

It was still early enough in the day; they felt they should be able to reach it in the daylight. Once there, they would rest at the edge of the garden before venturing in. Delilah pulled out more snacks from the bag Whitney had given her. Squeaker wandered over to a nearby fruit tree where he'd noticed small pears growing. Pulling one off with his front paws, he gobbled it down.

"Yum! Those are super sweet and good. Come eat some, Delilah." Together the two gorged on the sweet sickle pears, along with some of the berries and roots in her sack. Rejuvenated, they headed off, keeping their eyes peeled to either side of the path as they walked. Neither one wanted an encounter with Abaddon or any other serpent. The warnings they'd heard caused them to walk together silently. No reason to alert any nearby predators to their presence.

As the grassy hill loomed closer, Delilah heard a rustling in the grass. She stopped short, straining her ears. Seeing her pause, Squeaker followed suit. But

all they heard was the swaying of the grass in the breeze and the warbling of some swallows in a small grove of bushes.

Wandering in their direction from the east, they saw a group of wallabies grazing. Continuing on while picking their way carefully, they suddenly heard the swallows cheeping loudly, the call an obvious signal of near danger. Then, without warning, Squeaker saw the huge head of a snake, with a dark red and brown diamond mark, rise up and pounce on one of the wallabies. It sunk its teeth into the startled creature's flesh to help itself hang on, providing leverage so it could wrap coils of its body around the wallaby.

Delilah shrieked at the sight of it, the wallaby's eyes bulging as the python squeezed its body tighter around its neck. After less than a minute, the animal hung lifeless within Abaddon's coils.

The terrible fate of the wallaby provided the distraction necessary for Squeaker and Delilah to race ahead since Abaddon was preoccupied with swallowing the entire body of the wallaby whole. They hoped, with the sun still overhead, Abaddon would settle down for a long while to rest and digest his meal.

Feeling like fate had intervened on their behalf, Squeaker boldly led the way forward, with Delilah following closely behind him. They had now halved the distance to the lush area that Daisy told them was where they would find the garden.

But as they moved swiftly, the grasses rippled. Another serpent, one of Abaddon's entourage, approached Delilah, coiled, and leaped upon her. Squeaker heard Delilah bleat in a strange, muffled voice. Turning, he saw the constrictor trying to coil around her body. The honey badger snarled, with teeth bared; then he bit sharply into the snake's back, near its head. The force of his teeth shocked the snake. It dropped from Delilah and prepared to relaunch, hissing at Squeaker as it eyed Delilah's neck. Before it could strike, Squeaker pounced again, this time further back on the snake's body, a narrower section that allowed him to fully grasp the python's body and pull it backward. He dragged it as far as he could before the python attempted to strike at the badger. Its teeth just grazed Squeaker, but the snake was unable to free his body from the badger's fierce grip.

Delilah bleated as she anxiously watched the battle. She urged on her valiant partner, hopeful he would defeat the snake without being injured.

Squeaker again dragged the python backward while it flailed, digging his teeth in more deeply to inflict maximum injury. But then Squeaker momentarily relaxed his grip to catch his breath. In reaction to that slight release, the python was able to escape his hold, hastily retreating into the grasses and out of sight. The snake had missed the meal he had hoped for; now the python would need to look for something smaller, an easier prey, to get his food for the day.

Delilah rushed over to the badger.

"Oh, dear friend, I thought I might never see you again!" she cried, "and all because you came to my defense. Thank you, thank you!" She nuzzled Squeaker's face.

Proud of his victory, Squeaker puffed out his chest at Delilah's praise. "Aw, it was nuthin'. That pipsqueak was not going to ruin our day!" He beamed at the lamb. "But we better get moving, as fast and as quietly as we can so we can get through these grasslands before any of those python's relatives find us."

Delilah nodded her head vigorously as they resumed their journey with a new sense of urgency. Fortunately, other than a few grazing gazelles and the chatter of birds from the shrubs, the pair did not encounter any other predators as they traveled closer to their destination.

Midway into the afternoon, they saw they were approaching the densest thicket of green trees and rambling vine-laden bushes Delilah had ever seen. Huge honeysuckle bushes emanated their fresh, sweet scent. Lilies of the valley sprung up all along the line of bushes. Red poppies peeked out from behind the roots of the trees.

Amazed at their discovery, the friends examined the sight before them. It was the garden Whitney had described, then confirmed by Daisy's description. But where was the entryway? "I don't see where we should enter," Delilah said.

"No prob," Squeaker said. "Follow me. We'll find the best entry point together."

As they skirted the thick greenery, Delilah felt almost a physical tugging at her feet, pulling her east along the edge of the garden. No clear entrance emerged until they reached two monstrous willow trees, each one arching slightly in opposite directions.

There, between the willow trunks, lay a vast corridor of low-growing periwinkle, yellow buttercups, and a huge stretch of pure white lily of the valley, together forming a dramatically carpeted pathway. The friends gaped at the entryway to the garden, so inviting as the sun kissed each petal, adding its luster to the luscious landscape.

Delilah wandered in, munching on the choice clover as she entered. Honeybees swarmed in a hollow log, which caught Squeaker's attention. Nosing his way into the log, he chomped down on a large section of honeycomb, downing it with gusto as he smacked his lips (as well as batted away the angry bees).

Delilah chuckled at the sight while inhaling the incredible fragrance that wafted up her nostrils. Truly, this was a paradise the little lamb never imagined knowing.

As her eyes became accustomed to these new surroundings, Delilah took in the awesome setting around her. True to what Whitney had told her, the colors of the flowers in the garden were breathtaking to behold. She realized she and Squeaker were surrounded by every color in nature's palate, from vivid fuchsia to the palest silver lavender to bright pinks, reds, and violets.

As she listened, she heard a comforting noise in the background, a gurgling sound. She beckoned Squeaker over, who had just polished off his honeycomb treat.

"I hear water nearby," she said. "Let's explore and see if we can find the source." The friends wandered deeper into the garden, their eyes rewarded at every turn with gorgeous trees and vegetation, much of which they had never seen before.

As they walked, they spotted creatures peeking out at them from the trees and bushes. Several hedgehogs stared at them and then hurried on their way. A large hare and his partner hopped out of sight while warblers sang in the branches above. Delilah saw several foxes in the distance. None seemed perturbed or even too interested in the pair's presence. A gazelle came up to them, nodded, and greeted them.

"Hello! Welcome. What are you looking for here in our garden?" he asked, one eyebrow raised.

"We're thirsty," Delilah answered, "and I heard the water, but we haven't seen it yet."

"Sure, follow me," he responded. They did as instructed, tagging along behind him. The gurgling sound grew louder until soon they saw a roaring river several meters ahead.

"Thank you!" Delilah said, and the gazelle nodded and continued on his way. The friends rushed over and drank until they could drink no more. Delilah thought she had never tasted water so pure and delicious in her life.

As they lay along the riverbank, Delilah and Squeaker rested. A spirit of contentment rose like a mist from the water, causing them to fall into a deep sleep as they lay on the soft green moss that covered the ground. The nighttime hours flew by as the pair slumbered.

Chapter 44

LURING APART THE FRIENDS

At daybreak, Squeaker stirred. He thought he had never slept with such peace before.

Soon, Delilah awoke too. She stretched her legs as she stood up, shaking out her soft wooly coat. For a moment, she forgot they had any purpose other than basking for a day in this dreamlike garden. Yes, she thought, I could imagine living here forever.

But as that idea floated through her brain, the image again rose up of a beautiful ewe, this time plaintively calling her name. "Delilah, where are you dear?" she thought she heard. It was so real in her mind that she was startled out of her daydreaming.

"Squeaker, we need to continue our journey and somehow find the far side of this garden. I don't know how we will know where that is, but Whitney told me the only way back to Ataraxia is by reaching the other side of the garden."

Squeaker didn't respond right away. He was staring into the water, admiring the image staring back at him. He could see a handsome and bold honey badger with a sleek dark face and underbody. Across his sides were white stripes that melded into light gray hair across his back. Proudly, he bared his teeth as he stared at his reflection, which revealed sharp white incisors that glistened in the morning sun.

As he examined his image, he saw next to it the reflection of a beautiful female honey badger. She batted her long eyelashes coyly at Squeaker. Startled, he looked beside him on the riverbank, but no other creature stood alongside him.

Had he imagined it? He looked back at the water. No, he hadn't; there she was again. Yet there was no sign anywhere around him of another honey badger. He rubbed his eyes, staring back again.

This time, the captivating creature beckoned him to follow her. He heard her, as if in a dream, whispering in a velvety smooth voice, "This way, brave one, I need you to help me. You're the only one who can! You're so strong and fearsome," she said while smiling.

Delilah wandered over closer to where Squeaker stood. "Squeaker! We need to get going. What's up with you?"

Squeaker barely heard Delilah's voice. He felt as if he were in a trance, captivated by this exquisite female badger with her alluring voice.

"Leave me here for a while," Squeaker muttered. "You go on ahead. I'll catch up with you."

"No way! C'mon, you're teasing me, aren't you?" The lamb gave him a friendly nudge with her nose. Instead of his usual jovial response, Squeaker shouted at her. "Leave me alone! I told you to go on ahead, and I meant it." He made a hissing noise at Delilah to register his displeasure. Quickly, he gazed back at the water. He didn't want to lose sight of his newfound friend with whom he was enamored. After all, she said she needed *his* help because of his strength and bravery.

He thrust out his chest with pride. Finally, someone who recognized his talents. But he saw her reflection floating further away down the river, so he rushed away from Delilah along the water. It was as if that beautiful honey badger had looped an imaginary leash around his neck. He felt himself drawn to her with infatuation, unaware of his surroundings or of the fact that he was deserting his friend.

Delilah's smile drooped into a frown. She couldn't figure out what was going on with her friend. Sure, he could be a bit of an egotist on occasion. But his behavior was making no sense.

He was the one who had told her no matter what happened, he'd be with her until they could get back home. "Squeaker!" the lamb shrieked plaintively. "What am I going to do without you?"

Delilah stood staring in disbelief as Squeaker's image became smaller and smaller. She was dumbfounded. But as she stood, trying to determine her next moves, she remembered the warning Whitney had shared about the spirits who inhabited the garden, spirits that preyed on their victims' vulnerabilities.

"That must be what has happened to my friend," she lamented. "Now what?"

Delilah fretted to herself about whether she should try going after Squeaker—about what direction she should choose at all. She had no sense of how to reach the far side of the garden. There must be something or someone to help her figure out how to reach their destination.

The lamb decided that since they had entered from the south, she would use the sun as a guide and try to head in a northern direction. Before heading on her journey, she grazed in the meadow by the river with an abundance of alfalfa and clover. With her tummy full, Delilah downed a final guzzle of water and headed north.

As she trotted along, her eyes were overwhelmed by the dazzling colors. Shrouds of morning glory dangled from the trees. Wisteria hung thick among the increasingly dense, forested section of the garden; its purple blossoms greeted her as she passed. Vivid red and yellow roses climbed up the low-hanging branches of junipers and maples.

A nearby redbud tree beckoned her to stop and sniff the drooping clusters of double lilac and pink flowers that blossomed from thick, green vines wrapped around its branches. A huge raspberry bush covered with sweet berries grew wild along the flower carpet Delilah was following, so she paused for a snack and then headed on her way.

Occasionally she would stop and look behind her to see if Squeaker, true to his word, was going to catch up with her. But so far, there was no sign of the honey badger. A faint breeze fluttered the leaves of the trees that filled the garden. Delilah strained her ears. Was it just the whisper of the leaves? Or did she hear a voice calling her?

Delilah had reached a part of the Garden where the dense forest had thinned, leaving a path trampled by various animals passing through, so she now easily stayed on the path.

Again, a whisper of a voice called out.

"Delilah, come this way. I've been looking for you for such a long time!" Astonished at hearing her name, the lamb peered in the direction of the voice. Beyond the bushes, she thought she made out the form of a large ewe. She shook her head in disbelief, never expecting to see some of her kind here in the Garden ruled by Abaddon, much less a ewe calling out to her by name.

Is it possible I might find my family here? Perhaps I don't have to return to Ataraxia after all, she thought. She continued in the direction of where she had a glimpse of the sheep.

Once she got past the bushes, she noticed a mist over a small pond not far from the path. Because of the mist, she couldn't make out what she saw, but it looked like a small herd of sheep on the far side of the pond. She hurried her stride into a trot as she headed toward the mist.

She walked around the pond to the far side after hearing the ewe's call, but once she arrived, she did not see her. *Is it possible*, she wondered, *that the spirits Whitney told me about are tricking me in some way? Perhaps the figure I saw from a distance was an illusion.* But because it reminded her somehow of the mother she longed for, Delilah continued to search the area for the ewe.

Chapter 45

ORIGIN OF THE SPIRITS OF THE ABYSS

The spirits, of which there were three, reported to Abaddon, king of the Abyss, who deftly utilized them as lures for unsuspecting prey. At one time, many years ago, the Garden had been a mecca for creatures sentenced to the Abyss, animals of all sizes and species who had discovered this idyllic place as they roamed searching for a way to return home.

Slinking one day across the grasslands, Abaddon discovered this garden paradise. He saw it was providing cover for some creatures who, he thought, would make delectable meals. As he slithered along the river that briskly flowed through the Garden, he heard voices that seemed to be emanating from the bushes that grew along the riverbank. Sliding closer, he could hear their voices more clearly.

"I've been imprisoned here in this Garden now for three generations! It is ghastly that there's no escape," exclaimed the voice.

"But Lorna, we should be thankful. Gorgeous colors everywhere, perfect weather, and creatures we get to chase after and tease. What could be more fun?"

"You've only been banished here for a decade. C'mon! What do you know, Gaffy? You wait and see. In a few years, you will wish you could escape too."

"Who is speaking?" Abaddon asked in his deep, mellifluous voice. "I hear you, but I don't see who it is."

He peered ahead, his black eyes darting back and forth. Then he spotted them.

Abaddon saw the spirits eyeing him. He could see they were aerial creatures, spirits in their natural form, with a misty, cloud-like presence, so they were not easily detected. They also seemed to be gifted with the ability to disguise themselves by taking on the forms of other creatures in the Garden.

As Abaddon stared at the spirits, one of them, Lorna, swirled her form into the shape of a dark green female boa constrictor, with attractive chartreuse lines setting off her eyes, and slid down the tree trunk into Abaddon's view.

"I'm Lorna, and I'm chatting with my friend, Gaffy. We're spirits of the Garden, sentenced to abide here. We were unruly—I guess you might say rebellious." She giggled. "We have been sentenced to stay here forever. We can morph into the image of different creatures, which is why you can see me now."

Abaddon learned as he spoke with them that these spirits had been banished to this place from another kingdom for their refusal to be obedient to their Creator. The Spirit of Agape Love who ruled over all creation had banished them to here, which imitated the perfect home He had once created for all mankind and creatures alike.

Abaddon considered this state of affairs for a moment before speaking. "Perhaps you could help me. Let me explain . . ." The devious python went on to propose they become lures for him. In essence, they'd be partners in his schemes. By taking on a similar form to creatures passing through the garden, they could cajole, confuse, and exhaust them, making them vulnerable prey for the nefarious python.

"After all, it would give you some entertainment," Abaddon said in his honeyed voice, raising his huge gray-green head as he stared at them with his beady eyes. "You must get bored. Why not have some fun and add intrigue to your tedious lives?"

Lorna and Gaffy whispered together for a moment. "We have another friend, Mr. Abaddon, named Myrna. Can she join us as partners with you also?"

"Why, of course," Abaddon exclaimed. "Of course. That would be ever so helpful."

Myrna was even more irked than Lorna with her banishment to the Garden. She was moping near a weeping willow when Lorna and Gaffy spotted her. Having spiritual eyes with which they could sense each other's presence, the spirits easily detected each other.

The two enlisted Myrna for their newfound partnership with Abaddon. Myrna had inhabited the Garden even longer than Lorna, often whining to her spirit friends about her frustration.

The first assignment from Abaddon was for the spirits to search for a small mammal, specifically a wallaby. Back then, Abaddon had seen a few of them in the grasslands, but none were close enough for him to attack.

When that mission was accomplished, they would let Abaddon know. He told them he would linger in his favorite spot, camouflaged by the flowering plants along the forest's edge, near the river.

"Oh, this will be entertaining!" Myrna said. "We'll have to be clever. Once we find it, what will be our strategy?"

"Let's all take the form of something frightening," Lorna said. "How about large red foxes?" she laughed. "We'll position ourselves in three directions. When he starts running, the others must be ready to pounce on it. We'll have it exhausted in no time."

The game was on. Lorna, Gaffy, and Myrna soared over the Garden, scrutinizing every possible place where a young wallaby might graze or wander to rest. On a soft, mossy verge, Myrna saw it first: a young male wallaby resting in the shadows of a tree.

She alerted her companions. They quickly morphed into the perfect images of red foxes with toothy jaws and huge, bushy tails. Lorna pointed east, indicating she'd come at him from that direction; Myrna headed south and Gaffy to the north.

The wallaby was first alerted by a rustling sound. *Is it the breeze wafting through the saplings?* he wondered. Or was he dreaming? As he lay still, listening, his eyes caught an image at quite a distance. As he stared, he could make it out now.

It was a red fox, racing toward him! He knew danger when he saw it. But he also knew of a cave in the opposite direction that might afford a hiding place for him. He loped fiercely, propelling himself forward at the fastest pace he could manage.

As he got closer to the cave, he jumped backward. A second red fox appeared, jaws open, revealing sharp, pointed teeth. It stood between him and the cave. He gasped, pivoted, and shot in the opposite direction. Perhaps, just possibly, he could reach the river and get across to the other side where a thick overgrowth of bushes and vines created an effective refuge.

By now, the poor wallaby's heart was beating so wildly, he thought he might collapse. But he knew he was getting close to the river; just a few more leaps should have him there. As he reached the edge of the forest, he paused for a moment, glancing at the most likely spot where he might be able to cross.

At that moment, Abaddon struck, sinking his teeth into the wallaby's neck, holding on tightly to it while he wrapped his huge coils around its neck. In a matter of seconds, it could no longer breathe. Its legs stopped thrashing, and its body went limp.

Abaddon held on, not moving until he was sure he had squeezed all life out of the creature. He then opened his gigantic jaws, scooping the wallaby artfully down his gullet, turning and twisting it in his jaws until he had managed to consume the wallaby whole. Then he laid and rested as he enjoyed his repast.

The spirits found this "game," as they called it, entertaining. It lifted them from the ennui they felt and appealed to their troublemaking natures. After all, they had been banished here for a reason.

As time passed, Abaddon rewarded them by lavishing praise upon their efforts, applauding their cunning tactics. Without any apparent conscience, the spirits were willing partners in Abaddon's deathly plots. After each mercenary escapade, they giggled as they observed the monstrous python gorging himself until he was unable to move, sometimes for an entire day. It was an ugly sport with dire consequences for its victims.

Chapter 46

SJ's Message

While SJ had won a few races at school, he had never run a cross-country course, which was essentially what he was doing now as he tried to maintain a steady, fast running pace, heading back from Malvelnia to deliver his message to Solomon.

He tried to ignore his left leg where the snake bit him, but it was now red and swollen. Every time his left foot hit the ground, he felt a pulsating pain. Realizing the urgency of his mission, SJ kept running. Everyone back home had always told him he had a photographic memory, so remembering the path back to the Ataraxia Amphitheater would not be difficult. Ignoring the swelling leg was much harder.

Focused entirely on his mission, SJ didn't notice a dark shadow above him, which was growing larger. Suddenly, he heard the wind rush from a pair of gigantic wings and felt prickly feathers envelop him as two humongous condors lifted him from the ground.

Each bird had one side of SJ's jacket held tightly in their sharply taloned feet. The jacket was a tough canvas material and zipped shut. SJ shrieked once as the massive birds soared above the treetops, and he saw the ground moving further and further away.

The condors had been directed by the wily Ashok, who had disregarded his brother's wishes. He was unconcerned about Kibou and figured his clownish nephew would eventually make it back home, one way or another.

On the forefront of Ashok's mind was revenge! He was seething over the demise of his two favorite co-conspirators in the evildoings of the kingdom: Diablo and Phinehas. He intended to make the Ataraxians pay for their deaths.

He figured if the condors took out the measly boy, the message from Wendigo would never reach Ataraxia, and the war would continue. In this scenario, Ashok saw Malvelnia as the victor. In the aftermath, he would have a key role, he surmised, in further subjugating the Ataraxians to do Malvelnia's bidding.

SJ's mind raced as the condors continued their journey. He was thankful he had his jacket on and tightly zipped because he felt cold currents of air whip across his face as they neared their apparent destination, a craggy cliffside where he saw, atop one of its highest points, a gigantic nest.

As the condors descended, SJ could see the nest was empty. But it wouldn't be for long. As the winged pair dropped SJ from their claws into the hovel of twigs, branches, and straw, things worsened. His first impression as he somersaulted was of a terrible smell of death. As his eyes focused, he realized why.

At one far side of the nest lay the remains of something, perhaps a rat or a mole. All that was left were bones and some fur. He tried to suppress the gagging reflex he felt rising in his throat. Turning, he scurried over to the other side, putting as much space as possible between himself and the mostly consumed carcass.

To SJ's surprise, after depositing him in the nest, the condors flew on to an unknown destination.

As he raised his head to look out around him, SJ realized there was no uncomplicated way for him to escape. The nest had been built on top of a rocky spike that was virtually inaccessible to most creatures.

Fortunately, the nest seemed solidly built. He walked around the side of it, testing for any weak spots. But the twigs, branches, and dry grasses had been woven together by the condors into a tight mesh. Only as he tested the stability of the nest did he notice how swollen his leg now looked. He rolled up his pant leg partway and saw an angry red welt around the bite. His leg throbbed.

"Help!" he screamed. "Somebody, help me!"

His cry echoed against the rocky cliffs. SJ sighed, his eyes misting. *I've totally failed my mission*, he thought, *and there's no one in sight to help get me out of here. If I don't get my message back to the Guardians, the war will continue, and it will be my fault*, he fretted. *And Wendigo may do something terrible to Allie! Oh dear, what should I do?*

Feeling panicked, SJ leaned as far over the edge of the nest as he could to explore any viable option for escape from his lofty prison. The surface of the rocky cliff had been rendered smooth from the wind and rain buffeting it over the years.

SJ couldn't spot any footholds whereby he might attempt a descent. After half an hour of peering down from all angles of the nest, he sat down to rest. He remembered his dad telling him that when everything looked bleak, to call out to God.

"He will never leave you nor desert you," Will had told his son. "That's a promise in God's Word."

Remembering his dad's words, SJ called out to God. "Help me!" he shouted. "If you're there, like my dad said, help me now! The lives of many depend on me!"

Tired and hungry, SJ sat dejectedly. He thought of Allie, by herself, counting on him. And here he was, unable to do a thing to help himself or to help their Ataraxian friends.

As his mind raced with unsettling thoughts, SJ heard a faint noise from a distance. It sounded like wings in flight, so he peered upward, afraid the condors were returning and not wanting to imagine what they might do to him.

Instead, he saw a flock of birds, much smaller than the condors, and as they soared above his location, he could see some were white and some a soft gray in color. Perhaps, just perhaps, they might be friendly.

SJ waved frantically. At first, there was no response as the flock headed a bit further away. Then SJ remembered the talent his sister always teased him about: his ability to whistle more loudly than anyone, even his dad, who had taught him to whistle as a little boy.

Woohee! He whistled what sounded like a fox's shriek at night. *Woohee! Woohee . . . Woohee!* SJ kept whistling as he gazed at the now departing flock of mourning doves. But even as he kept making the startling noise, he noticed the lead dove veering to the side and then . . . Yes! It was circling back to the source of the noise.

"Who is that?" Moriah said to her younger brother, who was flying right behind her to her right.

"I have no idea," he cooed back. "Let's glide down and take a look."

As they flew closer to the huge condor's nest, Moriah saw the boy, still trying to whistle but now falling back against the side of the nest, seemingly exhausted, with no air left in his lungs to make another sound.

"It's Allie's brother!" she exclaimed. "How in heaven's name did he end up here?" Moriah and several of her party came down to land along opposite sides of the nest. She spoke to SJ. "You're Allie's brother, right?" she asked.

"Yes, that's right. I'm SJ, and I was rushing back to Ataraxia to take an important message to the Guardians from King Wendigo. While I was running there, two huge birds, condors I think, lifted me from the path and flew me here. I think it was done on purpose, to prevent me from taking the message to Ataraxia. You need to help me get it there fast. But how can I get out of here?" SJ threw up his hands in frustration.

"Don't worry, SJ, we're going to take you directly to Solomon. He'll know what to do. But first, we have to figure out how to best transport you. . . . Oh my, what's happened to your leg?" Moriah blurted out, staring at his red, swollen ankle.

"I was bitten by a snake on the ground," SJ said. But by pointing it out, Moriah could tell she had caused SJ to focus on it more than before. As he rubbed his sore ankle, SJ cringed. Moriah imagined he must be feeling helpless. Worse than that, she had no idea how he could get down from this scary place.

As they thought about escape strategies, they noticed an unusual sight. A throng of large birds came swooping toward the nest! SJ thought it might be the group of condors returning.

But as they came closer into viewing range, he saw that they had red heads and long beaks and were larger than Moriah's mourning doves but not as huge as condors.

"They made it!" Moriah exclaimed. "I had put out a call for our woodpecker allies in the region to help us out, and here they are."

Sure enough, not only could SJ see they were woodpeckers, but they were some of the largest ones he'd ever encountered or imagined existed!

"We've got several more of our group arriving shortly," the largest woodpecker of the flock told Moriah. "And they've found just what you ordered."

SJ looked upward to see a gigantic green lily pad seeming to float downward but held around its circumference by eight woodpeckers who gingerly placed it atop the nest, where it spilled over the sides.

SJ reached out and touched its cool, damp surface. It must have measured at least five feet across and the length even longer. It occurred to him that these resourceful birds were about to load him onto the lily pad, much like a carpet. As he considered this, four additional, larger woodpeckers arrived to aid in the effort.

"C'mon, SJ," Moriah coaxed. "Slide onto this lily pad, and our friends are going to fly you to safety. In fact, with that sore-looking leg, they'll fly you directly to Ataraxia."

"Please, let's get him to Graham. You know the way," she directed the woodpeckers. Moriah knew Graham would help get SJ to Solomon quickly and safely.

Off they flew with SJ seated on the lily pad, holding firmly onto its edges. He found, to his surprise, the woodpecker crew seemed to fly in perfect harmony so that their passenger was not tossed from side to side, but rather rode smoothly to the destination.

In less than an hour, they arrived near the grove where Molly and Graham lived. The woodpecker medley set SJ down on the ground and quizzically looked around. The boy winced as the pain in his leg welled up.

"Hallo! Anybody here?" he called out.

He paused. There was no sign of Molly or Kibou, but Graham and Luke apparently heard him and rushed over from the field behind their home that sloped down to the creek.

"What's wrong?" Luke cried out, reaching the boy first. Then Luke saw his leg.

"A snake bit me on the way to Malvelnia," he told Luke as Graham arrived. "It was okay for a while, but now it's swelling up and causing me some pain. Then, on my way, some huge condors kidnapped me," SJ said, sharing the entire story. "These awesome friends rescued me . . ." He nodded to the woodpeckers. "And just brought me here under Moriah's direction. But I need to continue to the Amphitheater to deliver a message from King Wendigo. It's urgent!"

"Hop on my back, young man," Graham said. "We'll have you over there before you know it."

SJ scrambled atop Graham's back, wincing as he did, and the trio headed off to the Amphitheater, with Luke trotting behind.

Graham was a tall ram, but the ride was much bumpier than the gliding leaps atop Aurora. On the way, they heard loud shrieks emanating from the monkey caves, where that battlefront continued to rage.

At the Amphitheater, Graham paused near an expanse of black sandy ground. He remembered that once, when Ethan was bitten by a snake, his mother had been

able to spit on the sand, roll it up, and put her son's paw in the muddy mixture because the dark sands were known to have healing properties.

He instructed SJ to slide off, spit in the sand to make a paste, then rub it on his leg over the snake bite. SJ did as he was told, waited a few moments, and felt the heat being drawn out of the wounded leg. As he sat, Solomon arrived. SJ overheard someone say one of Aurora's cousins had already reached Solomon to tell him SJ was there with news from Malvelnia.

"What news do you have for us?" Solomon asked, his eyebrows raised.

"Oh, thank goodness!" SJ answered. "King Wendigo is holding my sister until he gets word that his son, Kibou, will be safely returned to him. You will signal this by a flock of white doves in the sky, at which time a cease-fire will begin. The king said he would withdraw his forces if Ataraxia does the same, and he will temporarily freeze his edict. He is going to send Queen Eris and his brother, Ashok, for the peaceful exchange at the Waterfalls. When he receives Kibou safely, he will release Allie."

By the time SJ had finished the message, other Guardians had arrived, including Moriah, Zion, and Aurora.

"Quick, Moriah, gather your flock and fly high above the Indigna River, so high that all of Malvelnia and all on the battlefront can see you," Solomon instructed. "Do it quickly—quickly! This will signal a cease-fire, as we want no more bloodshed." Solomon knew so many lives had already been lost—and even one was one too many.

Making haste, Moriah flitted to the area where her flock of mourning doves spent much of their time.

It was a small field filled with sunflowers, wild grasses, and ragweed dotted by large, dense bushes that made suitable places for resting or even nesting, although more often, the doves preferred the taller trees surrounding the field for their nests. Several were recovering, having just returned from the journey during which they had recovered the stranded SJ.

"Friends, time to gather!" Moriah cooed, urging her flock to join her in the air. The soft sound of flapping wings echoed in the trees as they ascended, following Moriah as she steered them upward, higher and higher, at the same time heading in the direction of the Indigna River.

Below, they saw the reptiles of Malvelnia regrouping, preparing to strike the front line of Ataraxia's wolves and foxes, who had been waging a fierce battle to gain ground.

On the trees at the edge of the plateau, King Wendigo's army of vultures was poised to attack the honey badgers who had successfully taken out several snakes. The king himself appeared in the highest tree.

As he gazed upward, he saw the doves floating above the battleground. He paused, momentarily considering ignoring the signal he had called for, but the image of Kibou rose in his mind.

Despite his deceitful character, his fatherly instincts prevailed. He screeched noisily and waved his gigantic wing, signaling Diego to back off with his line of crocodiles.

Diego, anger draped across his brow, hesitated but then begrudgingly nodded and directed the battalion backward, with the group of constrictors following his lead.

Solomon, now flying overhead, observed the reaction of King Wendigo's battalion and signaled to the Guardians below to move back in accord. Jake, Helen, and Lucius nodded and stood quietly after stepping back. Solomon flew to the monkey caves, urging Albert and Orion to move their troops back from the caves. There, he spied Simon in the branch of the largest tree above the monkey caves.

"Simon, please, help calm your Heralders! King Wendigo has signaled for a cease-fire," he told the orangutan as he settled on a nearby branch. "An exchange is being arranged. The fighting is over—for now. And the king has halted his edict." Solomon stated loudly. "Ataraxia celebrates this signal for peace. My hope remains that the two kingdoms might find a way forward, free of conflict.

"Convey to the king that we will live up to our side of the agreement. Tell him we will plan to be at the Waterfalls at midday tomorrow for the safe exchange of Kibou for our young friend Allie. She and her brother have delivered a great favor for both of our kingdoms with their bravery."

Simon tilted his head, staring at Solomon; he was relieved to hear the fighting was over. But he was fearful of how the king would treat him after his inability to find and return Kibou. Perhaps with Kibou's safe return, this failure on Simon's part would be forgotten. Such was Simon's wishful thinking.

"I'll be on my way to Malvelnia," Simon said. "What time should we be there at the Waterfalls for the exchange?" he asked.

"Tomorrow, when the sun is at its highest point," Solomon replied. "The Guardians will be there with Kibou, who is in good health; tell the king we stand by our word. We will be there in peace with his son."

Chapter 47

OUT OF THE GARDEN

Squeaker gasped for breath as he scanned the river. He had chased after the gorgeous badger for at least a mile as she enticed him to follow her farther and farther down the river. He had been pulled by her magnetic face, smiling up at him, calling to him, beckoning him to join her.

On this particular day, Gaffy had taken on the form of the exquisite honey badger who had lured Squeaker far away from Delilah. She had created the hologram, an intoxicating image, to lure Squeaker away from his partner. It was a tried-and-true tactic that had worked countless times.

The spirit called his name again, annoyed that Squeaker had tired of the chase. *That honey badger doesn't know it,* Gaffy thought, *but our power is most effective when we are able to beguile a vulnerability, such as this creature's pride. But when he turned his focus to the welfare of his friend, it broke my spell.* Miffed at this development, Gaffy flitted away.

Squeaker rested by the riverbank and scanned the Garden in the area he had left Delilah. *What got into me? How could I leave my friend?* These questions rose in the sturdy badger's mind as he turned back to find Delilah. Squeaker shrugged off the distraction the spirit had created. Gaffy called after him, but he was now engrossed with finding his friend and making sure she was all right.

Trotting back into the grove of stunning colors that had captivated Delilah, Squeaker stood still for a moment. He thought he heard a noise in the distance, so he walked toward the sound, which, as he got closer, sounded like a lamb bleating. He moved faster until he saw the small lake and spotted Delilah on the far side.

She seemed to be searching for someone.

As Squeaker got closer, he saw a horrifying sight.

On a tree between where Delilah stood and Squeaker was the form of a gigantic snake, one larger than he had ever seen. Unknown to Squeaker, it was, of course, Abaddon, who had moved himself into position to attack the lamb.

Squeaker hissed loudly and rushed toward Abaddon, teeth bared. Startled, Delilah spun around in time to see Squeaker leap onto the back of Abaddon's head as the constrictor sprang toward the lamb. Abaddon wildly shook his head, trying to dislodge Squeaker's grip. As Squeaker fell off, he screamed at Delilah.

"Run, Delilah! Run!"

Heeding Squeaker's order, Delilah loped ahead. But after a bit, she looked back.

"Squeaker," she screamed. "Are you there? Squeaker, where are you?!" She took a few steps back and stood atop a grassy knoll.

Squeaker was still battling the gigantic constrictor. He had left a gash in the snake's neck and now was on his back, biting into the boa's flesh with his sharp fangs. Incredibly tenacious, the plucky badger had no sense of the full size of Abaddon compared to the badger's small stature.

As they fought, Abaddon unleashed a violent twist of his body to break the badger's grip. Angry over his wounds, Abaddon twirled and struck Squeaker's back, digging in his teeth to hold him while swirling his coils around Squeaker's body.

Delilah could see the battle from the distance. She sobbed huge crushing sobs that racked her body as she saw Squeaker go limp. Overcome with tears that blurred her vision, the lamb turned away and galloped beyond the lake to a clearing in the distance.

As she neared it, she saw an archway overgrown with vines and honeysuckle. It looked like the gate Whitney had told her about. She didn't want Squeaker's sacrifice to be in vain as she walked under the arch to find what was beyond.

Chapter 48

Peace

Graham and Molly awoke that morning with a sense of hope. Molly nuzzled Graham. They had been thoroughly exhausted the evening before—Molly from the range of emotions she had experienced awaiting Graham's return, and the ram from the daring escape from Malvelnia, followed by the rapid planning and negotiations needed to achieve a temporary stop to the battle.

The couple, with their son Luke and the royal son Kibou in tow, had quietly gone to their secret cave where they had slept that night. It was a precaution against any marauders trying to attack and take away the vulture. Truth be told, Kibou and Luke had become fast friends. With both having fun-loving natures, the two joked and teased each other just as brothers might do.

"Graham," Molly said with a smile. "There's something I haven't told you yet, what with all the excitement yesterday. But Luke is going to have a little brother or sister!"

The ram turned to her, tears filling his eyes. Graham was, at heart, very sentimental. It had been so difficult for them as they tried to recover from the loss of their daughter. He knew just how much this meant to their family.

"My dear Molly." He gently nuzzled her. Then the ram grinned from ear to ear, his chest puffing out. "W-w-what exciting news! I can't w-w-wait to tell Solomon."

"Dad, aren't we supposed to make a special trip today?" Luke asked. "You said so last night."

"Yes, son," Graham said. "But first, let's have some breakfast before our journey."

The family grazed in a nearby clover field that had an abundant amount of wild strawberries, which Kibou gobbled up. He also spotted a dead field mouse, which he quickly consumed. During his time with Graham's family, the plucky vulture had grown bigger, and his wing had gradually healed.

"Yum, that was a good breakfast," he said as he grinned at Luke, who winked back.

Several of the councilmembers of Ataraxia were heading to the Waterfalls together that day to attend the meeting that had been arranged. Following the launch of the truce, the Council had spent the evening assessing losses and counting the injuries of their troops.

Two wolves had been killed in fierce battles with the crocodiles when they'd received additional support from some venomous snakes. There'd been no casualties to the skunks or oxen, but at least a dozen foxes had sustained injuries.

Solomon and Graham would lead the way; SJ and Luke would bring Kibou for the exchange, and Zion, Helen, and Orion would attend too. Jake, whose brother had been killed in the battle, was grieving his loss and would not attend.

As the sun rose higher in the sky, the group gathered in the grove by Graham's home. It was a stately procession befitting the solemn occasion.

Moriah flew overhead, keeping an eye on the path. Luke had explained to Kibou that the trip had been organized specifically to return him to his family and for SJ's sister to be handed over to them, completing a peaceful exchange. Kibou told Luke he felt his heart beating faster at the thought of being together with his family again. Even though it had been a lively adventure away from them, he was ready to be home with his family.

Allie had learned the evening before about the truce and planned exchange. She woke up that morning in the nook where she had remained throughout her detention, where she had slept on the modest cushion of moss and twigs and survived on water, fruits, and nuts, which the vultures provided for her to eat. Other than a head of messy hair, a need for a hot shower, and a strong craving for a burger and fries, Allie was fine.

She ran her hands through her thick black hair, the blue streak now partially grown out, and wondered how SJ had done on his mission. Obviously, he'd successfully relayed the message since the meeting was now scheduled, but she still worried about his leg.

Ever since their dad had died, she had felt deeply protective of her little brother. She tried not to let it show so he wouldn't feel she was hovering or smothering him in any way. But always, her heart felt a twinge of pain when she thought about SJ growing up without his dad encouraging him, listening to him, cheering him on at future races or even just providing his comforting presence.

How could God have allowed this? She had that question on the top of her list for the day she'd be in His presence. She wanted to know how God would answer.

She stood firmly in her faith, and she realized she wasn't alone; many people faced formidable challenges in their lives that were not the result of their own doing. Nevertheless, the pain of loss had seared her soul. She'd recognized that her grief had opened her eyes to the suffering of others. It had shaped her perceptions in ways she did not fully understand, but one day she knew she would. Experiencing such a loss, for one thing, made her know she could never purposely inflict pain on another person.

Pain caused by others made the everyday world of being thirteen excruciating at times since that kind of behavior was intrinsic to her age group. She believed the insecurities of the kids around her at her school motivated a lot of the social interactions, from the cruel comments that girls could casually drop within earshot of their victims to the mindless insults boys cast at other guys to perpetuate their bravado.

As her mind wandered, she thought of Grace, who had welcomed her without hesitation, despite Allie being a new kid and an unknown quantity that first day in gym class. Allie resolved to get to know Grace even better when she returned home.

She had also thought more about her role with *Aviso*. She loved doing illustrations since it was something she had a talent for. But she also wanted to get involved with the editorial staff. Her time in Ataraxia had heightened her perceptions of good and evil.

She didn't want to be someone whose silence equated to indifference about issues that mattered to her. Not taking a clear stand when she saw someone being mistreated or discriminated against was the same as choosing to allow it, she realized.

It made her think of Ben, someone who did take a stand when it mattered, which made her respect him. She would think more about that later. But now, she heard a noise outside the banyan tree, a commotion near the entrance to the royal household.

"Outrageous!" Diego yelled at King Wendigo. "You've been seduced by the lies of those Ataraxia creatures!" he shouted.

"No, now listen, Diego. Calm down. This is an exchange—one the Ataraxians have promised will be peaceful and will result in the return of my son. Put yourself in my place. Kibou is my only son. I must ensure his safe return. Eris will never forgive me if I bungle this with a surprise attack of some sort."

Diego, still seething over the escape of the prisoners under his watch, had proposed that Malvelnia go through the motions of the peaceful exchange, and then, once Kibou was safe, perpetrate a surprise attack.

First and foremost, he told Wendigo that he wanted Ethan to pay for the losses they had suffered during the escape, especially for his compatriot, Diablo.

But Wendigo was adamant that they go through the peaceful exchange without any hitches. He promised Diego he could have a future opportunity to take out Ethan. They would strategize about it together later. But this day, the attack could not happen.

Grumbling, Diego backed down.

"But I insist, this messenger girl will be guarded in the front and the rear by my most seasoned fighters," the incensed crocodile seethed. "If Zion or any of his crew deceive us, they will be poised to take down the girl for good!"

Allie could not hear the specifics of what the huge crocodile she had spotted said to Wendigo after that, but she sensed it was not meant for her well-being.

Preparing herself for the day's journey, Allie ate as many berries and nuts as they had left for her, followed by a long gulp of water. She could see the sun rising higher in the sky, which meant they would be leaving soon.

"Wendigo, where are you?" Eris called, nervously. "Is it time for me to leave? Where's Ashok? Shouldn't he be here by now?"

"Calm down, dear," Wendigo answered, seeing that his wife was clearly flustered. "Ashok is talking to Diego. We are going to have two of his best go along to guard the girl. Everything will go fine. Solomon has promised us that this will be a peaceful exchange. You are to do as we discussed. Once you have Kibou with you, our group is to turn and head back immediately. No prolonged communication with those kidnappers. Just return here safely!

"And don't worry," the king reassured his wife, "there's going to be blowback on the Ataraxians for this. Mark my words. They are a rebellious, self-serving lot who will get their just recompense for this betrayal."

It seemed to Eris that it was Wendigo who had orchestrated the betrayal when he falsely imprisoned several of the Guardians at the conclusion of their meeting with Malvelnia. But he was happy to twist it around and place the blame on Ataraxia. It was one of the king's personality patterns: perpetrate a double-cross and then point the finger at the intended victim of his deceit. The vultures and reptiles didn't need to know the true details of Wendigo's skirmishes. If he repeated his version enough times, it became the truth in their eyes.

Ashok sauntered over to greet the haughty queen. Beneath his visage, Ashok was furious that his plot to have the condors kidnap the boy and prevent him from returning to Ataraxia had failed.

Instead, Ashok learned the boy had been rescued and was able to deliver the message about the truce. Ashok and Diego were already plotting for a future opportunity to escalate the conflict. But for now, Ashok would follow his brother's orders so Wendigo could get his son safely home.

"Are you ready, your royal highness?" Ashok said to Eris, with a note of sarcasm in his voice. Ashok and Eris had never seen eye-to-eye, but he was fond of his brother and for that reason, put up with Eris's antics.

"Yes, Ashok. I'm more than ready. Let's go," she announced curtly. She loved her rascally son and could hardly wait to see him and have him back home with her. Before soaring upward into the trees, Ashok glanced behind him as Diego and two particularly gigantic, leathery-skinned crocodiles lined up with Allie, one in front and one behind.

Ashok and Eris fluttered ahead from tree to tree, keeping a steady pace but waiting while Diego and the rest of their party on the ground marched forward.

As the Council from Ataraxia came around a bend in the path, several gasped at the sight of the majestic waterfall.

A truly dramatic sight, its waters plunged like silvery missiles of foam from rocks forty meters high that protruded out over the flat sheets of rock below. It created a wide arc of roaring spray, nearly deafening as the group moved carefully from the path, picking their way up to the natural platform that had earned its spot as a place for important meetings between the two kingdoms.

Solomon and Graham stood at the front of the line of Ataraxians awaiting the arrival of the Malvelnians. Zion, Helen, and Orion stood behind the two, while behind them, Luke and SJ stood with Kibou between them.

Luke and Kibou were in the middle of an animated conversation filled with jokes and laughter. The much more solemn adults waited quietly, their eyes searching the horizon for signs of the others.

A rustling overhead alerted them to the arrival of the vultures. The two perched on a large and low-hanging oak tree branch, awaiting Diego's arrival along with their hostage, who would soon be exchanged for Kibou.

Atop a rise in the path, Graham spotted the intimidating-looking crocodiles. He watched as SJ's jaw dropped when he saw his sister, dwarfed by the massive reptiles guarding her. SJ stared nervously, obviously afraid for her. Allie spotted her brother and Graham and gave them a quick thumbs up to let them know she was okay.

Eris and Ashok swooped down, alighting on the ground immediately facing Solomon and Graham.

"Let me see my son!" Eris demanded.

"Greetings, your highness," Solomon said, bowing his gray head. "Let's execute the exchange right now. Bring the girl forward to us, and we will bring Kibou to you. You will find he is in excellent health."

Excited to see his mom, Kibou fluttered forward, then flew upward over the heads of Zion, Helen, and Orion, landing right next to his mother.

"Mom!" he exclaimed. "I missed you." The young vulture stretched his head forward and nuzzled his mom's neck feathers. She made a gentle cooing noise as she cuddled him under her wing.

The crocodile in front of Allie had pulled back, allowing her to run forward. She ran past Eris and Kibou and zeroed in on SJ for a super-sized hug.

"Thank you, SJ. You saved the day with your speed, carrying that message. But how's your leg? I've been worrying about you, bro!" He grinned and lifted it up. As it had dried, the muddy salve Graham had directed him to place on the swollen leg had eliminated the infection. Allie used the bottom part of her T-shirt to wipe off some of the dried mud and smiled as she saw her brother's leg looking pretty much back to normal.

"Thank goodness," she muttered softly, gazing up at SJ's face.

As she did, a hushed murmur arose from all the attendees. Allie glanced quizzically at the councilmembers and could see their eyes were trained on the waterfall.

As she turned her head, she discovered why. There, from behind the waterfall, she could see a small, perfectly white lamb walking behind the crashing waters, wandering through the spray, squinting out at the sunlight . . . and now emerging on the rocky platform on which they all stood.

"Oh, dear," the lamb gasped. "What is this place?"

Chapter 49

Reunion

He lifted me out of the slimy pit, out of the mud and mire;
he set my feet on a rock and gave me a firm place to stand.

—Psalm 40:2

No creature had ever survived the Abyss, so when Delilah, grieving her friend Squeaker's demise, saw the arched passageway out of the Abyss, she had no idea of the feat she had accomplished.

Her combination of courage, sheer pluck in navigating the sinister swampland—with the help, of course, of Squeaker—and then withstanding the conniving maneuvers of the evil spirits that haunted the Garden, had earned Delilah release from the claw-like grip of the Abyss. Delilah's sense of a greater purpose, to find her true family and her home, along with her gentle spirit, loosed her from the Abyss's power.

As she stepped out of the Garden, she felt incredible warmth envelop her body, an overwhelming sense of peace. Then a spray of icy water awakened her from that moment of reverie. As she focused her eyes, it was like looking through a frosted glass. The pounding water obscured her vision, but she could make out the outlines of a host of creatures gathered on the other side of the torrent, which led to her exclamation upon walking out on the platform.

Before anyone else spoke, Kibou let out a loud shriek. "Delilah! Delilah! Hurray, you're alive!"

Hearing the vulture's outburst, Graham felt every muscle in his body go weak. Then, while the Malvelnians and Ataraxians stood motionless, Kibou flew over to the tiny lamb, laughing, fluttering alongside her, and nuzzling her cheek with his beak.

The crowd let out a loud gasp. Next came sounds of delight, and a cheer broke out, followed by exuberant clapping by Allie and SJ. Who could have ever dreamed that a young vulture and a gentle lamb would embrace, even with the wounds of the battle between their respective kingdoms still fresh?

Graham, however, still stood frozen—an unmoving statue. He was staring at the lamb, this tiny creature Kibou had called by his fallen daughter's name. As he stared, he saw it, unmistakably, the swirling cowlick on her forehead that created a perfect circle.

He collapsed forward on his front knees in disbelief. But then, a voice he hardly recognized as his own, whispered, "Delilah?"

Everyone watched as the lamb gazed past Kibou and toward the stately ram who had just spoken her name. They didn't know the thoughts running through her brain: *Could this be one of my lost family members?* Before she had time for another thought, Graham approached her.

"D-D-Delilah? I'm your father. We thought you were dead! We've been grieving for you ever since S-S-Simon took you away."

As tears of both joy and guilt poured down Graham's cheek, Delilah softly said, "Yes, you must be my dad. Why else would you call me by my name and cry at my presence?"

She sidled up to her father, burying her face in his wooly shoulder. The two stood as if suspended in time; Graham leaned down, nuzzling Delilah's nose and licking her soft coat and that perfect cowlick on her forehead.

"Today, you are going to make your mother the happiest she has ever been in her life," Graham told the lamb. "We must get home to share this incredible miracle with her."

Graham could almost himself feel Delilah's heart soar as she learned she had a mom waiting for her! He couldn't imagine it was something she had seen so many times in her dreams. Now it was going to be a reality.

"And you have a brother, Luke. He's right here behind me."

Luke, who had been standing in disbelief, now rushed forward, his hooves clattering on the rocks. A big grin lit up his face as he gently butted Delilah's chin.

"Wow! A sister." Luke smiled. "We're gonna have a lot of fun together; you can bet on that."

Allie and SJ joined Graham and Delilah, both looking just as astonished as everyone else.

Eris, meanwhile, was fluttering by her son and nudging him lovingly with her beak.

"You stay right next to me," she told Kibou in her sternest voice. "You are not going to be separated from me again! We are heading home immediately. Can you fly yet?"

Shifting his attention away from the reunion of his friend and her father, Kibou looked up at Eris. "Yes, I'm fully recovered," he said. "But remember that Delilah's family took care of me while I was lost. You and Dad are powerful, but please treat them with mercy."

Eris made no such promise to her son but abruptly turned away from the Ataraxians, shooing Kibou upward with one wing as they soared above the rocks, leaving the spray of the waterfall and the upward glance of Delilah behind them.

Ashok remained behind. "Our business is finished. Leave safely while you can," he said rudely to Solomon and Zion and the others, whom he barely acknowledged.

"Yes, our business is finished," Solomon agreed. "Let's make sure we all abide by the truce and the promise of Wendigo to abolish the ill-advised census. Hopefully, both kingdoms can live peacefully alongside each other."

Ashok snorted something between a scoff and a laugh. "We'll see about that," he announced as he signaled the rest of the Malvelnian group to depart. "In your dreams," he mouthed silently as he departed.

Solomon and Zion stared at each other, shaking their heads. They knew Wendigo's nature, which offered them no comfort as they prepared to head back to Ataraxia with Helen and Orion, the two human children, and Graham's beaming family.

Molly, who was experiencing early throes of morning sickness, had plopped herself down on a particularly soft pile of tall grasses outside the grove where they lived. It was on higher ground so she could doze but still glance up every once in a while, anticipating her husband and son's return.

Earlier, she had told herself there was no point in worrying. Graham had assured her this would be a peaceful exchange, since a truce was now in place. She was also pleased she would get to see their young friend, Allie, again who had been so caring and supportive ever since she'd arrived in Ataraxia.

She felt the ground vibrating with the rumble of motion. Raising an eyebrow, Molly could see figures in the distance. "It must be Graham, Luke, and the councilmembers returning," she mused.

Unfolding her legs, Molly stood and shook off a pesky dragonfly. She focused her sight on the approaching group.

As they came closer, she was startled to see not just two sheep, but three: the largest was Graham, of course, and Luke with his horn stumps was next to him, but who was that smaller figure alongside them? It appeared to be a lamb.

As Molly puzzled, she watched the little figure come trotting toward her. The trot turned into a gallop. Then the lamb bleated out, "Mama!"

The ewe stopped breathing. *It can't be!* Her eyes clouded, filling with tears, which she tried to blink away so she could see more clearly. "Delilah?" she cried out, a hitch in her voice as she stared incredulously at the lamb.

"Mama, it's me, Delilah! I'm home!" Delilah shouted, tears falling from both mother and daughter's eyes as they embraced, neck to neck, then nose to nose, hearts overflowing with joy.

"I've dreamed about this moment," Delilah told her mom. "I knew I'd find you one day," she bleated, unable to even begin to share the story that would take days to describe.

"You don't know how many nights I cried myself to sleep, longing for my daughter," Molly said. "This is something I never imagined could come true. Come here, come here. I'll never let you go," Molly cooed.

At that moment, Graham and Luke arrived after bidding farewell to Zion, Helen, and Orion. The four had a wooly snuggle for a moment, immersing themselves in the delight of their reunion.

Allie and SJ, standing back on the path, looked at each other for a moment. They shook their heads, basking in the euphoria generated by this miraculous reunion.

SJ grabbed the moment to tell Allie about his kidnapping by the condors and the amazing rescue by Moriah and the giant woodpeckers. It nearly brought Allie to tears at the thought of her little brother stranded up on a cliff in the clutches of the menacing condors. She was overwhelmingly thankful for his rescue, and she gave him a sisterly hug of relief, which he shrugged off. One hug for the day was enough.

But then, their minds simultaneously headed in the same direction. "We have to get home," they agreed.

"I'm afraid Mom will be worried sick about where we are," SJ said.

"Don't worry," Allie responded. "When I came here before and then returned, it was as if time had not changed on the clock. It's because we are in a different dimension."

After allowing Graham's family time to themselves, Allie quietly walked up to the ram to tell him that she and her brother needed to go home.

"Oh, yes, of course," the ram nodded. "W-w-w-we owe you a huge debt of gratitude. If it had not been for you and your brother, the truce might not have come about. And then we would not have been there at the very place and very moment our Delilah arrived! Oh dear, I cannot even think about that possibility," he said.

Allie put her arms around Graham's broad neck and hugged him. Then she ran over to say goodbye to Molly, Luke, and Delilah.

"You have to come back soon," Molly said. "We'll be a family of five, which I can hardly imagine, but it is going to be true!"

SJ, who had found a friend in Luke, gave the young ram a quick headbutt and told him he'd be back to see him. "Take care of Delilah," he told Luke.

"I'm going to walk you to the pasture where you arrived," Luke said. The three ambled over the crest of the hill and down into the deep green fragrant grasses that Allie recalled.

"Imagine in your mind's eye we're back in my room, getting ready to say good-night to Mom," Allie told SJ. "Close your eyes, keep that thought in your mind, hold on to me, and take a leap," she said.

She grabbed ahold of her brother's hand, and they jumped. Again, the huge sucking noise exploded, and next, they lay sprawled out on the rug in Allie's room. SJ was startled. But when he saw Allie smiling at him, he sighed a breath of relief.

"Oh man, did that all really just happen?" he asked.

"Absolutely," Allie said. "And look at the clock. It's still 7:05 p.m., just like it was when we left. I'll bet Mom is downstairs working on her speech. . . . Look, SJ, we're gonna have to review everything that just happened," she said. "But for now, we need to do what we told Mom we'd do. Finish up any homework and be ready to go to school tomorrow as if nothing happened. Do you think you can do that? Because nobody is going to believe us, and for the time being, I think it's best if we keep this as *our* secret," Allie said.

On this occasion, SJ immediately agreed with his sister. They nodded solemnly and did their personal dap to seal the promise.

But that evening, it was hard to focus on thoughts about schoolwork or anything else, for that matter. As he lay in bed, SJ's mind was flooded with images from his visit to Ataraxia: his new friends, Luke and Kibou; the lamb, Delilah, emerging from behind the spray at the Waterfalls; and all the interesting and diverse creatures of that kingdom. As he dozed off, he was soaring atop the back of a graceful gazelle through a mysterious forest bathed in a light from above.

Chapter 50

CHANGE IN PLANS

That coming Friday, the December dance was taking place. Allie and Grace shopped together over the weekend, helping each other find the perfect dress that complemented them.

"You look amazing, Gracie!" Allie said as she examined her friend modeling a white dress that featured dramatic black zig-zags, which she had paired with lacy leggings. "That fit is so on point!"

Allie had fallen in love with a royal blue dress with fancy cutouts on the sleeves and the side that Allie thought looked like it had been made just for her. The girls buzzed around the store, trying on fun hats and bracelets while they talked non-stop about Dak and Ben and the upcoming dance. Both of their moms had given them cash to pay for their outfits, so they knew the dresses they picked out fit within their allotted budgets. Bags in hand, they headed outside and waited for Allie's mom to pick them up.

Unfortunately, later that evening at home, Allie got a call from Ben with some unwelcome news. Ben told her his boss at the bodega was insisting he work on Friday, the night of the dance. She could tell he was nervous sharing the update as his voice creaked like an old rocking chair, and he hesitated for a moment.

"I tried to find a way to reason with Mr. Nagle," Ben told her, "but the problem is, Carlos, the man who usually receives the items coming into the store and stocks the shelves, has come down sick. It's a real contagious flu, so Mr. Nagle doesn't want Carlos to come in. He told me if I want to keep my job, I have to be there on Friday."

"Oh, my gosh! Doesn't he know you've had plans for Friday for a long time?" Allie said heatedly. "Can't you get him to find an alternate?"

"Well, the thing is, Al, I really need the job. And I *am* the alternate. There's no one else. My boss told me if I don't cover this shift, he'll look for someone else to replace me. Even though it's not a lot of money, it helps my family," he confessed. "My parents have a hard time paying the bills, so I feel like I can't let them down."

Allie had not considered this because she didn't know about the Lopezes' financial situation. Ben never complained and had never mentioned to her the importance of his job.

"Okay," she said. "I understand."

"Y-y-you do?" he stammered.

"Yeah, life doesn't always make things easy, so we have to adjust. I'll talk to my mom. Maybe we can have our own December dance at my house. Lemme talk to her, and we'll make a plan."

"Wow—thanks, Al." Allie heard a sigh of relief on the other end of the phone.

"Thanks for what?" she said.

"For being the kind of friend that you are. I want us to be friends forever."

"Agreed," Allie said. "G'night. Talk to you later."

Only a few minutes passed before Allie ran downstairs to tell her mom about her conversation with Ben.

"That's terrible! But I'm glad you could understand Ben's situation. That's being a true friend, honey. And yes, we can plan your event here. Ben could come over for dinner. And hey, he could help us do some tree decorating to Christmas music."

SJ, who had been reading a book in the other room, heard the conversation and chimed in. "Yeah, that'd be fun!

"Great!" Allie said. "Is it OK if I invite Grace and Dak too?"

"Yeah, sure, Allie," her mom agreed. "Why don't you get a date that works for Ben and then see if Grace and Dak can also come over? We could say six o'clock for dinner first. And a few hours after to hang out, play a couple games, maybe? And you could get Ben to help you put together a playlist of some favorite music we can listen to that evening. And we could ask parents to do drop-offs and pickups. Maybe 10 p.m. would be a good guideline?"

"That sounds awesome, Mom!" Allie grinned. "That really means a lot. I'll let you know as soon as I talk to Ben what date we would be looking at so you can see if it sounds good."

Allie ran upstairs and immediately texted Ben about the idea. Before she knew it, they had selected a week from Sunday as a possible date. Allie rushed to message Grace about it, and soon, the friends were all in sync about the date and super charged up about the idea.

Grace told Allie she was sorry they wouldn't be there on Friday for the school event, but she understood about Ben needing to work.

"We'll have such a fun time together at your house! It'll be cool to all hang out together."

"Thank goodness you're over that ankle sprain," Allie wrote. "And I'm super happy for you that you're making some friends on the cheer team and get to cheer at the games that Dak plays in."

"Allie!" she heard her mom yell up the stairs. "I need your help a minute."

"Bye, Gracie," she texted, "Gotta go. See ya tomorrow."

Chapter 51

THE HANGOUT

At school on Monday, Ben told Allie and their lunch table crew that he had spoken with the principal about their idea of having a place where students could come to relax, study, chat, and find helpful information.

Ben told the principal, Mrs. Anderson, he and his friends wanted to coordinate finding a room for this and were willing to work at getting it set up, cleaned, painted, and whatever else was needed. He told her that they wanted to also post info about resources, such as where to get mental health help, an 800-number for suicide prevention, and places where kids could talk to someone about substance abuse.

The principal had explained to Ben she was delighted that there were students in her school who were concerned enough to want to create a safe space for their fellow classmates. She also said she'd meet with school staff and see what they could come up with as far as a space within the school that could meet the need.

"You guys know the custodian, Mr. Jeffries? He said there's an empty room back behind the gym, which they used to use for storing equipment, but in recent years, it's been emptied," Ben said.

"The equipment that had once been in storage is now either in active use or has been eliminated. The room is just sitting empty! It's in bad need of a cleaning and a coat of paint, but otherwise, it seems like it could be just the solution we need," he continued, enthusiasm building in his voice. "It has windows along one side of the room that had been covered up in past years. But now, the cardboard that covered them has been removed. All we need to do is get it ready."

"This is awesome," Allie said to Ben. "We've already got a great team ready to spring into action," she said, as Matt, Grace, Dak, and another student, Chloe, all gave it a thumbs-up.

Ben grinned. "We'll have fun fixing up the space. We'll need to set aside a non-school day to clean it thoroughly, paint, and create a list of everything we think we need to make it comfortable to hang out in," Ben said. "Mr. Jeffries said he'd provide us with the cleanup tools we need, like buckets and mops and cleaning products. He said he'd get us paint, rollers, and brushes too."

Fortunately, the school had recently painted several classrooms and had a surplus of paint for walls in the soothing colors of sea foam and semi-gloss white for the doorways, windowsills, and the baseboards along the floor.

The students agreed they'd all stay after school that Wednesday to get the cleaning done and start on the painting.

As a few more friends heard about the developments, the group ended up with a dozen students that Wednesday.

They swept and dumped old pieces of wood, an abandoned bird's nest, rusty cut-up wire, and lots of dust and dirt into big bins Mr. Jeffries said would be rolled out when they were finished. The work went much faster than expected, so they went on to clean the windows and wash the flooring with the buckets, mops, and cleaning detergent the custodian had provided.

Later on, a surprise came in the form of several parents who arrived in the afternoon with paint rollers at the ready. It was a gargantuan effort. By early evening, they had rolled out the bins, given Mr. Jeffries the leftover cleaning supplies, and helped the parents finish one coat of paint on the walls.

Mr. Jeffries came back to announce he had the go-ahead from the principal to pay for a couple of assistants he used from time to time to come in and do a second coat of paint and all the trim. When he made that announcement, there were lots of cheers and high-fives all around as those assembled went and washed up in the bathroom next door to the gym and headed home for dinner.

"So, what are you gonna call this place?" Dak's dad asked as they walked out to their car.

"We decided while we were cleaning to call it The Lakeshores MS Hangout," Dak said. "So we agreed on that official name, but as we started talking about it, everyone was just calling it 'The Hangout.' So that's what it is."

His dad nodded, as if to say, "Yeah, that makes sense."

The next day, the following appeared on the editorial page of *Aviso*.

The editorial staff of Aviso is pleased to inform the Lakeshores MS student body of a new development, made possible by Principal Anderson and her staff. Soon, a space will be dedicated specifically to all of us, the students of Lakeshores MS.

It is the space behind the gym, which we all have wondered about since the windows were covered up and the doors were always locked. Going forward, it will no longer be the scary place behind the gym.

One week from today, the doors will be open to "The Lakeshores MS Hangout." It is meant to be a safe space, somewhere students can stop in to rest, study, and take a break.

The Hangout will also be a place where we can find resources available to us as we deal with stress, the uncertainties of life, and those challenges many of us face.

A large bulletin board near the front doors has a list of people here at our school who can help us too—whether for a mental health crisis we are going through, difficulties with substance abuse, or a family situation we need to talk to someone about. We will also have 800-numbers posted, such as a suicide hotline and one for anyone who's been a victim of abuse.

These are serious subjects, but all of us know these are issues happening among students our age, so we need to know to whom and where we can turn for help.

Likewise, it is a time to consider our actions toward each other. We're all in this together. We need a kinder and gentler world. A good starting point is something simple: treat other people the way you would like to be treated. If we do that, we won't be passing on negative gossip about someone else at their expense to make ourselves look good.

Let's all make The Hangout a place anyone and everyone can enjoy and make their own. Looking forward to seeing you all there!

Chapter 52

Answer to a Prayer

December had brought an unusually cold start to the month. There had already been several frosts, which usually didn't arrive until January. But on this particular weekend, the sun was out in a cloudless blue sky and unleashing rays of warmth that softened the nippy morning into an afternoon where a thick sweater was enough for a trip to the mailbox.

Despite the sweater, Allie hugged herself to warm up as she ran across the stepping stones to grab the mail. As she did, she noticed a letter addressed to her in lovely cursive handwriting. When she saw the return address was from Darshana Verma, Sophia's mom, her heart felt like it stopped beating. She gasped for breath, afraid to read the contents of her letter.

Allie raced up the walkway, up the porch steps, and into the house. Running to her mom's office by the kitchen, she grabbed a letter opener and slit open the envelope. Inside was a card decorated with colorful flowers from Sophia's mom. Allie opened it and began to read.

Dear Allie,

I have to share with you that something miraculous happened this week: Our lovely Sophia woke up from her coma! Even though the doctors acted like this would probably not happen, it did!

They did many tests, but to their surprise, Sophia's mind is functioning well. She will need physical therapy to build back her muscles and regain her strength, but the IV tubes were unhooked, and she ate her first regular meal in seven weeks! I have to pinch myself to make sure this is real.

After she woke up from the coma, she told us she was aware when you were there in her room. She could hear your voice, she said, like something in a dream.

But she said she could remember you reading to her and praying to God for a miracle. She insisted I write to you to thank you for your kindness in visiting her, but also, she wanted you to know that your prayer was answered. Her father and I and her sister are in a state of joy. Sophia will finish her school studies from home and then will transfer to a private school.

You are welcome to our home anytime, Allie. Thank you again. We hope to see you soon.

Allie gasped as she let out all the breath she had been tensely holding in suspense.

She read the letter three times. A miracle! Sophia was awake! It was almost too hard to imagine. And she could remember hearing Allie's prayer for her! This was so incredible—Allie could hardly wait to tell her mom, but she had gone out on a quick trip to pick up a few groceries.

Allie would have to wait to share this news until she returned. She went upstairs to her room and leaned back on her favorite green pillow shaped like a frog. It was her best spot to think and where she often puzzled over the things in life that she didn't always understand.

"Dear, God," Allie prayed. "Thank you for hearing my prayer for Sophia! I am so happy . . . no, I'm *ecstatic* that you are here and real and listening to me and answering this prayer, which was really, really important. Forgive me for sometimes doubting you or wondering whether you are listening. I know you are. And help me," she concluded, "to work at being a good friend to Sophia, who will need that after all of this stuff."

Tonight, God had spoken to her heart.

She made a mental note to call to see if she could stop by and see Sophia next week.

As her mind wandered, she thought about having Ben, Gracie, and Dak over for the party. She could hardly wait to share her home with the friends who had become an important part of her life in Lakeshores.

As the word *friend* entered her mind, she couldn't help but think of the opposite. To be reminded of those who purposely hurt others. Why did there have to be bullies in life who persecuted the weaker ones, whether the victim was a gentle girl like Sophia, or a humble creature like Graham?

Staring at the painting on the wall, she wondered how Molly, Graham, and Luke were doing.

She imagined they were all basking in the joy of Delilah's return. *And are the Overseers keeping their word about dropping their plan to number and mark all the creatures of Ataraxia?* She hoped so. And she wondered, *Will we go back soon?*

As she daydreamed, she told herself she'd talk to SJ about it that evening.

Steep Cliffs
Caves
Mt. Kukulkan Home of King Wendigo
Indigna River
Malvelnia
The Grasslands
The Abyss

The Amphitheater
Mango Grove
Riverside Reptile Dwellings
Monkey Rocks
Ataraxia
Graham
and Molly's
Home
Fertile Fields and Forest
N
W
E
S
Meadows where
Allie & S.J. Arrive

Acknowledgments

This book would not have been possible without the invaluable contributions of a number of individuals. My heartfelt thanks to my sister, Paula, whose encouragement, support, expert feedback, and detailed edits led to solid improvements in the book. Thank you to my granddaughter, Emily, my first early reader, whose thoughts and feedback were so helpful, and to Lisa Carlisle, for her encouraging feedback. Sincere thanks to Julianne Long, whose inciteful comments and suggestions led to productive revisions to the story.

Wholehearted thanks to my adult children: Wendy Robertson, Robin Presley, and Nick O'Connell, each of whose unique talent, character, and personality inspire me to want to write with imagination and purpose. Thank you also to Nick for his help on aspects supporting the presentation of the book, from cover art ideas to the website. My granddaughters, Emily and Serinda, continue to motivate me to write more stories.

Special thanks to my editor, Cortney Donelson. Her skillful edits and guidance heightened the impact of my story and improved its flow. The map created by Terry Johnson gives readers a bird's-eye view of the other universe that Allie and SJ traverse. Thank you, Terry.

The cover art, created by talented artist Samantha McInniss, captures the feel of the fantasy world while visually bringing to life the Lee children. Thank you, Samantha, for taking on this project and delivering such a remarkable cover.

Above all, thanks to my Lord and Savior, Jesus Christ, my guiding Light amid a world often shrouded in darkness.

About the Author

Nancy Gravatt is an experienced writer who has contributed to publications such as *American Libraries, Today's Christian Living,* and *The Washington Post.* She has written web features for the Fairfax County Public Library and *The Compass,* a global missions newsletter. As a travel spokesman, she has appeared on various media outlets, including *CNN* and the *Today Show.* Her dedication to global missions has brought her to many places around the world, including Cambodia, Myanmar, Papua New Guinea, and most recently, Jamaica. She holds a graduate degree in political science and an undergraduate degree in journalism. She currently resides in Ashburn, Virginia, located twenty miles outside of Washington, DC. Her faith in Christ has been the foundation of her life.

A free ebook edition is available with the purchase of this book.

To claim your free ebook edition:

1. Visit MorganJamesBOGO.com
2. Sign your name CLEARLY in the space
3. Complete the form and submit a photo of the entire copyright page
4. You or your friend can download the ebook to your preferred device

Morgan James BOGO™

A **FREE** ebook edition is available for you or a friend with the purchase of this print book.

CLEARLY SIGN YOUR NAME ABOVE

Instructions to claim your free ebook edition:
1. Visit MorganJamesBOGO.com
2. Sign your name CLEARLY in the space above
3. Complete the form and submit a photo of this entire page
4. You or your friend can download the ebook to your preferred device

Print & Digital Together Forever.

Snap a photo

Free ebook

Read anywhere